W9-CNL-351

WITHDRAWN

OUR FATHERS

ALSO BY ANDREW O'HAGAN

The Missing

Our Fathers

ANDREW O'HAGAN

Harcourt Brace & Company   *New York   San Diego   London*

© Andrew O'Hagan 1999

First published in 1999 by Faber & Faber Limited

Library of Congress Cataloging-in-Publication Data
O'Hagan, Andrew, 1968–
Our fathers/Andrew O'Hagan.
p.   cm.
ISBN 0-15-100494-3
I. Title.
PR6065.H18096   1999
823'914—dc21   99-25486

Type set in Centaur MT
Designed by Lori McThomas Buley
Printed in the United States of America
First edition
A C E D B

For
my father Gerry
and my brothers:
Michael, Gerald, and Charlie.

Be not too hasty, to trust, or to admire, the teachers of morality:
they discourse like angels, but they live like men.

SAMUEL JOHNSON,
Rasselas

Contents

OUR FATHERS

I

The Sea Shore

I know nothing of the house I was born in. The look of the
town is all I remember. And yet I can hear the sound of
the door as we closed it behind us for good. I sat by myself
on the train leaving Berwick: six years old in long trousers.
Jamie the boy with the watery eyes. That was me. And something of me will be sat there still. My eyes looked into my eyes
in the glass. The town of Berwick was out of reach, beyond
the window, and quiet at last. Under the mound of the railway station the sea lapped up on the brown sand. Every wave
brought forgiveness to the shore. And now I am left with the
thought of that day. The English town I left as a boy: the
closing door.

The houses looked into the North Sea. They peered at the
saline darkness: a world of algae and sea sounds. As a child I
wondered where it all went. Miles of sea and miles of dark.
They say that nothing goes on for ever. Even the tide goes
somewhere in the end.

Mrs Drake lived in the manse at Berwick. She was old in

her carpet slippers, pinning her sheets to the line that day, a skirl of winter down among the rocks, and I thought of how pleased my friend had been to teach me good books, a payment in kind, for odd jobs done in silence, with no fuss. I had learned a bit of life down there. The smell of chimneys still giving out to God. The smell of mackerel. All the small graces in Berwick town, where the river meets the sea, for someone seeking out gladness, exploring the sand, and knowing these things for the first time. The train pulled out and I never saw the town again. The North-East of England slid away in a rush of greenery. But more than a splash of time lay among those rocks I then abandoned for the North: my own first voice along the sea-front, the river's memory of salmon and corn, a notion of something good in that childish basin. I knew that day I would always miss it, and I always have.

Mrs Drake had given me a book to take away to Scotland. The book was for me alone. The book was mine. It had a strange blue cover, the glint of the old woman's eyes; and the words on the spine were printed in white, the spell of her hair. My book had belonged to someone else, but now it was mine, and it carried the trace of someone else in its tea-tinted pages. I could take it with me. I held the book in my hands as the train slowed at the signal box. Surely Mrs Drake would remain this while, her good hands clasped over mine, her piano-playing fingers with their slackened rings, holding me tight in the afternoons. Her voice with those fishing songs, softly sung, more spoken than sung, the kiss she planted in my mess of hair, her sweet perfume in the winds of Berwick. My old friend: in no time at all she was round the corner and out of sight.

I could see St Abbs lighthouse in the distance. It made me think of lamps and night-times and weather. I felt just then how the day was all movement: the beat of the heart, the clattering train, the tides out there, the light. I unfolded the book from my jumper. It was in my thoughts all the time. *The Sea Shore*, by C. M. Yonge.

She'd pressed down the corners of two pages. I took my time sounding out the words. The first page, 'Barnacles and Molluscs of a Rocky Shore'. I read out the big words circled in pencil. Her note said, 'Copy out, my dear, and try to remember.'

Limpets possess an undoubted 'homing instinct'. The exact nature of this has so far defied analysis; it does not seem to reside within the restricted powers of sight, smell or touch. As shown in Fig. 35, limpets browse in a rough circle around their homes, travelling at most three feet from this and usually very much less, and are able by this sense of direction to regain their home when it is necessary.

Some of the words were hard to read, and they sounded new. Underneath was a picture of a limpet stuck to an English rock. The second page marked down by Mrs Drake was near the end of the book. In her own writing it said, 'Learn this one, Jamie. Near your new house, on the other coast, you might notice these things as well.'

On the coastal lands of Ayrshire seaweeds are extensively used on the potato fields, where up to thirty tons are scattered per acre. As a result of investigations at the Marine Station at Millport (underlined), methods were worked out for the successful preparation of agar (arrow: 'jelly, good for all the experiments') from *gigartina* (arrow: 'red seaweed'), of which large supplies exist on the coasts of Wales and especially on the west coast of Scotland (underlined twice).

Mrs Drake so loved to write things down. She had taught me to love it just as much, though my favourite part was the digging part, the measuring part, the walking part, and the milk and the toast at the end. As well as the marked pages of *The Sea Shore* my old teacher had written something on a square of paper – a slip of paper with a black edge – and she had placed it inside the back of my book. As much as the book itself, the writing on this paper would always remind me of Mrs Drake, and without notice it would bring me back to her living room, the open fire, the record player, and those jars of hers, high on the shelves, filled to the brim with cockles and whelks.

Dear Jamie,

Please remember to round your letters and curl your tails. You are a good boy and I will miss you. From now on I will think of you as I go along the shore. Work hard at all your reading, you are very clever about it. Here are two fine books you will enjoy as soon as you feel ready. Try to find them if you can in the good library. One is by John Graham Dalyell, and has a funny title, Rare and Remarkable Animals of Scotland, represented from living subjects: with Practical Observations on their Nature. *The other is by Philip Henry Gosse,* A Year at the Shore. *These will help you. Say ta-ta from me to your mummy.*

Yours faithfully
Mrs P. Drake

On the back of the paper she had written out some words. ' "Who can say of a particular sea that it is old? Distilled by the sun, kneaded by the moon, it is renewed in a year, in a day, or in an hour." Love, Pat.'

My father returned to Scotland in a flurry of hatred. My mother soothed him over the border in a Bedford van. They put me on the train and then limped away to their big people's business. The train took me first to Glasgow, and my grandfather Hugh, who made a point of never asking about my ailing father, and never knowing our proper address, though now and then he would wonder if my mother was 'coping'. He took me from the station to one of the new building sites at Ruchill. He threw an envelope of papers at the face of the foreman there. He peeled money from a roll. From the back of the car, in the pouring rain, I could see my granda shouting the odds, throwing up his hands, handing money to the men in the yellow hats. He climbed in and out of a visiting truck. With that strange fury on his face he looked like my father.

I lay down in the back seat. You could see the concrete layers going all the way up. Metal rods hung over the sides; they went up so high you couldn't believe it was so. Sawdust came down with the rain. My mind went soft with the weather, and the journey, and the thought of the deep green sea. Everything was mingled now: the world at my back, the sea shore; and this building site in the north of Glasgow, this field of mud, with its new clanging. My ears were filled with the roar and the clang. I fell asleep with water running down the car window.

My father took drink. He was an alcoholic, the kind that rages and mourns. His long-haired flight to England was all about drink. Nothing meant anything without drink. It was all drink.

He had thought he might drown himself in Berwick. Leagues away from his father's ideals. Good miles out from his mother's patience. Six-fathoms-five from the glory of his dead grandmother and all her Utopian dreams. My father sought an end to the question of himself in Berwick. In the rivermouth of Berwick he tumbled down, drinking the waves, a floating tribe unto himself, and wet with loathing, he drifted out, no high-toned relatives to temper the sway of his blitzed afternoons. My father was an alcoholic. The kind that rages and mourns. He never meant well, and he never did well. A blind-drunk bat in love with the dark. There was no feeling sorry: he took down too many days for easeful sorrow; he glutted on ruin.

And books became the only breath in that foreign room he kept us in. The only soothing language known, and all the kindness of printed words just taught me to hate him more, and to pity him, and to see a day when all would be loosened, or gone, and no one left to feel sorry. This is what I thought then. My father was a maniac. He frightened away the best of our health.

I would sit in a chair by the window of our new Ayrshire house – birds twittering out there, diving for the grass seed – and watch him drunk and asleep by a three-bar fire. My damp eyes bored through him. I could take the lighter and set fire to him as he slept. I stared at him. I knew I could do that. The twittering grew louder. Somewhere over the burn, in the thick of the housing scheme, an ice-cream van was selling good cheer. The sound of that music. I stared at him. I tried to make him go, and thought of him disappearing, and sliding away, being no more in our lives, and dead, or part of a place that was meant for badness, and right for the cruel, and endlessly quiet.

My books kept me living. And the thought of my grandparents. I was in love with what they knew, my semi-estranged granda and nan. They knew about trees and Robert the Bruce; they knew about rivers and buildings and stones. And without their thoughts, my mind turned slowly on the blaze in the armchair, one day coming. I sat at the window. I watched him to death. Down a slanting column of light – high window to living-room pile – a million tiny rags of dust came floating down, a million specks of chance, turning there, reflecting, turning again, each one a whisper of something peaceful. A million lessons in calm, part of a hateful day.

My father did not resemble himself as he slept. And that too was a part of his danger. He could have been somebody else. Somebody else in that raging skin – easy-going, a cool forehead – and dreaming of sunshine. So good inside, and with hope of being happy, and all his suffering due to stop, if only we'd let him breathe. He seemed a different Robert, much more wounded than wounding. He failed to resemble himself in that chair. Our candy-striped wallpaper behind his head, a long ashtray by his legs. Feet crossed at the ankles; cardigan buttoned up the wrong way; his chest breathing softly, like a baby in its cot. He could have been good as he lay there. Mindful of all our strange days, our hurried lives, and keen to make everything right for us. Our guardian. A madman who slept with an angel's smile. He could have been better, and that made it worse.

I sat by the window with the books he detested. The pages turned over. *Don't wake him up, and rustle his bed, and turn him into himself again.* The shadow of new-begun leaves came past the venetian blinds and crossed his face: 'To me my father should've been as a god. Composing my beauties, making of me a form in wax, by him imprinted . . .' So on and so on. '. . . within his power to make me good or bad, a well-made figure or more like him, disfigured.'

I closed the book. I wanted him to pay attention. Stop

shouting. I dreamed he might rise and prove himself great. Improve the world, make the days work, and add some shine to the new Ayrshire day. He lay for hours in a malicious slumber – his face as calm as milk – and opened his eyes as the day went out.

'Get me a beer from the fridge,' he said. 'Hurry up.'

In my father's anger there was something of the nation. Everything torn from the ground; his mind like a rotten field. His was a country of fearful men: proud in the talking, paltry in the living, and every promise another lie. My father bore all the dread that came with the soil – unable to rise, or rise again, and slow to see power in his own hands. Our fathers were made for grief. They were broken-backed. They were sick at heart, weak in the bones. All they wanted was the peace of defeat. They couldn't live in this world. They couldn't stand who they were. Robert's madness was nothing new: he was one of his own kind, bred, with long songs of courage, never to show a courageous hand.

Into the arms of oblivion they ran like wicked children. Their pretend love of freedom: we all learned the family business. We all knew the shame. His Scotland was lashed, betrayed, forgotten. That was our happiness; that was our song.

'How would you know about us?' he snapped. 'You English bastard.'

In Berwick my father gave vent to his troubles by punching my mother. His life was hidden behind floral curtains. In Ayrshire he went into the open air with his burning valour. No one was safe.

Cunts and fuckers and bastards and slags.

Ordering a cup of tea in a café, or buying a newspaper, or

paying a bus fare: a season in hell. My father's theatre of war.

A hopeless cunt, a useless prick. The fucking idiot. See that arsehole.

'No,' I would say. 'Just pass by.'

Total wanker. Dickshaft. A right good kicking he's needing. See you.

The newspaper seller had better be nimble and accurate with the change, or else he might find himself, or his mother, being raggedly abused in a giant voice . . .

You stupid fucking tosser. A good slap you're needing. Get the fuck out the road. Wankstain.

The confectionery display being brutally disarranged.

'Sorry,' from me. And in silence: *I'm sorry. I will always be sorry.*

This was the person who lived in our house. He broiled inside his own deep anger, keen for reasons to writhe and scream. He loved his own strength. He missed his own weakness. There was nothing he wanted to know, or not know. From the petrol-soaked armchair he aired his views. Minute by minute he lost the plot.

Hitler: *tried his best for the people, so he did.*

Churchill: *a pure wanker who kissed the King's arse.*

Books: *a load of shite, only good for boring bastards who don't know how to enjoy themselves.*

Cooking: *if the meat is any good, you don't need anything in it, just water and salt. Fuck all that poofters' sauce shite.*

Churchill: *kept the people of Scotland hungry, so he did.*

Women: *fucking pests.*

Racehorses: *slow cunts.*

Shopkeepers: *thieving Paki bastards.*

Cricket: *English fuckpigs.*

Hitler: *at least his soldiers could fucking march.*

Person with chequebook: *a pretentious middle-class twat.*
People with gardens: *time-wasting, no-use tosspots.*
Churchill: *not a clue. The thick tosser. Complete wanker.*
People on the dole: *layabout sponging cunts, most of them.*
Traffic wardens: *fucking lowlife scum.*
God: *a load of pish.*
Politicians: *bastarding liars, just like your granda.*

So on and so on.

The world, for my father, was a thing to be hated. And dreaded. And vilified. And one day left behind, as he sank to a kingdom of his own, where drink could be his friend, and like the best of all friends, could dull all sense of the enemy. With the can and the bottle he fought the good fight, and kept himself from himself again.

My mother and father had never seemed young. Early in their lives they made ready for decline. I had imagined it would come early to both of them. When I was a child he had sandy whiskers. His hair was short and orange; his eyes were green. He sounded young enough, but he walked with a deepening stoop at the age of thirty-two. His trousers and shoes predated his father's. Robert didn't want to be young – he wanted to be past everything. He wanted to live out of time. He never wore denims, went swimming, rode a bike, or ate greens. He didn't dance. He sought out the company of pensioners, and would shine among them, his young wisdom ringing true, his lively complaints, his barefaced cheek, his scattercash.

My father took no pleasure in buying things for my mother and me. There was nothing in it for him. He was generous in the pub; he believed in that sort of kindness, where near-anonymous men could think him free, and think him great. He didn't care if his family thought him great. He didn't want that. His wife and his child were his mother and father: a constant drain on his sense of himself, a pain in the arse, a bundle of bills, a wrongful call to responsible action. I can see it now: so much he resented our claims upon him. How sick that made him feel. The men in the pub could ask for nothing, and therefore anything was theirs. All the men in those pubs were the same. And they clung to each other with their sense of freedom. My father was the sort of man who would criss-cross the country, on behalf of a drunken pal he'd met twice, in search of some phoney tax-disc going cheap. Yet never once did he sit down with me and my homework. Not that I would have wanted him to. My homework was my own secret. And homework is a different kind of sickness.

So my father was using a walking stick before he was forty years old. And my mother had all the singing and dancing knocked out of her before she was twenty-five. She was an only child, her father dead in the Second War, her mother remarried and living in Australia. As a teenager she wanted the man who might take her away. She wanted a musician or a fast driver, someone to make her all over again, to take her places, two weeks a year on the Isle of Man, and the promise of laughs, and something new. And after all that an easy life, a series of days quite filled with colours. Goodness in the kitchen, the children in their beds. Some day there would be one of the new houses to make orderly. Other mothers, and bikes for Christmas, a lager-and-lime on a Friday night. The chance of hire purchase, a three-piece suite, wall-to-wall carpets, no time like the present. There'd be sex with a man called your husband. You would lie beside him night after night. A man who loved you. A man with his faults and no angel, but loving. She dreamed of the world she could just build up. They all dreamed of it. They could piece it together with time and love, and call it their own. The life they had made out of nothing special. The life they had made, their own small victory.

But my mother was half in love with chaos. She liked my father's hatred of his father, and encouraged me in my hatred of mine. With all her yearning for the ordinary life, my mother was born to admire outsiders. You could see she felt enlarged by drama and trouble, by the electric pulse of things going wrong, and her vision of the easy life remained in most ways a recurring dream. Though he killed half her life, and always took his hand to her, and never listened to a word she said, there was a part of my mother that found in my father's listless turmoil, his seething rancour, the features of a vast attractiveness. My mother and me, our little alliance, lay somewhere among the backroads, a place to run to in the uncoupling hours, those times of sense or savagery.

My mother was in love with him, and I never was. There was nothing in my heart for my father then. That is what I said. And my mother liked me detesting him. It left more of the lovable him for her, and made me a stranger to their understanding. Sometimes she would come to me at night, sit on the edge of my bed, and look at my models of engines and trains, stacked on the floor beneath us. 'We could go to Australia, you and me,' she would say. 'I want to leave him. He's a bad bastard.'

'Mum,' I would say, 'don't upset yourself.'

She would dab her eyes on the bedclothes, laying her head down next to my feet. The red on her lips, her old-seeming face, would shine, the light coming in through the top of the door. 'Jamie, you're a boy that likes history and flowers, and that's unusual. You build these wee engines and take them apart. I bet you'll end up planning houses like your granda. Your father was never good for anything.'

My mother would sometimes try to drink, just to be more in my father's world. But she would never try to read a book, or come along the beach, or take me into a towering building, just to be more in mine. And who could blame her? My mother was willing to let me go. She would rage and scorn, and hold me close for a minute, and promise to leave him to rot away. Yet she knew herself better. She would always go back in the end, and I would be left, quite happy alone, uncovering peace among boyish things, planning a future without my parents, in a world that believed in the things it said. My mother told me she believed what she said when she said she would love him in sickness and in health. She would say that, and would be right to say it, and would one day allow him to unsay the lot, and divorce her by Royal Mail. That is the sort of kindness my mother believes in. She's a better person than I could be. There are no vows between parents and their children.

The top of my shorts was made of elastic. It dug in. There was always a ribbon of red-ruckled skin appearing just over my hips. There was a summer's day, not long after we came to Ayrshire. I played at the door of a pub called The Unco Guid. The smell of the sea and the smell of the pub came on like one thing.

I remember my arms were out of the arms of my jumper. My hands stuck out the bottom, busy at Five Stones. I was more than good at that game. One stone up in the air – pick up two — catch the fallen — put them aside — nick off each pebble — scoop up the lot — toss them into the air again — good boy — and make them come down on the back of one hand. Good boy. My hand darted about the dirt as I sat against the brown tiles of the pub. The Spillers dog-food factory across the way.

Dogs were bad.

Saliva.

They were made to be just like their owners. Angry, barking, with stuff on their teeth. Men in Scotland make dogs be like them: aggression machines.

In Berwick you never saw people kick dogs, not like you did in Ayrshire. My father said he loved dogs. He would bring one in from the pub — docile, lost — and thereafter train it to bite people. He liked terriers most. Scots, cairns, wire-haireds, West Highlands. Little dogs with sharp teeth. Every one we ever had would pee itself at the sight of Robert. He beat them so much, and taught them the rule: to be scared of him. Any that peed would have their noses rubbed into the wet carpet, lashed with the leash, called all the names. The yelps and whimpers of those poor dogs. And yet how they'd dive up, and lick and kiss him, as soon as he showed some sign of affection. There was something of soft Judas in each of those terriers. By and by my father would take each of them away. He got sick of them. One day we'd wake up and the basket would be empty, the tins of dog food stacked in the bin. My father would go off with the shivering dog. A drive to the countryside. He would lose it there.

The dog-meat factory was over the road. Spillers, they called it. Spillers: 'The Happy Choice for the Happy Dog'. Cars went past in a hurry to somewhere. A little way off, under the clouds,

I could see cranes moving. New houses going up. People came along the street with their pushchairs. Some of the women would stop and bend down.

'You all right there, son?'

And yes I was all right thanks. Every hour or so I'd go on tiptoe and look through the glass, the wire-mesh glass at the top of the door. My mother and father sat in the corner, brown tumblers on the table, a jukebox hung on the wall behind them. That day I saw them kissing in the corner. She rubbed her hands in his hair. She kissed his neck. There was blue smoke swaying around the room. The noise of glass upon glass, and songs tailing off inside. And voices overlapping in the dark place. Big laughs. Coins crashing. Then suddenly someone pushed at the door. A man tripped into the day with his trousers loose, his red face shouting something.

'Away ye go,' he stumbled and said, his eyes all watery and wrong, the steps unsteady, his fingers yellow. 'Oot the road.'

My mother came out now and then. A packet of crisps and a tumbler of orangeade. 'Me and your dad are just talking, son,' she said. 'And we'll no be long.'

Salt and vinegar. My mouth was spiky and raw with the taste of them. My eyes watered. The tumbler smelt dark. I sat there for hours, the sky changing over. All the headlamps came on the cars. Blocks of light running past on wheels, the local buses, and the faces of people looking down from the upper decks. Some of the people spoke to each other, some snoozed gently against the window, and others looked down, with their big eyes vacant, passing the pub and the pavement and me. I thought who all of them were, making up names and jobs for them, and thinking of birthdays, and places they went on holidays. Where did they live? I thought of each person going now to a faraway place. I thought of them arriving at a well-lit kitchen, with children there, and the TV giving out the regional news.

I thought of them remembering me. Just as they lay in bed. The boy they passed on the bus through Barrhead. He sat at the pub door. Only a second. He sat there looking up, and waving a hand in the Esso-blue evening. The smile on the boy, a life not my own, and over the top of him, on the other side of the trees, a graveyard stood on the sloping hill. You could see the stones. You could see the light pass away through the branches of wych-elm, the green-winged samaras spinning down to the roof of the pub. Under it all was a smiling boy.

In a second gone.

I walked up and down to the bus stop. The smell of pies came down from the houses. We would go home soon. Some wind collected in the bus shelter. Cans lay about with their pictures of girls. Samantha. Terri. Joyce. The shelter was under the lights on the nearby flats. They were naked yellow. I sniggered at the way you could see the girls' tits. My eyes got fixed on some distant spot – a crush of lights I could see through the perspex wrap of the shelter.

A thought came down my kaleidoscope.

Here: me being in this shelter, at this time, holding on to these crushed sexy cans, the wind coming through, the lights as they are, the smell of pies. No one but me has been in this moment. No one is living my life but me.

Saltcoats was made up of lumpy steppe. A fading of fields, bleeding away to the Firth of Clyde. The sound of progress was shrill in those days. New main roads were gouged from the dirt tracks. Battalions of houses were drilled on the grass.

The new shopping centre was loud by the shore front; young folk clustered at the Amusements, a jangling all year round. And people came down to the broken sea wall for air. They came in buses every half an hour.

The town had always felt sleepy and late: a place of quiet endings, and lost industry. No more salt-pans or fishermen; little of coal or the iron smelt. A place of grass sidings that once were canals, a place of beaches, with ice-cream booths standing idle on the prom. The ghosts of Edwardian holiday-makers chattered in the breeze. Saltcoats had played its part in wars and explorations; it was apt to whisper its own small stories. We were full of its quiet backwaters, its drowsy hymns to the god of indifference.

Saltcoats was becoming somewhere new; no longer could it stand as it was, back from the world of great events. Old fields were filling, day upon day, with new-style flats, and model schools, and endangered families from other places. Mulligan's Pool, where children had swum on mild summer days, to the menacing sound of tractors and crows at their backs, was now engorged in a factory and car park, a company flag up a slippery pole, and local workers doing Japanese breathing out in the yard of a morning.

The name of the pool was a secret among the children. Mulligan the Irishman. He had drowned in the pool one night. Just after saying goodbye to the pigs. He had fallen in drunk. The new assembly workers hadn't heard of Mulligan. To children he was a known ghost. He lived underwater, in the moving shadows of all that was new, and all day and all night he tumbled down in the evil drink. The Japanese nation built a shed the size of the Pacific Ocean; everyone worked there. They flew in bosses and clocks from Osaka. But none of them knew about Mulligan's Pool. They dressed it to look like an Eastern pond. But we knew better. Mulligan span in the rootless dark.

The valley had once been a cup of old life. Not any more. Every day of my boyhood it was littered with something new. A glimmer of loading bays. Private golf links on the outer bounds. And giant superstores, fastened to the by-pass, and built in the style of the farmer's hut. The windows looked out on the road, and the girls inside had overalls and hairnets; girls in checks who were hurt by their boyfriends, and lazy or tired, they swayed all day with their price-guns. Beyond the windows were Barratt houses, and the seaside dead, and the Isle of Arran, some way off, like a silver smock laid over the horizon.

Yes, life went ahead in the mess of our town. From the head of it, on Ashgrove Hill, you could believe the heart of progress was hereabouts. The place was losing the look of old photographs. Reinforced concrete was gaining the light. But a single spire was still bold at the centre; it stood on its own, the Coade-stone bricks of the grey church spire. From our house on the hill it was eye-level. The other churches were bungalows. How very lonely that grey spire seemed. How very old. How old with its face of grey weather. And all round the town new houses came about. The harbour was closed, the quarry was flooded and spoiled. But there it was. Every day it was something new. And one grey steeple under the sun.

Breeze-blocks. The approved school at the Ferguson Loch was built with those bricks. And in my memory, in my heart of hearts, the common wind that whistled there is whistling still, and it fades to a moan in the corner of my dreams.

A few years after coming up from Berwick my father got a job as the cook at Ferguson. We moved into one of the company houses. It was built with the same bricks as the school itself. The rain was pouring that day we moved in. Our bits of carpet, our single beds. To my father that place was all of heaven. The house came along with the job. And the job came along with his romance of chaos. It gave him a home in the land of his fathers.

The school's governors loved him. To them he seemed street-wise. The kind of man who had understanding. A man ill-at-ease, who might easily handle the poor thugs there, the scrambling boys who needed his eye. The bosses loved him. They took his instability as a guarantee of experience. And sure enough the boys loved him too. He was just the father they'd sooner have had. Swore like a trooper, drank like a pagan, smoked like a bomber descending to earth. Like them he had a talent for resisting the everyday: all his delinquent nerve was ripe for those boys. He became a hero. My father had at last found his home and his station. It was a place where his vices could make him heroic: the Ferguson List 'D' School for Boys.

I used to waste time watching fish in the Ferguson burn. I'd guddle away the afternoons, in Wellington boots and a scarf new-made by my granny. It was there I would sometimes see the boys. The burn was full of old prams. Down at the bridge the flow was clogged with rotted leaves, and dammed with sticklebacked branches. The burn fell thick with cement; the water was dark under a hood of trees.

Dods of cement going by.

The boys were called absconders. Berry was one of them. He ran from the school every chance he got. The first time I saw him he was hiding in the castle, an old building next to the water, a pile of stones in grasses and bin-bags. He told me he was fifteen, and showed me his stings from nettles. He was someone I'd seen in my head before: one of those bundles of shivers in books. He said his father had tried to strangle him thirty or forty times or more. His house was in Glasgow. The old man had put his hands around Berry's neck until he nearly died. He would faint as his father did it. Now he said he had epileptic fits; sometimes, when I was with Berry, he would just fold up on the grass, and go like a piston. He was tall and lanky and his hair was black. He showed me a tattoo he cut into his knuckle with Indian ink. It looked sore. He was always running away. His father hated him. Berry told me he got sent to the school because he had run from his normal school in Glasgow. And he said he sniffed the glue sometimes. His mouth was all scabby.

Berry had a supernatural look on his face. He seemed that much older than he was. In another place, with other chances, he might have been a boy playing rounders in the evening, or learning the piano, making model planes, or seeing the point of sums. Berry was the first friend I had who was different from me. But our secret was the same. We shared it between us. We knew that our fathers hated us. Berry and I would meet at the burn. We'd walk to the beach, with me saying stuff about lugworms and weeds and the lobes of shells, all the news from that morning's ocean. A lot of times we sat in the dunes and looked out. Berry always said the same thing: he said he wished he could go on a boat, and sail it far to another place. Out past the lighthouse, in its unmanned calm. He said he would never look back.

'You could have a magic time in another country.'

Sometimes, when it was getting dark, we'd plan how to get him as far as Glasgow, where he could go and stay with a girl he knew, and one time I stole him a bottle of milk, and a handful of silver for the train. But they'd always bring him back to the school. Sometimes my dad would go to the police station and pick him up. And I saw how Berry thought my father was kinder than the others. 'At least he would hit you only for something bad,' he would say. 'And he buys us things.'

From my bedroom I heard noises. I would sometimes hear the boys shouting from their windows. The night would be dark, the water of the burn trickling in pitch blackness, the castle no more than a lump of cold stone, and the lights of the housing scheme over there a blind temptation, a cluster of unnamed hopes. The boys would scream for their mothers quite often. You could hear their cries across the fields. As if no one would hear on this distant night, they cried up high, sad words for their mothers. I couldn't believe all those boys in the school, so similar in distress, with eyes so like one another's. Their cries all sounded the same as well.

One night I came out of my room. I wondered if one of those voices was Berry's. I put on clothes over my pyjamas. A blue cagoule, and Nature Treks, my shoes that pinched, too small. I remember everything of that night – an owl we called Morgan up in the tree, the moon a red forewarning, the grass on the playing fields crunchy underfoot – and I made my way down to the school with a flashlight. Berry stood up at the window in only football shorts. I could see his face was melted with crying. The flashlight shone into the ground. Berry couldn't tell who I was. 'You are all bastards,' he shouted. 'I'll burn this place.' He shouted it over and over. 'I'll burn it to fuck.' It was like he didn't know what to do with himself. He banged his head off the window. He screamed like hell. And at the end of it all he just sobbed in his hands. 'I want to go home,' he said.

'Bastards,' he said.

The school's boiler room was a den of mine. It was always warm there. And on most Sundays I would go with a book. Just the sound of bubbling hot waters. Thick pipes ran around the walls and over the ceiling, alive with pipes and meters. It was dirty and loud and it smelt of oil. A cooling tower rose like a periscope from the back end. There was always a yellow and fizzing light. A single bulb. This night I turned the wet handle and walked forward with my flashlight. All the pipes seemed to rumble together – fired with a task I could only guess at – the humid air enclosing me, softening my hair, tingling my skin. An old school desk, half-jaked, lay in the corner. You could fix the bolts and make it good enough to use. I sat there contented a minute that night, quite lost in the maddening rumble. A host of questions danced in the greasy dimness: *What if none of us can leave this place? What are we doing here?* I thought and thought and wondered at it. *Can you ever go back anywhere? Can you ever go back?*

'Are you dreaming there?' said a voice behind the oil drums. 'Just remember: you're the daddy now.'

The voice was my father's. It dangled a cigarette in the black of the corner. 'Yes you're the daddy now.'

And the rumbling of the pipes seemed to fall away – just his voice in the heat. 'I bought you a rabbit, Jamie, you remember that? Your rabbit in the garage. I don't think you've been taking care of it now, have you? Your mother put it in the garage; you know it was a pest in the garden. It's in there by itself. And the ferrets, you know, have been sniffing around the edge. Tonight they might have found a way in. Your rabbit, Jamie. I don't think you've been looking after it the same. The ferrets are there. You ought to be a better daddy, Jamie. The wee bairns. Pitch black. And you with your books. Your shells around the lamp. Your maps. Your granda's tales of dead bricks. But the living things, Jamie. The wee bairns. Pitch black. And them depending on you, Jamie. I think the ferrets are in among them. Too dark in there. And you with your flashlight in this hot place. It's a shame, son. It's just no bloody good.'

Down fell the cigarette on to the oily floor. And nothing happened. He was gone. The sound of the pipes came back from beyond, and no one was there in the room. Just me and the heat and the naked bulb. And soon enough I was back in my bed. The owl shrieked in the tree. There was no rabbit of mine in the garage outside. The rabbit had died months before. One of us was lying. And yet my father was surely not out of his bed that night. He slept right through my bad dreams, and was silent there in the other room, his bed next to my mother's, as he followed nightmare shapes of his own. I had been alone in the boiler room. I only imagined he was near me. Or maybe he came to me later in a dream. I'm not sure: he seemed at the time to creep so easily into my head. His atmosphere lurked there. His cigarette burning in the dark; his mouth a malignant shadow.

My mother had a dog's life then. These were the years of our best alliance. She could never be true to me — I knew that already — but still we could stand together in the higher winds, side by side, making laughs out of nothing.

Every morning, from four until eight, she worked on the line in a baking factory, the Superloaf, and we'd meet halfway down the hill, and stand at an iron gate, rain or shine, to have our breakfast. This was our most open and peaceful time: a family moment for both of us. She would always have two hot rolls in her bag. A biscuit or two. A carton of milk. 'Never you mind,' she said more than once, 'you're just passing through here, Jamie.'

She would always say such things. And sometimes we would just laugh against that gate, the absurd business of our lives suddenly filling us up with hopeless mirth, and all our talk was of the daft things that happen. But she looked tired in her headscarf and cheap furry boots. 'You're a sketch,' she would say.

'You shouldn't have had me,' I said one time. 'You and him would've been fine then.'

'You're kidding,' she said. 'Some day you'll see what he was like with his own father. Problem with Rab is he can't understand people who aren't like him. You're your own boy already, Jamie. Never bother with him. But mind, he has a lot of time for you in his own way.'

Maybe I thought I could make my mother happier. I've never considered it much since those days. I allowed myself to think she had made her choice in life. Maybe she never really did. But the truth is my mother was something different from my father. She had all the simple courage that good people have. She went to her work; she brought me rolls; she stood by her useless husband. She was bright enough to see the point of other people's lives. She wanted them to do well. She believed that things would be all right for me, that time would be good. Only sometimes would she stop, and look at me, and see that I'd said a childish thing. And she'd know I was next to nothing underneath, and hug me for a minute, and then all my helpful intimations of adulthood would come to the rescue of both of us.

We laughed beside the gate. The mad things that happened

in our country, in our house. I always had questions about the last war. She didn't remember much. She told me no one would settle for that life now. 'The wars made us buck up our ideas,' she said, 'not that everything worked out.'

Every family was the same, she said. You had to make the best of it. 'Your dad's people were always very heavily into that. Politics and that. They used to give out leaflets in the street.'

The cows seemed to watch us with their big brown eyes.

'Tatty-bye,' she said. 'Sure and see you get good marks in the class. We don't want any dunces about the place.'

With a smile my mother would pad over the red-ash playing fields towards the school. I walked away. Now and then I would stop in the road. I picked leaves off the trees, held them up to the light. Sometimes I bit into them. Now and then I put a few in my schoolbag. The bag was full of leaves and things. The cows rolled their eyes. A drunkard was no big thing. Kids just had them at home. And sometimes teachers would offer a word of concern. But mostly they said nothing. Usually they'd come and ask if you'd had breakfast that day.

'*Si, al fresco.*'

'And is there a light in your house all right?'

'Well there's usually a fire on the living-room carpet. That tends to keep the bats out.'

That was the sort of thing I would say to them. Just to keep them off. Teachers would leave you alone after that. And also, because my father worked at an approved school, they somehow imagined that he himself might bask in a pool of approval. At any rate I would never say a word about him. Some kids would burst into tears in the class. Some would get themselves suspended, then toddle home for a beating. At my school there were two kinds of kid with a wasted parent. The first kind, the much more common kind, would sniff glue, chew mushrooms from the grass banking, break windows, sell their free school dinner tickets for cigarettes, never do a stroke of work, would end up in remedial, and dog-off as many days as possible. With glee and worry they would set fire to half-built houses, and attack girls in the playground, and eventually strike a teacher, and would one day find themselves expelled.

That was one sort at St Bridget's. The other bunch would stay in the library during the interval. They would ask for extra homework. They would run errands for the teacher. The smallest extra-curricular task would be theirs. They hid themselves in chores. They would see the teachers outside of school, and read them poems in the public parks. They would take out their vengeance and fury on exam papers. They would learn about computers and home economics, planning the life they could live one day, the day they got up, and got out, and away from all this. Any old thing that offered the chance of not being their parents. They would grasp their lives to themselves. Their voices stayed small in the class. They missed every party. They never had girlfriends or boyfriends or dope, they never crossed teachers, and feared any cause for a note to their parents. Those kids knew it was only a matter of years. Each one bided his time for the grand escape. They had heard of deliverance, and they tried to bring it on with an eager pencil.

I made a name for myself in Biology. The teacher was chestnut-headed, lipsticked, and wise. Her name was Miss McCardle. The boys insisted her name was Bunsen. I quite lost myself in her classes: in photosynthesis, in geotropism, in reproduction, in the intricate process of respiration. She was something, Bunsen. She let me see that the world was mine. Not mine alone, but mine too. She would choose me for experiments. She once pricked my finger — a gentle, hilarious spearing — and took some blood for a lesson on cells. We crowded around the microscope. 'You have good blood, Jamie,' she said.

'Aye, right,' I said.

She smiled. Bunsen could know a thing without asking.

I loved the things she could tell me. We spent whole hours with our heads in plants, breathing the smells of creeping ivy, tracking the veins of a Busy Lizzie. It turned me about, to know how things had ways of their own. How plants could grow. And how they could live and breathe and make more of themselves. Bunsen allowed me to visit the classroom after four. We sat at the back with dishes of agar jelly. We watched life happen, replicating cells. And over the months we made our own wine. We added yeast and laughed out loud. At Christmas we sat in her office with plastic cups.

'How civilised we are,' said the excellent flame.

'How wise and true,' said I.

My childhood was dotted with lucky islands. Mrs Drake, and the cockles of Berwick. Miss McCardle, the siren of Salt-coats. And even now and then my father's father. My granny Margaret. They gave me much more than other children got. More of the seas and the way soil worked; more of their own dear health. But Miss McCardle was something new: her hair, and the sweet-looking smile about her. I wanted to kiss her right on the lips. She told me just to behave myself. And that was that. I turned to my maps of how the world was: H_2Os and CO_2s. Waters. Carbons.

After hours, the classroom lights burned on in the early dark. And cleaners came in from the housing estates, silent with mops, lifting chairs, thinking of dinners, emptying bins. But Bunsen and I went on. She led me awhile in the mysteries of Chemistry. I got the periodic table off by heart. We discussed this metal, that mineral, and gas. She showed me what rocks were made of. We talked of how strong things were. What uses they had. And after months she helped me to Physics.

'The study of pressure and time,' she said.

I don't know why. I still don't know why. But all those lessons I had in that class were like heady prescriptions against future pain. They soothed me with reason. Her carefulness soothed me. Bunsen was a tireless exponent of her primary subject, Biology. 'It makes sense to know how the world is alive,' she said.

'Physics is brilliant,' I said for trouble.

'Indeed,' she said, 'the study of pressure and time. But don't forget life, Jamie Bawn. Don't forget life. Ecosystems. For living is all that matters in the end.'

The English teacher disliked me. He knew I was born in England. He was all for the Scots and the language of his forefathers, 'them that fought to unsheathe the iron tongue'. Or 'thim that focht tae unshith the iron tongue'. That is the way he spoke. Our Scottish voices were canons and cutlasses to him. Our every word was an argument-in-the-making.

He refused to wear a tie. He proclaimed loudly of Dunbar, of Fergusson and MacDiarmid.

'The poets of the heart and the head,' he said.

Or, the poyets ae the hert an' the heed.

'. . . who put themselves against the placid mutterings of our neighbours.'

Or, who pit theirsels agin the placid muttrins ae oor nee-bors.

He was funny to watch, our seaside warrior, our nay-saying bore, Mr Buie. He wore pitted shoes the colour of mud. His woollen trousers hung as mail bags on string. He'd a baby's cheeks, ruddy and soft, and waves of hair, a coastal shelf, in steady retreat from his awesome brow. His greying eyes were always on us. They spoke of long ago. They spoke of lost ground, lonely evenings, and sins.

Buie believed in a grand commonness: he spoke of real people; he spoke of oppression. We had never known anyone like that before. He wanted us to know that the way we spoke was a political matter.

'They'll try hard to take your language away,' he said.

That was Buie. There was always 'they'. He could never understand our lack of taste for abstract resentments. We knew who 'they' were all right. And most of them — the 'they' that we cared about, and who haunted us daily — were never so far as the other side of the Border. They snored in the room right next to ours, or dwelled long and nasty in a parallel street, and some took classes at the local school.

I got into a bit of a mess with Buie. He banned Mac-Diarmid's 'English poems' from the class. He wouldn't hear of Robert Louis Stevenson, except for those stories in braid Scots. He thought Walter Scott was a fascist. Buchan was a swine. Muriel Spark was a 'turn-coat London harpie'. I had two girl pals in the class. Buie had christened them Cleopatra and Beast. He thought they were skiving hussies and pests.

'You're like the moon, Bawn,' he said one day. 'And these two are your satellites, spinning through the air quite canny like, transmitting mayhem and chaos and disastrous noises!'

We fell about laughing. Buie was mental. But the words that

29

he spoke were more than just words: he believed in them. One day, he stepped out of the class after a signature rant on the Treaty of Union, and he failed to come back that day.

A wandering supply teacher came to our rescue. She spoke of American things. She spoke of Norwegian plays. And next day too she came in with her strangeness. She had gathered something of our class's infatuation with the native voice. 'Speech is not all there is,' she said. She went to the board and held up a book. 'This nation was not always so obsessed with the way it *sounded* on paper. For many years it paid great attention to other things as well. To the way it *thought*. The Scottish Enlightenment shows us that there is more than one way to make English Scottish. More than one way to write Scottish English. *A strong Scots accent of the mind*,' she wrote. 'Discuss.'

Buie came in before the end of the lesson. He listened a moment. His face was grey. He dismissed the girl with the bangled wrists. He asked me to wipe the board of words.

'That is my blackboard,' he said. 'It belongs to me.'

And he told me to leave not a trace of her chalk. 'A very good example,' he said, 'of the English propaganda.'

He gave us a lecture on the meaning of Utopia. He said it was a word that meant everything in Scotland. 'We all want to live there,' he said. He told us this place was built of hard work, and 'a strength of spirit', and bravery too, and your own unweakened voice. It was a place with a government. A place without wars. A land where we all lived equal. Bring on the future, he said. Bring us ourselves, only better.

'It's a place to be built,' said Buie. 'You begin by building it with your own hands, in your own minds, in your own hearts. Our fathers wore themselves away to make this true. That is the history of this century, and of others before us, going back to the Industrial Revolution, and further. And it must remain with us.'

He looked at me. 'That is right, is it not, James Bawn? The work of our fathers might give us hope.'

I put down my eyes to the desk. Maybe he was right and wrong. A strong Scots accent of the mind indeed.

And yet much of Buie has stayed with me. I have loved the poems that he loved. I grew to perceive the beauty in them. They have been on my lips ever since. They will always mind me of my grandmother's yearnings; of all our yearnings. They bleed somehow, in their Scottish way, into my love of Miss McCardle, and now, with time, they colour the life she once pushed me to know.

They were poems of Biology and Physics. Poems of Geography. Poems of Breathing.

Mr Buie held fast to his ground. He never saw any other ground like it. He heard no words but his own rising up. Mr Buie was much like us. He dreamed of knowing the future, and he woke up knowing the dead.

My grandparents Hugh and Margaret had moved that year. They moved to the light of the eighteenth floor in a high-rise up the coast. Hugh was a famous Housing man. His whole life rang with the question of better housing. He was known as the man who had pushed the tower blocks. He believed they answered to people's needs. He believed in those blocks to the end of his life.

And he always said he could live in one himself. And as sure as his word he came one day. He joined the disgruntled people in the air. I was thirteen years old, and it was our third year at Ferguson, when Margaret and Hugh made the journey west. The journey for them was a long one somehow. But for me the journey was shorter: Hugh is the basis of everything I know. But that soft day of the annual fair, when the ancient burgh was throbbing in colours, and New Town lairds were ringing the changes, and each in their cups went across the moor, good Hugh Bawn came into his tall house, a pot of tea beside the stainless sink, a shore of clean air, a view from the window, a place that seemed like a palace to them. There were no red ribbons on the taps that day. My grandparents came as the band passed on. But the dauntless Hugh came up those stairs, quietly keeping his vision intact. These were the houses they had lived to build. And here his life was to come full circle.

His years as the Housing supremo were waning. His years as my godsend took over instead. We became separate halves of one another. He told me over and over again how I was his younger self. But still he believed in the man he used to be. No love was lost between his Glaswegian glory and him. That's what he said, and that's what we thought at the time. But Hugh had seemed to have the gumption to make himself new. Down he came to the Ayrshire coast with his bells and his books and his flow charts intact; he had old stories in his possession, and elderly hopes to burn. But he wouldn't retire. He would never retire. He came to the New Town with a mind to assist in the planning of all the new housing. He came like a king to a half-rural seat. I was nervous, but glad he had come.

I began then to visit in secret. I was learning Hugh's trade, and helping my granny with her flower stall at the harbour. During those years at the Ferguson school my visits to Glasgow had been too few. I was in their house there a dozen times. But seeing them had soothed me greatly in those wastes of time. Strange as it was, and given their age, and all Hugh's intolerance in the matter of ideals, it was these old folk who gave me my life, and who best represented the future for me. Their new flat was a mausoleum to future prosperity. Their feeling for the past gave me hope for the future, and awakened my sense of the livable times ahead. Hugh was to teach me what all of this meant. My father's illness had belittled us. He loathed all time. He saw only lies. My granda Hugh had his own desperate heart. His westward flight was not all it seemed. But that was for later. In the sorry glare of my first teenage years the appearance of my grandparents was all of a rescue.

It was the last year of my time at the Ferguson home, the very last months with my mother and father. Things were finally coming apart. My father's mind was not right. It was never right. Only the years would make me see this. But the job at Ferguson had seemed so hopeful, so right for him as he was. And even there, in the worsening light, we thought he might gain, and shake off the self that had raged near to death down in England. But the darkest time had arrived. It would pass, and then I would go, and all those Ferguson days would seem hopeless and grave. They would ever after seem cold. The unspeakable hours. Only now, with this distance of time, and my life in Liverpool, can I let those shadows cross to the page. My grandfather said I should tell our story. A summons to heaven or hell he said. And now I can see our days spread out. The way we were in that place of ours. The last days at Ferguson were the worst of our lives. And it was Berry too. Berry brought those hours to a head.

It was the day of my Holy Confirmation. I was taking the sacrament late. My father had twice set light to the form.

Hugh and Margaret took the whole thing over. It was important to them that I followed the faith, and somehow it mattered to me as well. I wanted it more as my father did less. I went in the morning to the high flat at Irvine. Margaret fed me porridge oats dusty with salt. She sang me her hymns as she unwrapped a new white shirt. 'St Michael's', it said on the label. Hugh came into the kitchen with his own talk of saints. He said he had given it some thought.

'Alexander,' he said. 'I think your Confirmation name should be Alexander.'

He said his mother would have liked that. And there was the end to it. None of us thought it a bad name. Margaret drove me down to Affleck, down to St Joseph's, in her sweet-smelling car. 'You're an angel among us,' she said. 'Give your confession first to the priest. We'll be back along in time for the Bishop.'

St Joseph's was a modern chapel. The roof slanted way to the floor. Everywhere was concrete and pine; the lights were electric. The faces on all the statues were odd. A crooked mouth, a bold eye. None of them was smooth or hallowed or ancient, none like the saints we'd seen in books. They looked like people we knew. They were not mighty faces, in just repose, or caught there purely, in serene rapture. They were faces cut with modern woe, or fixed with some current passion. The statues were all sharp lines. Long-fingered, large-haloed, bleeding from all the small wounds. And Mary was not like the Queen of Heaven — she looked like the girls in supermarkets, with her hair gathered up in the regulation way, and worry all over her face. But the smell in the church was the smell of old time. The electric lights hung apart from the candles, which burnt the last of their wax, under the altar's canopy. They were wagging tongues of flame. The yellow fire just licked at the air and was gone. A new candle was placed on the altar as I stood at the door.

Father Timothy took confession in a room. We knew him from school. He was young for a priest. A wave of hair rolled over his forehead, a glade of Scots pine stood green in his eyes. He was in love with the boys. We all knew that. He would kiss you at confession and nobody worried too much. You would sometimes find yourself kissing him back, and opening your mouth, and liking it then, when his tongue was warm and spreading all over your lips. At other times you would think it was bad. There was no alarm in the thing for me. You just sat on the chair, saying your sins, and he touched his body in a soft-seeming way, your act of contrition going out for the both of you. But it never felt like harm with Father Timothy. Not to me anyhow. He always smelt so nicely of soap. The kissing was nothing much: a quick lie-down in the laughing grass. And many a thing could be worse. There were worse things than being secretly kissed in the small afternoon by a young priest shaking with nerves.

'Don't say to Father Healy,' he said, his pupils black as the Calvary sun.

I don't know. Father Timothy was kind and bad all at once. But at least he was kind. His nice way with words made me open my mouth. And sure as all that I had wanted susceptible hands on my face. For years he always had two or three boys he called special.

'I haven't been to mass since Christmas.'

'I smashed a crate of milk bottles into the burn.'

'I called Mrs McIntosh an old fat cow.'

'I said fannies and tits to the janitor.'

And often enough he'd say that was all right.

'That's all right. Take off your tie.'

And he'd kiss your neck a dozen times and lay his head on your shoulder. Often enough my arms went around him. I'd pull him in closer.

'Everything's all right,' I'd whisper. 'Everything's fine.'

Father Tim was there the day of the confirmations. He sat in his room with his clean smile. His face was glowing with hard prayers and lust.

'You're the elderly boy here today, Jamie,' he said. 'And how's tricks at home?'

'My Confirmation name's Alexander,' I said. 'Is that not a good one?'

'Good as any,' he said. 'But that'll be later on. Let us start with your Prayer Before Confession.'

He drew his head in close. 'James Alexander . . .' he breathed.

I didn't want his kissing today. I picked up the sheet with the Order written on it.

'James,' he breathed again. There was a smell of after-shave on him.

He pressed his face down into my neck. 'Don't,' I said.

But there had been other days when I'd held him there. I remember the first time it went further. He was kissing me in the way that he did. I let him loosen my tie and kiss my neck. The slow seconds caused a change of some sort. A moment's heat. And then, with no less care than command, I placed his hand on the front of my trousers. He took down the zip. He brought me out. With tenderness, with a steady hand, he began to stroke me there in the room. I wanted to laugh. I thought I would cry. I pushed the hair out of my eyes. I wasn't sure of the room that day. But I didn't move, and the father went on, and to fill the silence I read out the prayer from the Order, and strained away from the young man's kisses, but let him go on with my cock in his hand, and the words growing louder, my eyes going up to the brightening window. My faltering breath. I read what I could.

'. . . behold me, O Lord, prostrate at Thy feet to implore Thy forgiveness. I desire most sincerely to leave all my evil ways, to forsake this region of death where I have so long lost myself . . .'

My breath was filled with worry. It came out in shorter and shorter gasps.

'. . . and to return to Thee, the Fountain of Life. I desire, like the prodigal child, to enter seriously into myself, and with the like resolutions to rise without delay and go home . . .'

His eyes were closed. The light from the window fell on his hair. 'God,' I thought. 'God almighty. What am I doing here?'

'. . . to my Father, though I am infinitely unworthy to be called His child, in hopes of meeting with the like reception of His most tender mercy. I know Thou desirest not the death of a sinner, but that he may be converted and live.'

But on my Confirmation day I held him back. I didn't feel threatened by Father Timothy; I just felt there were other things to be thinking about. I was getting older. Things were sad at home. And this was the day of my Confirmation.

My grandmother was my sponsor. She was certain I knew what I had to know, and was ready for the Church.

'It's only a life of total commitment, being of the Catholic faith,' she said.

Hugh sat at the front rail as I walked up. He smiled at me in his black tie.

'Alexander,' I said.

The Bishop touched my face.

'God be with you,' he said.

A small smell of after-shave hung about the air. James Alexander. Walking back to the kneeling bench I was pleased with God and myself.

Our house at the Ferguson school had become all damp. Water rose up through the floorboards; blackening fungus crawled over the walls.

A house of paper and powder and weeds.

It smelt of dead carpet. You could watch your breath in every room. It went to the ceiling in corpulent puffs. Woodlice nested in the skirting boards. Slugs would drag along the bathroom floor, trailing their vestments of brown slime. Every room in the house at Saltcoats was thick with alien spores. Nature had come inside.

The net curtains were planets of watery growth. The Japanese lightshades hung from the ceilings, spinning with cold, greenly alive. Spiders made caves in tiny brass ornaments, and fieldmice licked at the kitchen-damp fruit, wild mushrooms and fungal berries, which bled poison from the soaking plastic of the plug sockets. I didn't like the cold there, but the daily encroachments that came in with the cold, and rose with the water, were fine with me. The chaos of plants added some grace to that house of disaster. The animals were vile.

On Confirmation Night my father went over the edge. The house got robbed. I was lying there in my bed; all the bulbs were cold. Darkness crept over us. But for all that dark there was something of the moon. A glow that came down over the trees, and picked at the burn, and spilled through my bedroom window. For hours I lay there awake. The damp patterns on the wallpaper held me there, bright-eyed, unsleeping. The patches looked like the shapes of countries. There was India. Japan and France. The whole of Ireland a black furry smudge. Dublin dense on the paper's seam. The North blinking out as the ceiling meets the sea.

A run of Crete on the far side. A dipple of Falkland Islands. I lay there not sleeping for hours.

A bark from my father's dog downstairs. A door is closed. I can hear my mother and father asleep as I move across the landing. The living-room window is open. I stand in front of it. My feet in a squelch of sodden carpet. The curtains are disarranged, and my mother's ornaments are smashed on the floor. Her glassy swans, her porcelain peasants, the plastic flowers that are held in arrangement, the base of their stems well trapped in a crumbly sponge.

When I look out the window I see in the grass a golden-painted Buddha. From its bed of green blades it smiles a smile of uncomprehending calm. The moonlight is there. It is down among us. I close the window and go up the stairs. Everything is wrong. Nothing makes sense any more.

I was frozen in bed. Scared to death. And up the stairs I could hear him coming. Footfalls deep in the other room.

I could hear my parents breathing as they slept. More noise came from the landing. My lips were exhaling milk-clouds in the dark. And then, with some gentle, inevitable sound, the door of my bedroom swung towards me. He walked to the table beside my bed. It was my friend Berry. He looked at me. His hair was blond at the ends and black at the roots. Different hair. His eyes were somewhere else. He put a finger up to his lips. Noiselessly he said the word no. He held my eye. I didn't move. He opened a plastic bag and began putting things in. Small binoculars off the table. He took a penknife. A clock in the shape of a tree. He took some football boots I'd never worn. He put it all in the bag. I remember the Indian ink on his hands. The smell of gas; his presence.

He turned to me just as he reached the door.

There was a far-away smile on him. It said goodbye. And it said other things too. 'Who cares?' 'So what?' And it somehow said that I'd never see him again. I put up my hand before he turned, and bent the fingers into the palm. 'Bye, Berry,' I whispered.

In the morning my father went mad. Someone had torched the boiler room at the school. And our house was robbed. The police thought it must have been the same person. My father couldn't believe we hadn't heard an intruder walking the carpets at night.

'We could all have been murdered in our fucking beds,' he said over again.

I just sat on the sofa with a book. 'You sure you heard nothing?' he shouted. I looked in front of me, shook my head. The fire brigade stopped an explosion at the school. 'Has no fucker you know been in and out the house?' he shouted again. 'They took stuff out of every fucking room. Think!'

There was nothing to do but shake my head. After the firemen left, and the police took fingerprints, my mother went about with a damp cloth, picking up ornaments, wiping them off. (The house might have been damp, a blackness of spores, but my mother was always trying to keep it tidy. She liked an ordered surface. Tidy meant much more to her than clean.) My father stood in the middle of the room. He was white all round his mouth. A bottle of vodka stood on the telly, and every time he broke from the shouting, every time he paused for breath, he would reach for the bottle and take another slug.

'Fucking hell!' he kept saying. 'I'm going off my bastarding head here.'

I sat there all day. I tried to keep thinking of the words in the book. Reading the same line over and over. 'Sleep no more,' and 'Sleep no more.' Sleep no more.

My father beat up the dog in the kitchen. It screamed and yelped the morning away. The dog was first for the blame. It had failed to bark. It had let itself be shut in a cupboard. He beat it sore, until it peed the carpet. Then he beat it some more for that.

'People are trying to drive me off my fucking head!' my father shouted.

They stood at the top of the stairs. I was below when my mother asked him to calm himself down. He just slapped her hard, sudden hands hammering at her face. She put up her arms to cover herself, and asked him, so quietly, to stop.

'Don't, Rab. Please.'

Some horrible thing happened inside. At the bottom of those stairs, me standing full-eyed, the dense tinder of a dozen years and the spark of two strange days flew suddenly together. I was off the spot, and up the stairs, two at a time, and ready at the top with something of a punch, a roar of hatred, so mad to crush my father's bullying rage. A glass table overturned. A vase full of peacock feathers smashed to the floor. I beat at his face with two small fists. I spat at him. I booted his stomach once he was down. Tears and spittle flying towards him. My mother screaming between us. I could hear my own voice. It was out in the distance.

'I'll fucking kill you!'

Again and again the voice roared out. All the time it was me. My father lay in the corner among the glass. His mouth was cut. And I'll never forget that look in his eyes. It was seethingly calm. It was calm, but the gleam of murder was there. And it was with me as well, my father's son.

Coldly he lifted a part of the broken vase.

'I'll be waiting for you,' he said. 'Your sparrow's punches are nothing to me. I'll be waiting.' And he jabbed the sharp edge into his arm.

On the vase, on the wallpaper, gouts of blood.

My mother screamed but I couldn't hear her. Everything slowed to a pulse. There was nothing there but my own heart's sound in my ears. My own heart pounding. My father's blood all over the broken glass. My father mad in a pool of blood. My own heart's sound in my ears. I ran down to the garden and threw up.

It's the eye of childhood that fears a painted devil.

For weeks after the robbery my father would hide in the bushes. After dark, with a bowie knife, he'd sit and wait for the thief to return. Concealed there, alone with the vodka, his rabbit's eyes all pink-rimmed and ready, and no one came to vindicate his mood. He would never get over it. They had come into the house with us all asleep. He didn't believe that I knew nothing of it. The robbery affronted him. My father thought himself smarter than that. To be robbed in your bed. What an insult. That was the sort of thing that happened to other people.

'To cunting idiots.'

He himself would hear the latch if it was lifted. But no he didn't. Berry was next to his bed. And the thought broke him in two. It was one of the odder things about my father when he was younger: he was a threat to us all those years, and yet he couldn't tolerate the thought of others threatening us. We were his to threaten. We were family. And we were his. We belonged to him. Didn't we? It drove him mad to think of a stranger standing next to our beds at night, and him asleep. It drove him mad.

The Ferguson List 'D' School for Boys was a failure then. For some of those years I had thought it might hold off the crack-up. But at the time, with my dad as he was, there might have been no such place on earth. The school fairly helped him at first – imagining those boys thought well of him – but he knew that our house must have been robbed by one of them. He knew that. Only boys like the ones at Ferguson could carry off such an affront. Nothing, though, nothing at all, had let him believe they could do it to him. But one of them did. And his own son helped him.

Although I was soon to run from all this, from the Ferguson school and my father's sickness, I won't now stand apart from those days, and say I did well, and made proud, and think him the only bastard. In one way or other we all did badly then. And the school was a rotten world in itself. The searchlights kept us all bleached and lonely. We all cried some from our windows. Behind the trees, the dark water flooded its mucky banks, the castle stood behind fences, its dungeons a lesson in history. At the end we were all so small-voiced, so lost. I don't know how it happened. That season of mirk would take years to thin out.

The rain came hard on the red-ash field one night. The water lapping under our beds. I walked out the front with my slippers on. I put my hand in the bushes. 'Come on, Dad,' I said. 'Come inside, it's raining.' And how he trembled as I drew him away by the hand, and how he spoke to himself. His raw rabbit's eyes. Yes I know that too. Robert went up to his bed that night and slept the coldest sleep of us all.

All my life I have dreamed of the sea. Our waters. And the long walk around the coast of this island. I feel the difference in the rocks; I see the sand and its glinting deposits, the play of weather on land and sky and spray. They live in my memory: the colours of Scotland and England. With a bucket and spade I walk the length of Hadrian's Wall in a silver shower. Salt on the lips. My sandals wet. Every stone broken and loose. A fresh song rises to nowhere and nothing. I make my way to another beach.

My thirst for the sea. I know of a home I have never known. A liquid bed by some easy beach. I know it well in my sleep. The coast is unclear. The landmarks are ruined or new. Yet water knows nothing of nations. It is called after them — is claimed by them — but water is only itself. The pure green sea in my dreams is all the world I have ever known. And yet I have never been there. It is only water. It is only a dream. And still I drown there each night in my sleep. And still I look out for the coast as I wake.

I went a lot to the beach in my last week at Saltcoats. My father was worse every day. It was odd to see the sand under snow, as if the sea-foam had stepped from the waves, and it lay here and there, a white crackling on the rind of the coast.

Mrs Drake had been right those years ago in Berwick. I wondered was she still alive. Was she sighing and breathing yet? Or did she one day fall with her spade, the North Sea ripping the air about, a squall of kittiwakes marking the shore, and the old woman dead, like nothing was nothing, and breath just slipped away? The thought of her lying there. Her hand across the shore she loved. Her skin cells flaking in the sand.

Her ink was still clear in the note at the back of *The Sea Shore*. I kept it to hand. Her favourite line from Thomas Hardy: 'Who can say of a particular sea that it is old? Distilled by the sun, kneaded by the moon, it is renewed in a year, in a day, or in an hour.'

I walked up the town from the shore that night with a sense of coming change. Aldo's chip shop aglow in the early dark. Young men gathered at the window-cage. The sound of their heels as they bashed against it.

You followed the towpath that came from the shore, where our Ferguson burn ran into the sea. You stuck to the path at the housing project, and found the old bridge, the castle still, and up through the trees you passed towards the school. The path was all ice as I walked along. There was sometimes a silence on the housing schemes at night. Every house glowed orange. You'd hear a dog's bark. A baby crying. Somebody whistling to a bedroom window. But mostly it was quiet on a night like this. The washing lines, the whirligigs, were hung with icicles, and the roads were slurried with grit. One or two chimneys blew smoke at the edge of the scheme. But hardly any. The hum in the air was from pylons; a cold and nervous electrical hum.

After all this time I took in the street names. I stopped and looked at them. I had passed through the housing scheme blind until then. A grid of twelve streets. I wandered that night from one to the other; wandering slowly, the pavement all ice, a deep-lying chill in the tarmacadam bones.

Keir Hardie Drive.

John MacLean Drive.

Sandy Sloan Drive.

James Maxton Drive.

Arthur Woodburn Drive.

Helen Crawfurd Drive.

Tom Johnston Drive.

Jean Mann Drive.

Hugh Murnin Drive.

William Gallagher Drive.

John Wheatley Drive.

Campbell Stephen Drive.

I had thought I would never know those names, and soon I would never forget them. My coming years with Hugh made me know them, and the years since then have made them strange.

But that frosted night I wanted to know them. The cold in our house made it clear all at once. I looked from the window at that sudden paradise of sodium yellow. The housing scheme. My grandfather's plans. There was my new life out there. Our modern housing. There it was, yellow through the trees. Street after modern street, named for the receding glory of dead socialists.

Our new windows. They deflected none of my father's old

pain. He was coughing up blood and refusing the doctor. He was so much younger than he liked us to know. But there he was, in that swamp of a house, spitting up blood in an ashtray, calling out names with his chin on his chest. My mother was white. The staff at the school just passed without blinking.

One night a policeman brought him back to the house in a van. They had found him down in the centre of town, lying in the snow, his red hair frozen to the pavement. The police had taken him to Casualty, and one of them brought him back. The officer said they had to cut his hair. They cut his hair to get him off the street. He was frozen to the ground. He was lucky to be alive, he said. Nearly lost him, he said. Must get help for him, before it's too late.

My mother sat him down on a stool in the living room. She brought in all the fires she could find. He was shaking like nothing. She sat him there. She gave him a can of lager.

'No more whisky,' she said.

And then, with all care, with all the patience there is in the world, she evened up the hair all around his head. His red curls dropped under the blunt scissors. Red leaves down to the carpet. I thought of his hair still frozen to the pavement. Down there, in the town, those frosted hairs where he nearly died.

Fear is what remains of Ferguson for me. Cold fear. And the thought that we all might die in the night. And time was so slow in going out. My last day passed so slowly. Ashen-faced, unkindly, a morning after my own heart.

I was standing in striped pyjamas at the crack of dawn. Thirteen years old. Standing at the window in my parents' bedroom. No one was there but me. My mother was working

47

at the Superloaf; my father was out there tearing up space. The day cracked open like an oyster. There was salt spread on the road, and the grass was white with unmarked snow, like a field of pan bread. Nothing but likeness that grey-filled morning. Nothing but like.

Our trees like the movement of three witches' fingers.

The clouds like the man in Mulligan's Pool.

And me like my father in his father's boots, watching for nothing along the road, keeping an eye out, chittering cold in that upcoming Baltic sun. My head was different that day. And then I saw my mother limping up the path. A black knot she was – the white sky behind, the snow beneath – and she moved up the path with her scarf round her head. I could see there was something wrong with her.

I sat on the edge of his unmade bed. The smell of him about it. I could see the stairs from where I sat, and could hear her footfalls, one at a time, and the way she whimpered in her sore throat. She was crying on the stairs. A horrible dread came over me at I sat there. The sound of her trouble. I could hear it as she moved up the stairs, and could see it as she stepped on to the landing. Both hands on the bannister, the scarf around her head. It wasn't a sound I knew. Not anger or unhappiness, not disappointment or woe, not embarrassment, not resentment, not regret. The sound in the hall was the sound of pain. She was hurt. She was crying like a child. The slow, thick whimper of the suddenly injured. I rose from the edge of the bed as she came to the bedroom door. The look of her will bother me all my life.

She couldn't keep up with her breath. She drew off her scarf in the pale doorway. My own breath went out to soothe her. Her forehead was swollen and dark. Her cheek was grazed from the eye to the chin. Blood ran from a wound on her lip. My eyes were lost in the shocked space between us. Like a child she wept. Our eyes joined across the metres of festering carpet. A look unknowable. And some wordless seconds we passed there in hell together. 'He ran after me,' she said. 'It wasn't his fault. I argued with him in the road. He pushed me away. I ran and ran. It was dark. I fell at the rocks. My face is sore, Jamie. Get me a cloth. It wasn't his fault.'

I held her fast and weeping at the door. 'I'm going to kill him,' I said.

The rest of the day she spent in bed. I fixed up a lamp beside her. There was something numb about Alice as she lay on those pillows. She didn't say much, and didn't flinch as I cleaned her face, dabbing the sores with TCP.

'Why did you marry him, Mum?'

'I loved him, son,' she said.

In the afternoon he came back to her side. I walked up the stairs with a cup of tea. He sat on her bed with his head on her knees. A waste of tears. Her hand just stroked at his scissor-marked hair. I put down the cup by the bed, and he turned. 'It was an accident, Jamie. She fell on the road.'

'And you left her there,' I said. 'Don't look at me. We're finished.'

My escape came sooner than most. I woke in my bed one day with sore legs, just a kid with sore legs, and I told the parents I couldn't walk. An ambulance came to the school. They lifted me out of bed. My mother stepped into the ambulance too. We were never meant to return. There was nothing wrong with the legs. I just woke up, that's all, and the sun was coming through the net curtains. A fearsome promise in the sun that morning, scorching out the damp on the walls, the countries and glaciers and lost forests, burning through my framed certificates of First Communion and Confirmation, and in the vast white heat of the moment I knew it was time to go. I couldn't live our life any more. So I faked the legs. And in the Kilmarnock Infirmary I spoke to my mother in a new way. 'I'm off,' I said.

'Where are you off to?'

'To fuck,' I whispered, 'and don't say stay or anything else cause I'm gone.'

The doctor waited by the gurney. He looked like one who had spent his life just combing his hair. I spoke to the mercy of his white coat.

'I like history and flowers, me,' I said.

'Shut up,' he said. 'Can you not see that you're upsetting your mother with this talk?'

'And buildings with windows going all the way up.'

I felt sometimes like I wanted to die. My mother's grazes. We wept beside the choking lifts. I could think of nothing but the lunatic smell of the wards. 'I will go and stay with Granny and Granda,' I said in the end.

And my mother, she walked away. She always wore a nylon apron. Even when not doing the house, or tidying herself away from the world, she wore a checked apron. I don't think she had many clothes to wear. And as she walked away in tears that day, making off down the corridor, a wounded animal, I felt I might just freeze there for good. She couldn't help me; I couldn't save her. No longer could we even calm each other down. I stood on my shaking legs, my head on the public phone. I wanted to smash those walls, or dial God, or fling myself down the lift shaft, shouting last things in a loud voice. But there was nothing to do. My granda's voice came on to the line.

'Jamesie, my boy,' the old voice said, 'that's right. You're somebody who likes our new buildings, and you liked Nana's flowers. Remember? Come here to your room.'

He said I would do my exams some day.

'You'll be clever about it. Come to your room. You know your nana and me, we love to show you all the things. We have your chemistry set here. And new books.'

That was more or less the end of my mother and father and me. I wouldn't see them for many years. And it has taken these years to begin to know them.

It was that simple, and that hard. Mother going down the corridor, her apron covered in hospital light, my father sick at home, killing us all with his sadness. The sight of her walking away that day. She was a young woman, and all the fine strings of her being drew her back to the man we had once agreed to hate. And now she might lie beside him until the clocks had stopped. Of course I knew nothing. She couldn't just leave him alone with his bottles. And so there I was: my first grand act of selfishness complete.

I stopped all the crying. The polished tiles under my feet suddenly shone upwards, and I could see my face glowering back at me. My teen jeans and Lions' T-shirt. All the distant hospital noises came at last. My mother would be on the bus now back to my father. A steady breathing came back to me. Something was settled. There was no way I could ever miss that house of ours.

That was how I came to live in the flats at Annick Water. My grandfather's home was bright. The radiators burned in the evening, and wood-chip paper covered the walls, clean from ceiling to living-room floor, and white, a high room over the New Town, books and pictures and an early start. There were no pretty poisons or fungal walls, none of that old creeping darkness. There was only the past of Hugh and Margaret, the past of their people, the country, and buildings. I thought I knew what the country was made of. They said no, no: come along with us. 'There are ruined buildings in the world,' said Hugh, 'but no ruined stones.'

Hugh then called me his project. He gave me his books, his tools, and his names for everything. He spoke of the busy years that had made our day. All the secrets of Scottish housing came to me first hand. Not all of them – not Hugh's stone privacies – but the tricks of the trade, and the tale of our family's bid for Utopia. I heard of trades unions. I heard of saints. But mostly Hugh told me of building bricks, of clays, and slates, and cements, and steel. He told me the cupola of the Church of San Gioacchino was covered with aluminium sheeting in 1897. He told me how asbestos tiles clad the Empire Stadium at Wembley in 1923. He drew me a map of the bitumen source, the great Pitch Lake in Trinidad. He spoke of plastics, and resins, and 'rainwater goods'; he spoke of plasterboard. Hugh showed me love, and he showed me the scope of his love, of Margaret, and me, and reinforced concrete.

Three miles or so from the Ferguson school I found a place in another world. A place of disciplines and hopes. A valley of information. A well-lighted room. And Hugh and Margaret were people of no small understanding. We went to the rivers, and over the hills of Kyle and Carrick, the ferns and trees all listening like me on the headland, and Hugh with his words, full flood on the moor. Gran Margaret corrected his names for the families of flowers. And down below us the coast of Ayrshire was mute. The sea and the coast were quiet below, there in the lights of old January.

2

The Night Stairs

So the moon is up there. I see it fine. And know that an eye is looking down. It must see the earth that we can't see, and also see me, a stranger slumped on a racketing train, a yellow train on the marshes this night, gathering speed, and Ayrshire out there, a moon-drunk whore in the dark. This light from the sky, it travels right down the years to find us.

And years had passed since the train out of Berwick. Here I was on a different train. There was little of the boy I used to be in the face that stared from the darkened window. I sat alone in a charcoal suit. A thirty-five-year-old man on a train. I was coming back to Ayrshire to see my grandfather. The smell out there, the shadows. They were all that I knew and remembered. The fields were black. The trees were crooked past a gauze of rain.

The word in my head was carbon.

The vegetable origins of coal. The decomposition of old trees and shrubs. You imagine you smell it in the Ayrshire fields. The breath of everything; the black seams underground. The layer upon layer of carboniferous fruit. And as I

54

grew up there were men still mining the land of its antique load. But now they live on the surface again. Except for our fathers now planted. The ones now dead, and carboniferous fruit themselves. The ides of geology — a memory of loss.

Carbon. It led out my thoughts as the train came down.

The racketing, racketing train.

I thought of the carbon exhaled in the breath of those living. The stuff absorbed by those meadows outside. The atoms deep down, in the coal out there — pressure and time, pressure and time — which had gone from the tiny expanse of our lives. I thought of the carbon in crude iron ore — burning away, burning away — but keeping enough for to make it good steel. The train and the fields and the houses and me. Of course we were one on that journey back. The slow train's rhythm sending me out. Pressure and time, pressure and time.

The sight of a Gorbals tower block had put me back with the carbon again. The metal beams; my grandfather's hopes.

I breathed out hard in the empty carriage. You could see the breath like cotton in the air. I was going home.

Carbon combines with sulphur and hydrogen. With iron it forms steel; and it unites with copper into a carburet, as observed by Dr Priestley.

My mind fell back with the heave of the train.

Our fathers were made for grief. I could see it now. And all our lives we waited for sadness to happen. Their sunny days were trapped in a golden shag box. Those Scottish fathers. Not for nothing their wives cried, not for nothing their kids. Cities of night above those five o'clock shadows. Men gone way too sick for the talking. And how they lived in the dark for us now. Or lived in our faces, long denied. And where were our fathers? We had run from them. We had run and run. My life had been miles and miles away. Until this October.

The train screamed into a black tunnel.

Scotland again. We all sprouted up in these valleys of mirth. Possible fools with bigots for fathers, losers for husbands, and mean, mortal hours. And only the prospect of living in their wake, and one day becoming just like them. And how we were taught to wear our endowment lightly. A purple thistle sewn to the pocket of a school blazer. But hard drink had ever been the only promise. The only promise, and nowhere named in our history books.

I was coming back home with a hope to escape again soon. I thought it could make no difference to me. This other country. This place of the past. It couldn't detain me long. Outside the train I could see the lights, the spangled bands of once-modern houses.

Carbonaceous.

A heap of bones, a wrecked carbuncle. Flooded with streetlamps: the Hutchinson Charity School at Paisley. In a second we passed by its ruins. My granda Hugh Bawn once named him the only poet, a man who had taught in that school, John Davidson. And Margaret would have none of him. Davidson, the devil of Barrhead. The antichrist. The blether of science. 'God through the wrong end of a telescope.' The self-killing man.

But to us John Davidson had the modern soul. 'What does that man tell us?' Hugh would ask, out of my grandmother's hearing. 'What is it he's saying?'

'That man is made from the same ingredients as the universe,' I said.

Hugh would smile. 'Is that what it is?'

'Oh yes,' I would say. 'He says it here. He turns his back on Victoria . . .'

'Yes.'

'He makes a great deal of the common clerk. He says that science will make our joy.'

'He's the modern boy,' said Hugh.

And there I would read the secret verses. The man who could take his father by the beard. 'What did you in begetting me?'

Hugh loved John Davidson. 'I've no time for poetry, but for him all day.'

> Forms of ether, primal hydrogen,
> Azote and oxygen, unstable shapes,
> With carbon, most perdurable of all
> The elements . . .

The old school was back there. Davidson's dwam. And there on the train I felt a gust of his carbon-curdled vapours.

The house of my childhood was there in the dark. A light behind the trees. All winnowing tide, and early frost; winnowing tide, and eyes as big as the moon. Our house was out there somewhere. I wondered if it had a memory of my father.

The nicotine smell of his troubles once hung in the air. How it licked over the new ceiling. And all the days he would sit by his twisting fire, the television loud, saying nothing on nothing, and him with a tumbler of drink, the Ayrshire rain crashing at the window, and all his sad blood running its course, half mad with the sound of it moving inside.

The train stopped a while by the hill of Misty Law. Cold leaves on the line. My eyes were down in the rows of houses.

I had left my parents to their own ruin. I was too young then to see what it meant. How that image of my mother walking away would settle down in the mind.

What she did, what I did, what he did.

It would all grow silently with the noise of time. But what a great virtue I had made of avoiding their names these last few years. I had long been gone from the site of these memories. I had put much of it away. But time had brought it all forward. My granda was dying in his bed.

My mingled thoughts went out to the stars. The train into Ayrshire. Ten years since I last came down that track. And nearer twenty since the day in Kilmarnock, the day of the sore legs, when I moved in at last with the senior Bawns. And what had become of us all? I can only say I had once been happy there. Hugh was not disappointed at first. I followed his example. Then I grew up. Hugh was obsessive, as his son had been, as each of us was, in his way. Hugh then was keen to shut out the world. Margaret and me he wanted alone. A world of nature, and things gone by, and Margaret and me, his only tribe, the last of his good society.

Then my legs started aching again. I left the flat for university. Since those days he has called me a wrecker.

The train rolled forward on its beams of steel.

I remember that journey to Ayrshire now. I remember my thoughts that night. The sense of loss at the flashing glass. The sense of death and carbon.

When I set out for Ayrshire, that October day, I risked all my ease, my fine English solvency. I knew how my shored-up peace was at risk. Ayrshire for me was a far gone world, a puzzle of ragged affections. But my grandfather was dying. And the time had come. I held my breath. I packed a bag. I kissed my girlfriend at the bedroom door. I left my car. I took credit cards, and keys, and a brace of shirts. I stood in the kitchen waiting for a taxi. The morning was Scouse.

A notion of old things rained at the station. How well I had held back the years. I stood on the platform, stroking my chest, smoothing my jaw, the bristles there an orderly garden, a place where time could not stand still, or rage. I had come to manhood carefully. My body was pleased to outgrow that boy. At times you forget him, the person who lived in this skin. You find a nick on your thumb. An overlaying of white tissue, like anaglypta. You remember the story of a boy who once cut his finger on a rock. You hear something of his voice. You think of his books and his pencils. You remember the way he looked out through his eyes. And then you see they are your eyes too. Your vision clears. You were that boy. Every room of his house is here. You can never demolish him. He will never leave. Unless you find yourself leaving yourself. The boy is not back there in Ayrshire; he's here. He is always here.

I stood on the platform. The thought of home made me shrink in my shirt.

But calm. I had wanted to make this journey. The time had come. My head was light with other places. And Lime Street fell away, a small memory.

The train was enfolded in darkness. The burning train, the field out there; the fish alight in their pools.

Paisley then Johnstone. The farms of Wester Gavin and Newton of Belltrees. The train was a strip of yellow light. It shook up the moss and Herb Robert, and running at speed on the wires above, it rackled the moor, and lifted the wind to the rowan trees. A furrow of broom and bracken fern lay snug at the waist of Lochwinnoch.

Up and down the empty aisle, a bottle of Irn Bru.

To arms, old Ayr, to arms again. The drums of vengeance hear.

We passed Beith then Glengarnock. Over the silt of the Powgree Burn. I saw what I could. A loch of bashed prams and old batteries. The town of Dalry, with the chemical works, a cluster of lights, and night hours. My eyes were lost in the sparks and the solder. The men at their work. And fumes spreading over the Garnock Hills. A cap of smoke: sulphur, azote, ether.

Ayrshire moor.

The bottle rolled at twice my speed. A song lay low in my head.

> A brighter meed, a broader frame,
> Await our gallant toil;
> We hold the hearts our fathers held,
> And will preserve their soil.
> To arms old Ayr, to arms again,
> Her eager warriors cheer.
> And Carrick, Coil, and Cunningham,
> Together charge the spear.

Ayrshire out there.

A county shaped like an amphitheatre. Bent like the crescent moon. The only Scottish shire with a face towards Ireland. My mind ran out to the tops of the hills as the train moved on. Up go the eyes of rabbits and owls. They peer from the uplands of Kyle and Cunningham, and so do the eyes of people in their high farms, who are mad for the sea, and who applaud the roar from their rocky seats, their island view from the upper tier. I felt them near to me. I felt their breaths at the window.

And the rivers too come down from the hills.

The Garnock, the Irvine, the Ayr, the Doon Water. The Nith and the Stinchar. The Girvan, the Lugar.

How they bend and they turn, with the help of the land, the lift of the wind, and by and by they open their banks, and spill at last, a short collapse in the Firth of Clyde. And still it moves on, south and west, to the bittern graves of the Irish Sea.

At the back of those Ayrshire hills were broken castles. And under them, the putrefied hearts of great men. The open moors now bore the names and the marks of their Covenant spirit. Many a song stood still in the long grass. Over the top of those idle crannogs you might hear words on the south-east wind. The burr of reform still rolled in the Garnock Valley. Out there, in the dark places, men and women had died for Melville and Knox, and the ground was sewn with beliefs. And now it seemed but whispering grass. The old stories gone, of ministers and miners, of Union men, of troops, and now the land had been cleared. Japanese factories would be coming soon.

Those fields of blood and carbon. They became the sites for the newer wars, our battles for houses and redevelopment, fought by the likes of Hugh and his mother. The names of those dead warriors, Wallace and Eglinton, Maxton and Hardie, were now known as streets on the council estates, the former glories of Ardrossan and Saltcoats. But some of those houses, built on ruins, were now no more than ruins themselves. In fields they lay as rubble again.

I knew they were out there still. Beyond that bracken our dilapidations lay about in the grass. We had built houses after all. And we had torn them down with our own hands.

The train had slowed.

Kilwinning and Irvine. The lights down there. Once upon a time people crowded into those sandstone houses at the market cross. I could see the remains of those buildings from the moving train. And a plume of smoke here and there. The people with fires were burning the last of the local coal, to stave off the first bit of winter.

Over the orderly parks lay the housing schemes. The televisions beat out their sickly light, from house to house, from block to block, like some kind of dizzy semaphore. Bonfires were got up at the gable ends. Kids ran down from their dirty-white houses with burning sticks as the train rode past on the embankment. I sat with my head against the window. Light and life now blocked out the stars. The train buzzed slowly to its station stop. The bottle awoke. It rolled down the aisle. I lifted my bag and stepped to the opening door.

Outside you tasted salt in the air. Salt and sulphur and gutted fish. A nervous wind skirled above the station. I could see right down to the harbour lights. The village of Affleck; the church of St Joseph's. The sound of the sea over rocks.

My hands were freezing as I lit a cigarette and smoked it there on the platform. I quickly kissed it down to a stub. I wanted to feel thick with smoke inside; upped with that buzz of deep inhalation. Cigarettes, they make you feel like a super-breather on a cold night. You feel alive smoking them. You feel deeply alive. In the grand smoke you wonder at the depth of your organs. You feel a quickening in the undertow. The grand smoke. It makes you feel healthy on a cold night. Lungs and heart, liver and kidneys.

You feel all right. The lips' tender vent: a jetstream of smoke and icy air.

I dropped the fag on a wet copy of the *Ayr Advertiser*.

The station was the tidiest in Scotland. It said so on a brass plaque tacked to the wall of the ticket office. The station clock was no secret-keeper either. It whacked out the seconds overhead. The station brae was full of taxis with nothing to do. I was the only one off the Glasgow train. The town behind the carpark was quiet that night. Nothing too mad about the steeples or disco bars. A slow night at the bingo no doubt. Autumn sleet over the tower blocks. All the people who weren't in their beds, or asleep watching telly, or hunkered down in the backs of pubs, would have stayed by the door for the last of the children to come. The night I arrived it was Hallowe'en.

So there was my town for sure. I was happy to see it again. My time on the train had somehow brought me closer. The town had emerged like a place in a dream. Now it stood clear: the reek of fish, and sandstone cut with a Presbyterian trowel.

The unplaceable sadness of belonging was suddenly mine on that station platform. I saw that I wasn't here for much. To do the right thing was all. To put a cool hand in the world that had daunted my adult sleep. I wasn't looking for change or glory or madness or remorse. I don't think I was. I just came home to see my granda. But maybe I was blind. Maybe there is no such thing as an ordinary trip home, to a home as undappled as mine. But I know I had thought that it might be ordinary. It might just have been that I wanted it so.

I stood a minute more. Then I took Hugh Bawn's letter out my pocket. The paper might have been thirty years old. His writing was a mess. The letter was in green ink.

Dear young Jamesie,

You should hear I'm not well so there you are. I'm not wasting the time writing out all the stuff. Enough for you to know the score about me being sick up here and not very happy in myself at the present time. (But not dead and that's some mercy I suppose.) I am writing this now through a great sickness of body and everything and tired. I am not well enough to ring a telephone number. Anyway we don't have one for you. And there's no phone here to bother us.

You'll not keep away all the time, sure you'll not? I want to speak to you Jamesie. Not here in a letter (I don't like letters) but when I see you I'll see you. My throat is sore and my breath is not up to much.

*Most sincerely
Your Granda,
Hugh Bawn*

p.s. We don't know where your dad is and he's lost altogether I suppose but never mind him.

This Hugh was like Hugh at the end of his life. The letter even smelt like him. He had drawn more strength out of self-pity than is strictly typical in a man of action, but then again, he also had more skill in dealing with the facts of the world than do most people. At least that was how I remembered him. And that letter failed to unsay the hero of my childhood. It simply promised more of him. He had been ill a long time, but somehow I saw here an end to his illnesses.

A gust of rain had just blown about me.

Over the hill and the playing fields I went towards the housing scheme. The rain threw down its fine, soft web. I trudged across the sodden grass. It was after eleven. I stopped in the field's dead centre. I looked up at the towers and the whitened barracks of Monboddo Park. All the life going on in that citadel of worries and dreams.

The primary school was muffled in a barbed-wire fence.

But clear, late, further off, the song of an ice-cream van.

A giant Orion of satellite dishes. A constellation of box rooms up ahead. Most of the windows showed burning orange.

But not all of them. I thought of the people in those high rooms. Teenage girls in ultra-violet, trying for a tan. Old men bored in the nylon pyjamas. A teenage boy with a plastic guitar singing to a girl who wasn't there. A woman cupping a cigarette at the kitchen window. Her eyes going out.

Could she see me in the dark pavilion? Did she look down to where I was, there in the field, in the black of the field?

Nothing like October. A billion leaves in the mud. My favourite month was always that month of earlier darkness and the smell of rain. In Ayrshire at least, with the going of the light, the lawn-mowing evenings of summer, it feels like a proper return to the dark, to the older ways. October reminds me of pagans and poets, of days when the sky falls down among the people.

Gathering brows like gathering storm.

A boy once sat at the window in summer. A hay fever kept him inside. And he dreamed of wet leaves. He wanted his breath to make droplets on the glass. His hot eyes looked for waterfalls. He sat at that window with borrowed books, dreaming the smell of Octobers to come, when all shall be well . . .

. . . and all manner of thing shall be well.

The world that he yearned for was toffee and treacle. A banshee to yell at the back of the hills. A world of turning leaves. A Hallowe'en. And still we remembered the dead in our Ayrshire October. That was the month of the dead returning, the ghaists and bogles we tempted with fruit, and song.

Passing the goalposts at the far end of the playing field I could hear the dim bedlam of kids and dogs doing the late rounds. I could see them from the edge of the grass, messing about, and blethering among themselves.

Just doing the late rounds. Skateboarding.

A crowd stood at the mouth of Blair Avenue. Fire roared out of a metal drum at the roadside. A dozen steps and I was among them.

'Penny for the Guy.' All of them.

Most of the boys were dressed as old wives. The girls were made up as witches and punks. The boys were smeared with lipstick, old scarves tied in knots beneath their spotted chins. Some of them wore dresses with bulky trainers showing at the bottom. They all had the same glass eyes. Twinkling awhile with tonic wine and the light of the fire.

My hands made a fuss in my pockets. 'A bit early for the Guy,' I said.

'Never too early for the Guy, mate,' said the small one.

'And our Hallowe'en?' said another. He held a plastic carrier bag open by the handles. Apples and monkey nuts and a corner of coppers.

'You've done well,' I said. And I dropped a fist of silver in the bag. 'So mind and share that among the lot of you.'

'They're getting feg all,' said the small one, pulling up the sleeves of his dress. 'They mugs don't have a brain between them. Listen, mister, do you need an old lady to carry your bag?'

The troops giggled, and a taller boy slugged from a bottle of cider or something. He took a big slug. He spouted some into the flaming drum.

'Very good,' I said.

'This Hallowe'en is a pure mess by the way,' said one of the girls. 'There's no a party in the whole fucking . . . anywhere.'

'You should be in your bed,' I said.

'That an offer?'

They all started laughing again. The small guy was called

Caesar. And Caesar began to frug about in front of the fire. He spluttered a load of hip-hop banter as he danced around the drum. He sang what he sang in American.

'She's a *slut*.'

The flames licked out in some near-syncopation. His mother's scarf was beginning to slip.

'Fuck up, Caesar,' said the girl. 'At least the big man looks like he's got a ride in him.'

Some of the other girls cooed in mock horror. They twisted and laughed in their bin-bags.

'If Elvis was blond he'd've looked like you. No sweat,' said one of them dancing over.

'You're all mad,' I says.

'Well. Can you sing, blond Elvis?'

The Caesar one was nearly in tears. 'No stop it. No way. Just stop it or I'll piss myself,' he said, dancing in a circle, flapping his skirt.

'What were you doing over the grass?' said one of the girls in bin-bags.

'I've just come from the station.'

'We don't ken you. You don't live around here. What is the tie for?'

'I've just come from England.'

'The English,' whispered one of the tall boys looking up.

'The English,' I said.

'Fucking bastards,' said another.

'Not really.'

'You don't sound English. But you don't sound much Scottish either.'

I said nothing.

'Aye they are.'

'What?'

'Fucking bastards.'

'Are they?'

'Shite at football. Except Man U.'

'And Everton.'

'Away you go Everton. Pure shite.'

I started to laugh at that. The tall one seemed more interested.

'Is it good in England?' he asked.

'Some things are,' I said. 'Not everything.'

'See the Queen,' says the Caesar one.

'It's not that much different from here,' I said. He didn't believe me.

'No no. See the Queen.' Caesar again.

'In *London* you might see the Queen.'

'No, I mean. See the Queen, she's a pure fucking dog. Right? A pure boot.'

'Of course,' I said, 'if you say so.'

'Okay if-you-say-so big man,' he said. And danced around the drum again.

'We could beat the English,' mused the tall one.

'At what?'

'At anything we tried. You name it.'

'No you.'

'Me name it?'

'*Name* the thing.'

'Wars, like.'

'But we fight on the same side, usually.'

'But if we fought them again we *would* beat them, right?' the boy said. He sniggered and walked from the burning drum. He stood with a group that had drifted away. They seemed to pass the bottle more freely over there.

The boy Caesar walked with me to the hole in the wall. Someone had sprayed words on the stone: ENTER HERE ALL APACHES WHO DARE.

'Fucking half-wits, man,' said the boy, looking back at his friends. 'At least in England I bet they don't burn the Guy before they make a bastarding penny. They tossers burnt the Guy as soon as it was ready. No a toss-pot in England would have done that.'

Little Caesar, I thought.

'Here,' I said, giving him a big English note. 'Don't spend it all in the one shop.'

His plastic bag was swinging off his wrist. He stretched the note between his hands and then pressed it against his painted lips.

'Beauty,' he said. The light at his back. The note at arm's length. And the face of Charles Dickens stranded in space. A water-marked face, clearly there. Stranded in space between the boy's grin and mine.

'So cool. The Queen Boot.'

The boy was looking at the note's other side. A West Highland terrier leapt at his feet.

'See you, Elvis,' he shouted back. Tiny lights flashed on the heels of his trainers as he moved away to the guising crowd. And peeping past the buttons at the back of his dress, the green and white bars of a Celtic strip.

My grandfather's block was called Annick Water. It stood in the middle of a row of six. Twenty-four high. Reinforced concrete. Cement cladding. Balconies on four corners. Top of the line in their day. Each was built in a month and a half. Looking up, I heard Hugh's voice, his lessons on wind displacement.

'You can build a strong core at the tower's centre. Like the

69

one in here. It works like a ship's mast. The floors just hang off this central pillar, you see? It keeps the tower stable. Or you might want to think of a steel tube. The force of the wind hits the sides of the block, and down it goes, down a run of steel beams, until the force is displaced into the foundations. That is where the strength is: in the foundations.' He would point with a ruler. Show me a ship.

And the wind blew hard on the tower and me. Once that block had been pure perfection. Made by those modernist angels: the engineers. And my granda Hugh was the local Saints Peter and Paul. He just wanted towers stretching all over Scotland. Tower after tower, a legend of progress. Most of the high-rises on the west coast of Scotland were made, or inspired, out of Hugh Bawn's zeal, and his tireless days as a housing boss. A priest of steel decking and concrete was Hugh. And now he was up on the eighteenth floor. My eyes rose up. The lights were blue at the top.

At moments I still see the beauty in those towers. A thing of wonder, they stretch to the skies, and can seem for a time great catacombs of effort. They stand for how others had wanted to live, for the future they saw, and for hopes now abandoned. I had torn many down in recent years. But even to me there was beauty in them.

Proud like a Soviet gymnast. Flakes of snow in a smirr overhead. A face of iron looking out to the future, over the fields and the roads below, and so firmly her mouth was set on future glory. The high-rise future. A land of pure belief and honest work lay somewhere up ahead, where swooning towers would dot the land, as Annick Water and her well-built comrades. Our lives: a matter of fresh air and open space. Immaculate at last.

There it was.

We had studied hard. These towers had everything of us. My heart was there. And the need to destroy my heart was there. My granda, who lay behind one of those glowing windows, had devoted his life to these buildings. This was our modern way of life; we had said goodbye to the tenement slum, and rid the world of the single-end. And here was what he had taught me to live for. How beautiful and sad it looked to me then. With flakes of snow: our frozen aspiration. We shape our buildings, afterwards they shape us.

The sliding door of the 'Evens' lift was trapped in a mangled pram. The other lift was busted somewhere in the stratosphere. Some poor bastard's car windscreen lay about the hallway in nuggets.

Another day ended.

At the back of the hall the light was dim. The wall was plastered with glue. A red door rattled in the wind. The door was daubed. The words in black. A forlorn janitorial script.

The Night Stairs.

On the other side of the door, at the foot of the stairs, the light had near gone altogether. Most of it came in through the window. The floor was a carpet of aerosol cans, and crumpled bags, and tins of lager. The air was thick with glue and piss. It was 10.45. You couldn't hear much. There wasn't much sound, just now and again, the slam of a door far above.

The night stairs. They went up for ever. A small window on each floor let me watch the world receding, and see the far light coming to greet me. Holding the wall as I held myself, passing the tenth, twirled at the pin, and lifting my shoes, the fourteenth floor, the back of beyond, and into my eyes come the hanging stars, the sickle moon, the far-gone mysterious gust of thin air, the pop of the ears, and every ache of the heart goes out, the rush of the climb, a long lost memory of *terra firma*.

And over the sixteenth floor there are shadows to watch. Up there the tower seems to move as you move, and sway as you sway, holding on to your Liverpool bag. You pause at last on the eighteenth floor. Stop at the bannister, short of breath, and no longer yourself, but somehow thankful and somehow alive, yes deeply alive, and staring out there, a fearing of height, and all of your life has come to this.

The moon hung over the quiet sea. I don't know how long I waited there. I stood there a while. And then I turned. My grandmother's tin peacocks were fastened to the door. And underneath them a plastic nameplate: BAWN suspended in tartan.

I saw what is meant by time passing. There on the step my watch seemed to freeze. Maybe I'd never imagined this moment. Maybe I'd really imagined no other. But in that cold stillness at the door my own world seemed to turn and look back, and all the dead minutes of my life seemed at once to live, and to speak, and to justify this being at the door, on this wet night, with a man's hands and a boy's eyes, and those tin peacocks the very picture of faith.

Margaret near fainted at the opened door. She made me weak. She pulled my head down to her timid perfume, and she kissed me a halo. 'Jamie, my own,' she said. 'My plenty, you came right away.'

My grandmother's hands were always fixing herself. She could straighten her cuffs and primp her hair in the middle of any chaos.

'Look at the length of you, Jamie,' she said. 'And your hair that wet. You're welcome home here, son.'

'I've missed you, Granny.'

'Come here, son,' she said. And spread out her necklace. 'You have never been a day out of this house for me.'

And with that she drew me inside. The light was out in the hall. She took my hand. She tugged my bag free in her style. She led me not to the sitting room but through to the back bedroom. I could tell it was hers. The sort of world built by herself. Her own things quietly arranged there. 'And did you come from England the day?' she asked.

'It was easy, Granny,' I said, sitting in one of her wicker chairs. 'The train was good.'

'I was looking through the window,' she said. 'I never saw a taxi coming up.'

'No, I just walked it, over the pavilion. The gangs are out.'

'They've been at the door half the night,' she said. 'Looking for money and apples and whatnot. Let me get you a towel, son, you're soaking.' She turned up the fire. She closed the door at her back.

Yes Margaret, she breaks my heart. Just fixing herself all the time. Her hair is full of the Atlantic roar, and grey. Her head goes from side to side as she listens in to all you can say, and swift is the head-shake as she sits by the radio, a hard smiling about her, and listens to reels from the country dancing.

'My bones are liable to snap,' she said.

Coming in with a lurid towel she caught me watching her room. The bars of the fire glowed orange. Every surface was covered with mats of white lace.

Whitework.

Her small table. The backs of two chairs. The board at the top of her bed. Plaid rugs were laid out here and there. Little flowers in drinking glasses. She'd a mantelpiece clock too big for the room. The place was strange. Like a room for articles

73

saved from a flood. But it was orderly and clean. There was much evidence of her knitting. She seemed so calm in that room. Four books lay on the cabinet next to her bed. A Bible, an old mass missal, a Burns, and a tattered paperback, a Mills & Boon. The cover showed some brown-bodied Adonis in a bandanna scooping a girl on to a horse. I smiled at my gran.

'I see you've been adding to your library.'

'Oh that daft thing,' she said, picking fluff from her cardigan. 'Pure rubbish. You can read them in your sleep. The school has coffee mornings. There's a book stand, mostly rubbish, but you can buy them up for pence.'

We sat saying nothing for a minute or two.

'How is he, Gran?' I said to the carpet, and then to her eyes. 'How is he?'

'He's no got long left, Jamie,' she said. 'He is going to die you know.'

She too dropped her eyes to the floor. There was nothing to hear but our breath and the clock.

'But he'll no die the day,' she said. 'Dr Riccarton said two months.'

'Are the spirits high?' I asked. And then all of a sudden I felt how foreign that phrase would sound to Margaret. I paused and remembered. 'Can he . . . can he thole the pain?'

'Aye there's the pain,' she said, cleaning her nose.

'Can he manage that now?'

'He can thole the pain, Jamie son. The thing is no the pain. Your granda never worried about any pain. For a long time now your granda and me have been living at opposite ends of this flat. You know he's no for going easily? Hugh still wants the world to hear him, Jamie. The hearing of him . . . it's the hearing of him. That's what keeps him going, my plenty.'

'What is it he wants to say?'

Margaret stood up to make tea.

'I have willed all the saints down on top of him, son,' she said, 'to help him bide away from that question. And I canna answer you what he wants. I don't know what a man wants in his condition, except peace. His lips are dry. But you'll see yourself how he fashes and rattles on his stories, and his buildings and whatnot. Morning, noon and night, the devil is at him. Ofttimes he dreams it out loud. He speaks overmuch on the rent-strikers. You'll hear him yourself. He's made that room so's I barely go through, except to change him, and do for him, and take him his dinner. Not that he'll eat much now of what I give him. It will ease you none to hear of this, Jamie. But it's right you came. Stay there, and I'll bring you in your tea.'

I could hear his coughs in the faraway room. They had seemed to grow in size. He had one of those coughs encroaching on pain. His wheezing enfolded a deep and ominous rattle. Old Hugh was mired in decline back there. I could hear the warp and woof of his life. And now the wind in his arid chest. So what to begin to say of his end. We sat with the sound of his coughing. I was buried there, at the end of the hall, at pause with my grandmother's tea. I blew in the cup for courage.

I dreaded to see Hugh's wild, deserted face, or to hear his cracked voice, with all his words so long now baked in the family hatred.

He had once been a young man smiling and great. His voice was pure, and moist was his throat, for the singing, and for the talking. He could lift a crowd with a heave of his tongue.

Look, look, they might say, the mighty Hugh Bawn is gabbing the gab for us, singing the song for us, making the sound for us, young Hughie Bawn, look, look.

And up would go the eyes. Young Hughie Bawn's golden speeches to the people.

King Larynx.

Enlightenment, oh yes, and passion going together in the soft words of our good man Hughie of old and today.

The women's eyes.

And today. Who was like Hughie now? Were there men with high foreheads, with suits in the press, and larynx and love on their side? Was there a Hugh-like maker of bridges? But why would there be? Why should there need to be? We had our own ways now; our world had its different glories. It's just that Hugh's kind was so suddenly going or gone.

Hugh's young self was a self no more. Not just for him, but for all of us. There were no young men like Hugh any more.

They raised the roof, his battalion of coughs.

But weren't they trapped in their ways from the start?

A writing slate cracked from the beginning in a granite school.

An Indian summer of strong drink and Woodbines.

A young lassie drawn from her first things. Tutored in sorrow or the arts of support.

A family illness made royal and changeless. All new character swept aside.

A son who couldn't cook and could hardly breathe.

A daughter-in-law quite hated by the fine lad's mother. And all for her threat of future happiness.

And now a man like Hugh must lie with his regrets. The

lingering doubts about roads not taken; the fire in the heart; the necessary lies; the craving of pity, but not so's you'd notice; the deadening wisdom of the clan chieftain . . .

Yes, yes. *Our fathers all were poor, poorer our fathers' fathers.*

The clan chieftain. Going down now to a place where his certainties would finally be honoured. And the tears down below, the sadness of wives and weans who have come now, but only too late, to an understanding of the great man's worth.

Oh hell for them that couldn't show love without feeling loved themselves.

Oh hell is in their hearts all right.

And cast your eye to the mantelpiece. How crowded it is with pictures of our good men, whose hearts gave out to disease in the end. And here we are, alone, bereft in front of this metal fire, looking now at the pictures there, our grey-faced men in horn-rimmed specs, and wise cardigans, and hair lotion. And we think of them now as we look at them, and all around we are told they were right. They were right. Oh yes they were right.

And the smell of them about us.

One of these days you'll be old yourself.

'I'm sorry, Granny,' I said. 'I missed what you were saying there.'

'I was saying his cough can be better than that.'

'Oh yes.'

My granda was alive in the other room. Not going easily. There was no going easily from a life like his.

One day I saw my granda swim across the River Doon in spate. A thick-bodied man of sixty, he stood that day on the northern bank, his shirt and waistcoat, his woollen trousers, stranded among the yellow of the gorse bushes. And how he smiled into the onrush. The clouds overhead were black. On all sides the grasses were soaking wet and the air smelt of all that sodden turf and burnt leaves and people stood there in their rough balaclavas waiting for the old man to tumble in. The river was dirty and swollen. We knew it well. And that day all the eels and sticks and stray paint pots rushed past on their way to the sea. My granda stood there in his simmet and drawers. He had silver in his hair. Up went a roar as he plunged headlong into the stew. And right away his arms were thrashing; the water coming on with a mighty slap. He was carried downstream, a dozen yards at a time, but up he would swim on the diagonal, tumbling with the mad rivulets, pushing his body against the tide with a force unknowable. At times the water would seem to gain on him, challenging all his breath and ripping into his swimmer's art, and even with all that water so taunting his efforts, the crowd would holler and laugh at the cheek of the man.

But not me. I watched the river appearing from nowhere, and saw his face bob over the spray. The look on his face was partly of fear. He battled the scoosh and the onrush. He made it back each time he was forced downriver. But the look on his face was not as people said. They said he was only determined. I knew there was more than that. The fear was alive, the fear that was in me too.

The water was mad in itself. To me it seemed set on every revenge. The river was happy to play with my granda, but then it seemed ready to make itself known, and cover my da, to quieten those idle spectators. That day I thought it would rip him away, and carry him off to be lost in the sea. But the great Hugh Bawn would suddenly appear on the other bank,

his chest heaving in the gloaming, his hair spiked like porcu-
pine quills, and every person there present would be cheering
as if there were no tomorrow.

I hate tea. Its piping brown neutrality made me sick as a
boy and it makes me sick still. A swill of inane weather and
riverbank mud. Margaret would never give you tea and no biscuit. Tunnock's teacakes and Bourbon creams were spread on
a plate. Tunnock's: a nebulous, fondant dome of sugar, an
intense spot-welding of chocolate.

'He was asking who was at the door,' said Margaret.

'Did you say?'

'No,' she said, 'I told him Hallowe'eners.'

My granny drank her tea like it really soothed her. She
would always take it in a cup and saucer; the rest of the world
got a mug. 'It's good to get a cup of tea on a cold night,' she
said to fill the space, and then, 'In Liverpool, Jamie, do they
leave the tea-bag in the cup?'

'Some of them do, yes,' I said. 'They like their tea in
Liverpool all the same.'

'And do you call yourself James down there?' she asked, out
of the blue. That was my granny's speciality: soften you up
with a tea question, then hit you hard with something strange.

'Yes,' I said with a stupid laugh. 'They tend to say James.
But I don't know why you couldn't get through on the phone.
Maybe the accent up here confuses them.'

'But they can follow what you're saying?'

'Mmm.'

We sat quiet.

My granny took to her knitting, and we spoke a little of
everyday things. She liked to be quiet and she liked to be
watched. The common universe was really too noisy a place

for my granny. What she wanted was perfect peace. And sometimes I'd think her idea of order was there in the knitted rows she held in her lap, those staticky, coloured bands. A universe of virtues foretold in those gloss-paper patterns. The finished garments held all that was good to her mind. She stared into those fuzzy rows for most of every day, and there, I've come to think, she saw strength and goodness, and usefulness and purity. All through these long years, her ambition had slid down those pit-pitting needles, and day upon day her hopes had unfurled with the wool in the basket.

Knit one, purl two. Knit one, purl two.

My granny's days were invested in baby caps and jackets. The fruit of her private moments now went about in prams, snuggled softly against the skin of babies she never saw. And one day those clothes would sell on again, for pence, to other old women short of wool, with lives to unpick, and new hours to fill with this curious knitting.

Pit-pit-pit, pit-pit-pit.

'What goes around comes around,' she said from the depth of her chair. 'I've always looked forward to seeing you back among us, Jamie.'

I smiled across at her. The high rain was tapping around the window.

There was no light in the passage to my grandfather's room. Just a dark hall like some tunnel. But there was a strange blue-coloured glow at the end of it. Closer to his door you could see it was coming from outside: the blue searchlight on top of the block. As I walked down the hall his coughing gave out.

The door was open. A framed picture of Nat King Cole hung on the wall opposite. On the other side was a drawing of a beehive, a gold and pink hive.

All was dimmed in that blue fog. Shadows from the net curtains fell over most things, making cobalt patterns on the ceiling, and down on the carpet an electric fire burned away. The room was filled with an old man's smells: sweat and tobacco. Medicine.

And the strangest thing had happened to the walls. The plaster was bashed in around the room. Craters, at head height, were deep and cracked, showing the Gyproc underneath. Other holes, both higher and lower on the wall, were more in the way of small hollows or dents. My granda lay in a single bed in the corner. His eyes were bright.

We looked at each other for minutes. Yes, my granda's eyes they were bright, and humid, and scarce of a blink, and they scorched the air between us. The fierce blue light hung over him. His head way down in the pillows.

He stared over. His chest rose to meet the gathering cough. But even as he spluttered forward he kept his eyes up, only gripping the legs of his pyjamas, and he put a hand in the acres between us. He tried to give air to a laugh.

'You're good-looking all the same, just like me,' he said.

His voice was raw: a low, deracinated boom. You could tell he was once a big speaker, for the tone was there, though the vital gust was gone now. He was like a man without rooms in his former castle. The locks had been changed. The plan was altered. The servants no longer answered his call. He knew the place but the place no longer knew him. He had lost the power and the right to live as he once had lived in that place. His steps now echoed in the empty hall. Hugh Bawn's body made a stranger of his voice.

'Come over here,' he said. He moved his legs up the bed and pointed twice to the space he had cleared. 'Sit beside me. I'm sore.'

His eyes of druid grass.

He kept on looking me up and down. 'What's all that hair hanging about your forehead for?' he said. 'Do they no have barbers in England? I suppose that's the smart look.'

'You'd be glad of a strand or two yourself.'

'Aye, well. You're the smart one. Fair-haired like your mother. You'll all be in the Nazi uniforms in a minute.'

With this he paddled his hand in the bedclothes. 'I don't suppose you've sense enough to smoke?' he said.

I put my hand into my jacket pocket, felt for the pack, and pulled one out. I handed it over, and then reached in again.

'The good dentist,' he said, 'always takes them out one at a time.'

Never misses a trick, I thought.

And then holding the cigarette in front of his face he snapped the tip like some breaker of bread. He threw it down the side, and he licked a line down the length of the fag, then he burst it open, freeing the straggly bits of tobacco. He pulled half of it on to a Rizla paper. He rolled it up with his yellow fingers.

The whole operation was done in a spirit of perfect disdain. He put the rest of the tobacco in a green tin by the bed. 'Has Maggie been telling you all my secrets then?' he said, spitting some shag on the covers.

My first weeks back I was given to sneering. I thought it would make Hugh comfortable, and me less sentimental. That was before I knew anything. Before I saw the change in myself. But those first weeks my voice could be snide. I thought we would live for ever as us.

'My granny would only know a secret,' I said, 'if it set fire to her knitting basket.'

I rubbed my eyes. 'Did I ever tell you she's too good for you?'

'Don't start me,' he said. 'Any chance of a light before I die here?'

My granda was more comfortable with silences than any man I've ever known. He enjoyed silences. He just sat there, riveted. There was nothing he wanted to say, and nothing he was going to say, unless he was already saying it, in which case nothing else mattered. Other people's talk was just a distraction. Or a cue for something he could say himself. But I'm sure he loved the gaps best. He loaded them up with expectations: he thought that any good man he spoke to would use these silences wisely, to maturate the wisdom, and mull the genius, of the things that Hugh had just said. So he enjoyed them. He was always very generous with his silences.

We filled the air with smoke.

'You've no idea of the pain,' he said. 'It's no everybody that could stand it. This pain. But it's okay with me. The nurses at the hospital think I'm a great guy, a brilliant cunt. They say people usually get upset and scream blue murder and all that shite, but no me. I told them it was a whole new fucking ball game with this boy. Other people, they don't have the balls. That's the problem nowadays, Jamesie. No fucking balls. I'm sitting here happy as Larry. I know what the score is, believe-you-me. No fucking problem . . .'

As he said this he tapped his head with a long finger.

'. . . And you know me. Far too busy for feeling sorry. Holy fuck. Still too busy.'

He was eighty-something. But he still went on like this. One thing you could say: he had never outgrown himself. Not Hugh. All he'd been through and still he could speak like the lovable gangster. Always in a hurry, always busy, always smart about himself, easy with the facts, familiar with the territory, no time for the schmucks, forever dismissive of a world less attractive than himself.

Young Hughie. Jimmy Cagney.

Like all the men who liked to show how the world could never touch them. As children we loved those men. They could have told us the Clyde was all gold. They seemed so smart about things that scared us. Everyone outside their talk was a loser. They could doctor the world with their fists. And no one could force them — that was the message. They knew how to shine in this bastard mess. And they stuck with this knowledge. Even after the shine had gone. They stuck to their way of talking and seeming. Behind their doors those men could feel sorry. Some had always been sorry. But they marched ahead with their infinite bravado.

'This stupid cunt of a doctor — you know Riccarton? He asked me if I had been depressed. I looked at him. "Depressed?" I says. "Listen, fuck, where I come from people don't have the time to get depressed. We're too busy making things better." Is that no right, Jamesie?'

'That's right.'

'And you know what the daft cunt says? He says he thinks I'm in for a rough ride and I needs to be honest with myself. "Honest?" I says. "I was fucking teaching people to be honest in this country when you were fucking dribbling about your mammy's tits. You know what I mean, son?" Christ. Honest he says. Fucking honest. "Look, son," I says. "Never mind. Just you see to them that's sick, and I'll get away and get on with my business." These people think you've got nothing to do. I says, "I'll be honest with *you*, right? Things are fine. *I'm* fine. There's nothing the matter with me. Just you pay attention to them that needs help." He hadn't an answer. That was the end of him.'

Hugh had always spoken that way. He was ready for life as only he understood it. Everything else — even throat cancer, a stroke — was just rubbish. Nobody outside the family seemed to know anything private about Hugh. A big wheel in local government. People knew his face. Once upon a time he was Mr Housing. People remembered his slogans, his grand speeches, his swim across the open river as an old man.

The big wheel came round our way. He said he could live and die in these tall houses. 'Good for you, good enough for me!'

By the time I saw him he had slipped from the world, but not from himself. I wondered, as I sat on his bed, how long he could keep this going. Everything in that room spoke of his agonies, but he could not. Even this late, with his only grandson back to see him, with the illness far on, and Margaret at that small distance; with no great loss between us, with the heedless rain now heavy at that hour, he couldn't open up, or say he was frightened, or look at me straight in that blue light. Not for a second could Hugh turn his back on the public man. Later I might have understood. But that first night I was ashamed of him.

For an hour he spoke of his glorious well-being. Or he lay in silence. When I asked about the letter he said it was written in a hurry. He wasn't worried. He'd nothing to tell me. He wanted me to feel I had done nothing wrong. This is what he said. He wanted me to feel better about things. He wanted to see what I looked like now I was older. He was keen to hear me speaking.

But he spoke it all himself. In everything he said and didn't say.

'There's no point in self-pity.'

In that room he said it. And then he enjoyed the silence between us.

He slept a little. And then he would wake, with sudden, rambling tales of great buildings, major works. I began to recognise among these tales the speeches of the past. A line of Gaitskell and Wilson. A rag of policy; demographics. And slowly he bent his talk to the news of the coming successes. His eyes were swimming. He was lost to himself. At one point I began stroking his arm to slow him down. He was racing. He was stabbing the air with his yellowed fingers. And then he turned. His eyes seemed to snap to attention.

'Are you fucking about with me, son?' he said.

I said no.

'Cause if you are I'll fucking flatten you. Right? Like a ton of bricks. Flatten you, and your schoolboy's hair.'

'Granda. I've come here to see you.'

'See me? Not on your fucking nelly. I know you. What are you after? Have you come up the stairs to laugh at me? And I was here before you all. This is no Liverpool. Laugh all you like down there. This is my house.'

His voice was parched. But he was angry and crying as he said these things and I didn't break in. 'You're just like spoilers and Tories the same,' he shouted. 'Blacklegs.'

I rose from the bed. Margaret came down the hall.

'Don't upset him, Jamie,' she said. 'What's all this creating?'

'Did you bring this fucking turncoat here to laugh at me?' He was coughing and spitting at the bedclothes. 'Did you ask him his name?'

Margaret brought him something in a plastic cup.

'Still wrecking are you, stranger?' he said to me. 'You better lock him in, Maggie. He'll blow the house from under our arses before you know what's what.'

I wasn't surprised. I preferred this. There was something due in it, something honest. But the expression on his face knocked me back a little. I had quite forgotten the weights and measures of family venom.

'I came to see you, Granda. Just to see you. There's no need . . .'

'You took your bastarding time getting here. Fuck off.'

I sat quietly in a chair by the bed. My granny left us alone. Hugh rambled words and speeches for a while and then he turned his face to the wall.

'Just sit there,' he whispered.

The light was wrongly medicinal. The rain had gone to sleet again. I pulled the netting across the window, hung my jacket over the top. The minutes passed on the face of the digital alarm. And the hours. My granda's breathing grew low and coarse. He was sleeping. Sometimes he would gasp as he slept. His lips would go, as if to say something, and then he would fall away again, a mewling of sleep, and only his breathing filling the room. At 4.42 he said the word 'Thomas'.

Our high block swayed for an inch in the wind. Down among the orange lamps a broken car alarm marked out the time. You could hear its yell above the weather. I'd forgotten where I was. Hugh had taken all my thoughts. Watching him, it had seemed for those hours, for those darkened hours, that no one had lived but him and me. The thought of death made us entire.

But other lives would be taking place. Beyond these

troubled rooms, these tower blocks, and beyond the outskirts of our white-washed town, over the fields, the Ayrshire farmers would rise with the milk. Another sort of day was beginning. Men and women and children with lives of their own would be waking to reap their own dear sorrows. Some would be happy, as some could be.

It would soon be time for a change of shift at the micro factories down the glen. People going home to one thing or another. And down at the coast the fishers come back with their quota of cod.

That night was over.

The dark gave way as my grandfather slept, and some kind of mercy survived its quickening repeal. Hugh Bawn slept on his pillows. His old hands trapped in the cotton of the bedclothes, veins raised high and blue above his joints, the open plain of his chest now sparse of hair and ridged with bone. His dark throat lay inoculated beneath that hollow of wrinkled skin. Like beads of blood, the liver spots wreathed, and specked, the dome of his head.

That night was over.

Margaret had made me a bed in the box room. She came down the hall in a red gown as I crept away from Hugh. She handed me an extra blanket. She gave me a loan of her Burns.

'I'm fair glad you're home, Jamie son.' Her hair was all kirby-gripped and netted. She turned her back. 'Get your sleep,' she said. 'Things will be better now.'

The last of these words came along the black hall. I heard her closing the door to her room.

I went down to my shorts and under the blankets. There were seagulls now. They dived from the roof. I could hear them outside the window. Margaret had placed a tasselled lamp on the bureau beside the bed. Bundles of papers were stacked on the floor. Folders, cuttings. Hardcover books. A smell I had waited all day to smell – old and sweet, the carbon paper.

Keir Hardie adorned the opposite wall. A picture the colour of tea. That grim smile smuggled beneath his moustache; a temperance flag at his elbow.

Particles of dust rained down from the ceiling. A falling of dust. The sound of the gulls coming closer. My legs felt warm, and my chest was warm, and my cock, and my neck, and my face. Ghostly eyes peered down from the shelf.

Iodine-coloured photographs. Boys in muckle boots. Girls in soft bonnets. Crowds of people with banners and boards. Crowds to the distance, and under the banners their faces blurred, and the pavement wet, and all the suggestions of noise on that day. Crowds of unknowns. But a woman there at the core of one picture. A woman in skirts, a boy in her arms. The look on the boy saying something familiar.

The face on the boy. His eyes peering out. His eyes peering out on a future asleep.

3

Backlands

Hugh was born at Ayr in the winter of 1913. His mother, Euphemia Bawn, had lain on top of the bed – knees and belly and head like the peaks of Arran – until the day she was due had both come and gone. She wanted to see her baby on the first day of the last week in November. How she pained at the birth no one can tell any more. But a holy word went up at the sight of her first and last child. She had held to the sides of her bed until the break of that day, the feast of Alexander Nevski, her favourite saint. Both mother and son were confined at that time to a ward in the mental hospital of Glengall.

Euphemia had some voice on her, and she tossed her words over praying hands.

She memorised bits of obscure liturgy. Alexander Nevski's replies to the papal legates she had by heart. She took the liberty of rigging them up to her own broad Scots. A registered nurse once recorded her flyte with the sanatorium's young priest. She harassed his ears with the sayings of saints, words made good for her own use.

'We ken the law o' God fairly weel aboot here,' she said, 'and will need nae lessons frae the likes o' you.'

Her medical charts record nothing of the priest's reply.

Famie was a fan of the higher winds. You may be sure that no one spoke much of Alexander Nevski among the valleys of Ayrshire in 1913. He hadn't much been heard of, not since the abbots of Kilwinning had raised his name with their iron bells five hundred years before. The coming wars would make his name famous. But Hugh's mother had made it her own business. She was one for history. And in coming years she'd find other uses for all those whispered orders. Her political heart would always be softly divine. Even then, in her secret years of infirmity, Euphemia Bawn preferred to make good with the saints.

The husband, Thomas, was a fine singer and a bad farmer. A hopeless slave like the best of them. He loomed large in the life of the hereafter – people spoke of him after his death – but here on earth he was held in low regard, and often pitied. Thomas it seems was a lovely man, good at life, and making cheer; with never a rag of luck in his life, he was hopelessly bad at making a living.

Good at life, bad at a living. He could never pay his bills.

How some reputations improve in translation from this world to the next. Hugh was to speak of his father as a kind of god, or thereabouts a champion among men, who was only cursed with bad fortune and the wrong vocation. And other people remembered him well. He'd an older, bookish friend in Ochiltree. They drank wine together.

'Thomas had the sore gaiety,' his friend wrote in a letter. 'His nobility was deep in another time.'

Hugh never really knew his father. But he always had a

thought of him. A man with the spirit of goodness, and a habit of failure. Thomas became mythic with his blond hair, his eyes pinned over the hills.

But nothing went well. His days were filled with private unease. Up with the lark and its malicious twittering, down in the fields with his brown and white cows, which were famous milkers, but never for Thomas. And the idiot boys he grew up with would trot past the gate with their prize-winning bulls.

Jock the Lairds, Fairlie Geordies.

Tam had no luck in the world like theirs. His sad-eyed cows drank Carrick water in the snowy sun, and scarce made a pint he could sell. But it wasn't in Thomas's nature to blame a soul who wasn't himself. He kept his skinny animals like pets. And no one doubted Tam loved that hopeless land at his back door. He truly loved it. Every grass and hideous weed he knew by name; the hills had long befriended him. So no he never blamed the county of Ayr. It was all he had. Bar Famie and poetry and drink, his only loves.

Tam once wrote a letter to a cousin in Ireland, saying that he only stuck to the farm because of Robert Burns. 'My habits are bad in the field,' he wrote, 'but never mind, there's something to see in the battle for stuff over here, with the thought of the poet's hand there beside you.'

I would hear these tales of the distant Bawns. As a growing boy I dreamed of Thomas. I wanted to be that kindly man, who had wandered the fields, and loved his wife, and named the flowers, and wrote them lines by the burn. Even now, with all the years, and the spinning worlds of difference between us, I would still, sometimes, be happy to fail, if only to fail with his hand beside me. And just like his son, I never knew him. But I'd know his hand. I still look out for its shadow across the page.

The Bawn crops were dismal as well, and Thomas put this down to the evil luck of his ancestors, whose bones he knew were deep in the byres of Skibereen. In the worst of times, afraid in the night with a clattering shutter, he lay awake with those terrible faces, and thought in the dark of his father Lorcan. He had come to Glasgow, away from those ghosts, the green in their mouths, the common graves, and all that unholy black of the land. He had come to a Scotland free of the sickness of mud. Or so he thought. The face of Lorcan Bawn by the bed. Thomas's eyes. The clattering shutter.

The Irish water, running over. Running from Cork to the sands of Ayr.

The night shade.

Up in his bed young Tam would know how his father swore on the cross . . .

'Never another farm or shovel . . .'

Better we drown in the engine grease at Glasgow. But Thomas Bawn had wanted to make good the past. To make new life. And the soil at Ayrshire seemed good for the purpose. He came down to his fate on the Caledonia line. Coal fires burning along the way.

But some things worked out. Famie and Thomas were famous together. They laughed and laughed at the whole wide world. They filled the fields with tattered scarecrows. The frowning elders of the local kirk. Famie and Thomas were famous together. Admired by the young and scorned by the old. But legend knows they didn't care. Tam and Famie would love each other on the kitchen table (one of the things the old nurse said) . . .

'And never a loaf of bread on it besides . . .'

Tam made a kind of whisky in the barn. He sold it to worthies around the hills. And Famie worked when her mind was right. She was a steam presser in Newmilns. But often enough her head would go – she'd shiver and quake – and she'd slide on her nerves to the door of Glengall.

And Tam would turn up at the hospital like a wee boy. Tears in his eyes, with flowers he'd picked. Famie would rave and thirst in her bed. Ever so gently he craved her health.

'There's something the matter with my wife,' he said.

There was something the matter, but nothing wrong. He never judged her. She was, to him, like one of the saints, the blushing idols she coddled and cooed.

He once got expelled from the mental wards for singing a song. She was bound to the bed. He sang her 'The Belles O' Mauchline'. And just how that music made patterns on the wall, and wandered on air outside the wards, and lit across the gardens there, and over the sea, I just don't know.

I don't know.

But I see it that way. And I hear the words. Thomas putting Famie's name in the place of Jean Armour's. A song gone out of the window of the mad-house at Glengall, and over the fence, and into the spray, with the wild sea salt, and all the clouds, and the sound of waves, in a time we can never know.

> In Mauchline there dwells, six proper young belles,
> The pride o' the place and its neighbourhood a'.
> Their carriage and dress, a stranger would guess,
> In London, or Paris, they'd gotten it a'.

> Miss Miller is fine, Miss Markland's divine,
> Miss Smith she has wit, and Miss Becky is braw,
> There's beauty and fortune to get wi' Miss Morton,
> But *Famie's* the jewel for me o' them a'.

And Famie's eyes would fall about in distress and no doubt yearning. Thomas would sit there – the ward for a second the wide, wide earth – and the matron would come with her pawky regrets, the tale of her final warning. Thomas removed, as he was told, but not before he had slid the cloth band from his young wife's face, and there in front of the poor daft people of the parish, he licked her mouth and kissed her lips until her lips were trembling wet, and then he went on till the trembling stopped.

Famie's health improved when my granda Hugh was born. But money got worse. Tam was like to drink all the whisky he made at the still. And one day he wanted to be in Glasgow. He looked at Hugh, and cursed their lot. He wanted free of that hopeless farm, and away from the merciless tongues of the shire, and into the shade of St Mungo's cell, the only city he'd ever known. He knew he might drink to the last of himself. Glasgow was made for men like him. All his legible, calm days were over.

And this was a beginning in Famie's life. Her madness waned, her baby opened his eyes. But for golden Thomas the day was closed. The move for him was an end. He could see it coming, the bottle, or France.

In Govan the wars came early, with all-night work in the ship-yards, and massive cranes lifting high above the Clyde. And at every angle tenement streets, the buildings scarred and black as lungs, the backlands piled with ash.

But the Bawns came first to a Glasgow of lights.

They were left with a bit from the sale of the farm. Enough to get them started. They stayed two weeks in Battlefield with a second aunt of Tam's. The aunt was one of the 'good side'.

She owned a run of tobacco shops. A portly, puce, disdainful woman, she kept her money, and used it to bolster a curdled gentility. She let Thomas stay after someone called him a poet. He said that was right. She gave him a fortnight on the strength of his lovely hair, and put up with Famie, a 'slip of a lass', an 'Ayrshire daisy', but 'hardly marriage material'.

In that first week they inspected the shops, and they sat in Miss Cranston's Tea-room. Famie was jigged by the ovals and squares: the modern look of it all. At first she was scared of the trams in Argyll Street, the warehouse buildings so high off the ground. Tam would slow her down. He'd check her eyes. He'd calm her nerves. One whole day they stayed in Buchanan Street. Up and down with giggles and stares. Sometimes Tam would go off for an hour. Famie would walk, and say hello, and think of the life they could have in Glasgow.

My great-grandmother told her son a thing years later. She said that week in the middle of Glasgow was the happiest week of her life with Thomas. It would have seemed so. The sickness of the Ayrshire farm was behind them, and the trials of Govan lay just ahead. For a week or so, in the Kibble Palace, at the Broomielaw, on the grasses of Glasgow Green, they felt they were tied up with progress, with modern life, and the promise of health for Famie. Glasgow seemed like a foreign place. A city of bonnets and handsome braes, of slender teacups, and drinks at an hotel. But it all seemed over before it began. The aunt refused to extend their stay when she caught Tam in bed with a bottle of sherry.

The money ran out. Tam went to work at the Parkhead Forge, a place where they made battleship guns. It was all he could get in a hurry.

It was a cold day.

They moved to Govan with a bundle of blankets and the

map of Cork. Black rain running down the windows. Famie's heart just sank. The tenement at Grace Drive was over-crowded. And the rent wasn't cheap for a house so far from the Forge. Tam went out and bought a box of plates, and a picture in a frame, the great St Mungo, a salmon bending over his hands. Famie shifted. She cracked a smile.

The next few days she stalked the flat with a hot knitting needle.

Pit-pit.

She was out to kill wee beasties. There were roaches under the box-bed, bugs in back of the fire. Famie killed them all with her needle. She'd seen worse in the barns at Mauchline Moor. The baby Hugh was sat on the table. Big eyes for his mother. The Bawns were only in Govan a month when Britain went to war.

Tam would eventually go to Flanders. He said he would see the fields again. And drunk as he was, our Famie knew he would rise and go with the best of them. He wanted to fight for all they had known, and Famie cried, with nothing to say. This was the only nation they knew. And yet a distant reason ached at the back of their mouths. He wanted to fight for England? A reason rose to tell him no.

They stood at the sink; the air between them was silence, and whisky.

Yes. In the quiet of that moment Tam and Famie knew a reason. They knew why he shouldn't die for England. 'But it's Britain,' he said. 'We need to fight.'

They knew of reasons sure and strong. But just as sure, on that Glasgow evening, with few more words to come to their aid, they knew that neither songs nor dreams nor Irish boys would keep the rain from that sorry window.

'We need to fight.'

And so he did.

Years later, in the 1940s, in the months of her final illness, Famie Bawn would remember that moment in her Govan kitchen, with the taps dripping, and the look in Tam's eyes, and she'd never forgive the Dublin Irish for burning their lights as the German bombers picked out the route to Clydebank. She remembered his blinking eyes, the confusion in them, the thought of his fathers, the pain in his eyes, stinging already with the mustard gas. And she'd never excuse the Irish their lights. She never had time to. And God protect her, she went to her saints just hating every last one of them.

With the men away, and the bairns in their prams, Famie proved herself a great friend to the women of Govan. The war somehow changed her personality. She gathered strength from nowhere, from nowhere known to us. And even her look changed: her voice grew firm, her face matured to a kindly impatience, and her long hair was thenceforth wrapped in a bun. She was ready to look at the world and its troubles.

The Bawn family obsession with public housing really began with Famie. She was in there at the start. Her shyness, her general air of sadness, never held her back in that field. It was to become the great issue of her life. And what she achieved in these small years has rolled over time to scold and to haunt us. Hugh would live in the shadow of Famie's ideals, as I do in Hugh's, and might always do.

It seems Famie had grown close to her neighbours in 1915. She was well known not only in Grace Drive but in many of the streets surrounding. She had organised a rota for the wash-house – that was how the women got to know her – and then she took in ironing and kids, allowing their mothers to work more hours. She had little money for Hugh and herself. But she didn't seem to worry that much. She had been to worse places in her own mind.

She waved a banner of common sense over most things. But it was the evictions that created the Effie Bawn people still remember.

Effie. That would become her public name.

She was never political before that. She had never listened to politicians. She had only listened to saints. But the rent strikes brought her out to the world with her small fists clenched in a white-knuckle fury. But her voice was steady: she retained the energy that had once been her help in the excoriation of Ayrshire priests; yet her words had changed. She now spoke British English, with a Glasgow accent, with fewer Scots words than they used in Ayrshire, but a strong Scots accent of the mind, as we would come to call it sixty years on, in a Saltcoats school she would never see.

The free market was a bad ruler in Famie's day. Tenement landlords were cruel and invisible, hiding behind their curlicued, ampersanded companies, their ornate windows in St Enoch Square, from where they served as the bleeders of slums. The landlords had a good war. All they fought for was rent. They wanted more rent than people could give.

From her front window in Grace Drive Famie had watched the early evictions of 1915 with a sense of horror, a blossoming dread.

'It's not to be believed.'

The news of men dying in France, and those remaining in Glasgow working full pelt to send cannons and ships to their aid. Bullets, bombs.

Not to be believed.

Fathers dying in trenches, and their children and wives put out on the street. Famie was sick at her Glasgow windows. And standing there she saw other women, swaying sick at their windows too. Women stood on tenement stairs, covering their mouths, watching the bailiffs at their work below. Famie saw these other women, and they saw her. Their eyes would meet from house to house. Mary Barbour up the road was keen to get them organised. Famie joined her. Together they brought the women of Govan in league with women in other parts. They agreed that no one should pay their rent.

The field out there was an unknown land, with pain, and broken bodies. The thing to do was to hold your ground. The women's emotion rose up like smoke, and joined the air of political fact, as if somewhere they could hear the guns, and picture their husbands crying for shame.

The rent strikes began. Life would not be the same again. Not for those women, nor the babies they held. And not for the country either. The stuff of Mary Barbour's heart, of social change, would be bred in the bone, and Scotland would make a legend of change, of socialist leaders, and future bliss. A century of hopes would stand in our blood. We'd stir them up, and bleed them away. But Effie Bawn was in at the start. Her family would never leave houses alone.

'We Are Not Removing', the placards said.

So many of them painted up in Effie's kitchen at number 11.

The women who came to the meetings were not of the poorest. They had well-mended dresses and petticoats and boots. Once the strike was going, some of the women came to Govan from the groves of Kelvinside, their handbags heavy with the books of William Morris. They also carried the pamphlets of the Independent Labour Party. A ham hough for the soup. A tin of shortbread.

Hugh inherited those shortbread tins. They stood on a shelf in the spare room at Annick Water. Most of them were decorated with pale scenes from the first Empire Exhibition of 1909. But some were later than that: 1938. Beauties they were: The Palace of Engineering; The Palace of Industry; The Garden Club; The Dominions' Pavilion. They were stacked on the shelf. Hugh had stuffed them with insurance policies.

So the women would come to Grace Drive . . .

'Scandalised at the action of these awful lairds. How and ever, we will see them beat.'

Some days the women went down to the Burgh Court Hall with their babes-in-arms. The municipal buildings. Everything smelled of wood waxing. A nervous succession of tenants would rise before the baillie.

'Why do you not pay your rent?'

'My man's at the Front. No money. The wean's sick. A don't have it.'

'Three weeks to pay, or eject.'

Sometimes: 'Pay by Wednesday, or remove all articles.'

The women of Govan and Partick and Wilton Street would hiss over the bannister. They would hiss and bawl and shake their children at the magistrate.

She was Effie now. That's what the women liked to call her.

She started a system of watching. They would place their placards in the windows of all the tenants up for removal. And in every block the women took turns to watch the street. They stood with a bell. First sight of the bailiff's officer the alarm bell would ring out the strikers' angelus. And down the women would come from all parts of the building . . .

'Some with flour, if baking, wet clothes, if washing,' wrote Effie's lieutenant, Helen Crawfurd.

And any missile that came to hand. Helen wrote of how the bailiff would run for his life, fiercely pursued by the mob in their aprons, mad for justice, brandishing wooden spoons. The engineers and labourers would sometimes appear from the shipyards with their black faces. Out they came at the sudden behest of Mrs Barbour or Helen Crawfurd or Effie Bawn in their high dudgeon. No bailiff in Glasgow, for all his court decree, would dally on his heels when this pretty rabblement came tramping down the street. The rent strike held like a pig-iron gate.

Hugh was just over two years old. But the colours stayed. And the noise. The day of the rent-strikers' march on George Square.

He was there in the arms of Effie Bawn, and sometimes he walked on his first legs, leaning out from her hand, the big gold band on her finger. The morning was harsh. The Glasgow puddles held every oil and grime of the sky that day. Fog was everywhere. The Clyde had earlier spurned its banks; the Green was all mud. With a coat of frost on their backs, the leaves of autumn spun in circles in the public parks, and blethered about the statues.

Leaves all rotten and lolling like tongues at the feet of great men in their iron clothes of dignity.

There was silence in all the greenhouses, as the lamps began to swing on their hooks, the great crowd approaching, singing their song. The morning mist had swirled at the stanks, and then disappeared, clearing the streets, and the rumble of feet grew louder and louder. Up on the road they marched to a drum. The fences shook to the beat of them coming. A bad day for statues of Gladstone and St George, but not so bad for the women of Glasgow, who came in a tide . . .

An anarchy of parasols, or faces free to the open air.

They came in a tide. Elbow to elbow in their thousands.

'I was there,' said Hugh. 'And I hear the noise.'

Placards high for all to see, and down among the citadels of St Enoch's the procession passes, the clamour rises, brushing the fronts of those ornate buildings with their clocks insensible, and into Buchanan Street. The thousands of women were shouting now, and all the tramcars stopped in their lines, to roar them on, and roar them on, the wind coming in from the Campsie Hills to choke the streets, and drunken men they laughed at the roadside, hollering out at the very display of these women.

Yes and the housing managers hung from their high balconies on Royal Exchange Square thinking surely not. And surely not.

The watchmakers and jewellers they pulled down their shutters for fear of a riot.

The tops of buildings saw a snaking legion, saying no and no and no.

Hugh remembered the fur collars and black gloves of the women in George Square, and the easy smiles of that day, a metallic gleam on top of the Post Office building. Effie held one side of a banner: WE ARE FIGHTING LANDLORD HUNS. There were many others, drawn in her own home paints. THE WILL OF THE PEOPLE IS LAW. Mrs Ferguson's crowd from Partick passed out button-badges and pamphlets.

OUR HUSBANDS, SONS AND BROTHERS ARE FIGHTING THE PRUSSIANS OF GERMANY. WE ARE FIGHTING THE PRUSSIANS OF PARTICK. ONLY ALTERNATIVE — MUNICIPAL HOUSING.

Netta Laurie was one of the characters of the time. She held up the other end of Effie's banner. In those early days she smoked a pipe, she had bright orange hair, and deep in her frock there cowered a half quart of whisky. In years to come she would tour the temperance halls of the country. She would offer a personal tale of redemption, and include the news that Effie Bawn was the nicest person to live in Glasgow since St John Ogilvie. But before that day as a reformed woman, she would rinse her clothes in Barlinnie Prison, for other niceness, and other reform. She incited a crowd to riot, and was said to be behind the suffragette burning of Leuchars Station.

Netta held young Hugh in her arms. His mother climbed on a truck. She had words for the crowd, and was sure of them. But heaven knows she was shaking.

'We know the laws of God well enough about here,' she said, 'and we know that justice will be ours, and is harmful only to them whose business it has been to profit by ignoring it.' The women's faces looked up at her.

'My man is just now at the Belgian Front. God bless him. And bless them all, if we're ever to see them again. But whatna country sends its men to war and throws their wives and weans out in the street? The soldier fights for his country and the broker calls for his furniture. Women of Glasgow, see it plain. We will not be paying these higher rents. We are not answering to hun landlords. We are not removing. We know that justice will be ours, and we will pay the cheaper rent, and we will work, and our men will work. These tenements are barely fit to live among, never mind to starve in, for want of the extra rent. We have people to be proud of, and one day we might have houses the same. Come the day we have a room to live in, and one to die in. But in the meantime, we are not removing. God bless.'

The papers quoted her word for word. Effie on the back of that lorry. The crowd heard something of her Ayrshire vowels and saw the tears upon her. Some of them waved their good lace hankies then hushed to silence at the way she spoke. And they remembered her. A room to die in. Not many people had said that before. But our Famie's words went out to their hearts, and when she stepped down a roar went up, a women's roar to puzzle the sky. Hugh was oblivious to the meaning of words. But he said he noticed the Post Office roof. It shone for the world like a tray of diamonds.

Lloyd George got the message of that day. And the Rent Restrictions Bill was not long in marking the books. Famie liked to say they had given Lloyd George something to talk about. They gave him a subject: Housing. But Famie was like Lloyd George in that way. She had needed something too. The women of Govan gave her a subject, a reason beyond her own scarred mind. She always laughed at Lloyd George. But she carried in her purse a snip from a London newspaper. They quoted a speech in Wolverhampton.

'What is our task?' he said. 'To make Britain a fit country for heroes to live in. That is the first problem. One of the ways of dealing with that is, of course, to deal with the housing conditions. Slums are not fit homes for the men who have won this war, or for their children.'

Famie became a Glasgow councillor. After 1918 it was her own speeches she read in the papers. She was a builder of the Labour Party. She didn't want to go with her friends, the Independents, and she chose not to call herself a Communist. 'The Labour Party will show the way,' she said. 'We live in a socialist country, and that will never change.' And from this time on Effie worked all the hours; her days, and many of her nights, were given over to Health and Housing.

'Give the people fresh air . . .'

That was what she said.

'Fresh air. Windows. Gardens. Clean bedding.'

Famie was the Emmeline Pankhurst of Fumigation: 'Lady Panshine' herself. The new Corporation houses would be a part of heaven. Lightsome, immaculate, free of corruption. Fields of whiteness, boxes of air.

She made them believe it.

Boxes of air. The only movement: our own clean thoughts and limbs. And the breath of God, a sterile hush, that drops from the clouds, and winnows through trees, a rush of coolness over the lochs, and up from the Clyde, that comes to caress the souls, the lungs, of her people sleeping.

Thomas died at Ypres, that was all. They said he expired in a gas attack. To Famie he died on St Finbar's Day. A letter came from an Englishman. It said that Tommy had worked with the pigeons. Tommy got done for running away. They gave him the 'D' on the back. It was a liberty. Tommy was a good sort. One of the last men . . .

'You sounded so nice, what he said about you. We played at cards. I thought you would want these things. Some folk prefer the truth as well.'

They branded the 'D' on his back. All the men were sick. Tommy was a good sort. He needed a drink. Poor Tommy Bawn. They took away his pigeons.

Thomas had written a note to Famie. He never got it sent. But the man from England sent it to Govan, inside a bag, inside an army envelope.

A pencil stub, a St Christopher medal. Thomas's note was folded to nothing; the size of a penny black postage stamp.

My Dearest Famie Semple,

I'll tell you this is not the cow market in Dalry in this place. I shouldn't joke this paper is too wee. I fair miss you and the bairn. I hope you're taking your time and keeping all right Famie. You know I love you. The nights here I just think about us. Some day it will be just us. I bet you Glasgow has the good weather. Think about me. There are pipers here going up and down. A terrible din. Worse than shells.

Till a' the seas gang dry, my dear.

Love Tam.

From the age of four my granda Hugh would visit the socialist Sunday school. He loved it there. That was the place he learned all the songs. In a dusty room in the Pearce Institute the children sat round in a circle. They drew on slates. Young men in caps would come to talk about life in Russia, or show them the drawings of old men in beards.

Sunlight spread on the floorboards. An old piano was cracked in the corner. There was warm lemonade.

The weavers and martyrs were hung on plates. The past was held in evidence. But the world Hugh loved was a future world. A Scotland of turbines and giant engines. I asked him years later, a beard himself, to name what his favourite sound was. It wasn't a speech or a poem of Shelley's. It wasn't the sound of his wife doing Burns. That is not what he said that time. The sound that he liked was of metal on metal.

That's what he said: the hammering sound.

I'm sure Hugh got that from his earliest days. He would hear it going to sleep at night, and hear it again in the morning. His boyhood was filled with a study of progress. He needed to know how things could work.

He warmed to the empire of sugar and tea.

'How much can they store in the hold?' he'd ask.

He made a study, at eleven years old, of the watering system in Bellahouston Park. He followed the gardeners in the hours before school. He wrote it all down. He worked out the water; he looked at the times. He sent them a letter to tell them the system was slow.

His head was filled with abandoned canals and new reservoirs. He would try to work out the space they took up. He dreamed of ballbearings by the thousands of tons. And he went to John Brown's to ask them for samples.

'How many do you use in a week?' he'd ask. And then he'd take out his pad and pencil.

They gave him a handful and said goodbye.

He carried his steel in a football sock. But he wouldn't play with other kids, not at marbles or anything else. He'd carry his sock to a room of books. And he'd sit in the corner and learn about bridges.

Hugh's Glasgow was a paradise of train stations and carpet factories. The risen smoke. The people under glass. And the doors of trains and the gates of factories swang on hinges new-made in the workshops of Possil. People about their business, looking for groceries up the High Street, the pawn shops full of other people's watches, his best Sunday suit, and next door a pyramid of pies, bridies, eggs. The years would speed past those glass-fronted shops. Boys grew up. The fashions changed. But some things were ever the same in Glasgow: in front of the shop, some man would lean, breathing sourly on the glass, his eyes gone to heaven in a pea-green boat.

Hugh and his mother spent many weeks roaming the banks of Loch Lomond, enjoying her sufficiency of God's clean air, and listening to the temperance speakers of the day. He remembered the tang of socialist lemonade, the wisdom of tea above all else. The children would raise their songs, playing their fingers over water and rocks at the loch's edge, the sound of bullfinches, the ripple of fish, and the long grass so good to play and lie down in. The pictures stayed in his mind.

A man scything brown bracken by the shallows of Dunoon. All the light at his back. The waves slapping up to his waders. The children singing. The man blacked out against the yellow of the sun with his bottle.

'Wine is a mocker. Strong drink is raging!'

The silver buttons of the well-doing children glinting across the loch.

'Wine is a mocker. Strong drink is raging!'

Famie said to the mothers in their braw bonnets, 'Let us not forget our duty to the working people. Teetotallers of the world, run to their aid. There is nothing but glory and honour in the pledge. Children! You remember: "What may not a night bring forth?" '

And Hugh's gang would sing for the love of it, seeking glorification among the knotted whelks on the shore front. And sometimes a man with a bottle not far would see them and wonder, putting down his scythe, his hand over his eyes. The glinting buttons.

Hugh always made time for himself growing up. Days on which he would climb alone to the high graveyards. Among the baroque tombs of the Necropolis he made his way with Lenin and Marx. A bagful of books, the sun not far up the horizon of Dennistoun, the young Hugh would sit, alone with his futures. He'd laugh at the stories of Edgar Rice Burroughs, gawp at the swish of Jack London.

From here Hugh could see what the dead merchants at his back had made of the world. He could look down at the streets and buildings. He could think of the river; the ships preparing for India or New York.

My granda found his voice among the living. His all-time hero was John Wheatley, the health and housing minister. Hugh had cut out a picture of Wheatley, sitting at a broad desk, his hair slick, his hands clasped. He pasted it into his socialist scrapbook. There was nothing so beautiful as Mr Wheatley's plans for the new Glasgow cottage houses. Hugh had a picture of them in his mind. Glasgow cottages. Where other kids lighted their imaginations with Buck Rogers and Outer Space, Hugh's was taken up with pictures of his own back yard, a place of well-oiled engines, and green belts, with rows of sharp modern houses, white sheets blowing on the line.

This was the future. Mr Wheatley had plans for humanity. He knew how people might live. He was one of Famie's tribe, Scottish, Catholic, and filled with the sense of improvement, a sense that grew out of his knowledge of woe, a story of hunger, and dirt, and loss. Hugh went up to St Mungo's Academy. And Wheatley's new housing schemes rose in the north of the city.

Hugh made a father of John MacLean. Agitator, prisoner, the first Scottish consul to the new Soviet Union, MacLean gave classes in economics. Hugh was thinking about his father's death, and every day he had wanted a father to talk to, but the German war had robbed them all. Hugh went to some of those lectures. He would sit near the front, with his scrapbook, his pencils, his copies of *Forward!* and *The Builder*, and he'd look at his father, John MacLean, and wish he could help him off with his coat. The 'rightful hands', the 'means of production': MacLean let his finger dangle in the air. Hugh was only yards away. He could smell the soap off John MacLean. Hugh sat with his papers and his baffled eyes. He was only ten.

'The Irish are now part of what we are as a people. And here we must disagree with Mr Engels, and even further with Mr Carlyle. They wrote before the forces of history were ripe. Listen to the words of the former.'

Mr MacLean would open a book. His face would be gaunt. And starting to read he would point at the crowd in the hall. ' "These Irishmen who migrate for fourpence, on the deck of a steamship on which they are often packed like cattle, insinuate themselves everywhere. The worst dwellings are good enough for them; their clothing causes them little trouble, so long as it holds together by a single thread; shoes they know not; their food consists of potatoes and potatoes only; whatever they earn beyond these needs they spend on drink. What does such a race want with high wages?" '

MacLean would look up.

'But this is not true of our people now. The Irish are among the strongest arms in our struggle. Their children are our best counsel. They will bring about a change in the economic system that subjugates their class.'

Famie might not have liked that. She drifted in time from everything Irish. But Hugh listened to John MacLean that day. He was yards away. Hugh could smell the soap. He could smell the soap off John MacLean. And he wished he had John McLean for a father.

By the late 1920s Hugh was reaching beyond his political heroes, moving beyond his mother and his father. He'd had enough of most books. He wanted to build cities: monuments to what he already knew.

He spoke about bricks and concrete, steel frames, ceiling tiles. And even then he had contacts. People knew him as a fine young man – a person who came from good people. But he didn't want a job in an office. He didn't want elections and speeches. Not then. He wanted to know the trades; he wanted a hand in the building revolution. His early career he spent making a wage on the building sites. He took labouring jobs, as the bricklayer's boy, the plumber's mate, writing secret notes on the tram back home, about problems, and prices, and waste.

He described his young self in the fading hours.

He saw himself as a pioneering doctor, a hero of the age, who had dwelt with the poor, and drunk the bad water, and tried for cures on his own sick body. Like a brilliant explorer, he pored over charts, and stresses and levels, in the twilight hours. And one fine morning he would roll from his bed. He would put on his boots. He'd find the North Pole. Ten years he worked as a dreaming spy. He seemed like a failure to those who had thought him bright. But he mostly stayed quiet. He knew what he was doing.

He spoke of aluminium and plywood, asbestos, plastics.

He became a site foreman, a negotiator.

Tradesmen always liked Hugh. But he never drank. He absorbed everything, he forgot nothing, and he studied hard at the kitchen table. He was odd, and he never said anything about himself, but he asked questions, and made the men feel their answers would go towards some larger project, some unstated business, drawn from their honest principles. On a Friday night he would drink a pint of lemonade at the bar. He would buy a round of beers for the men, and then he would leave, and go back to Govan, to brew the tea and drink it with his mother. He would show her his plans. One day he emerged as the person in charge of everything. And by then there was no one surprised.

Hugh's enemies (and even his friends) would often laugh at the way he spoke. He would harp on certain words. And some of these words turned up in his many nicknames. Condemned Bawn. Hughie Decay. The Developer. Shug the Scheme. Mr Housing.

The Glasgow children in their classrooms would come to know these nicknames. Hugh Bawn of Govan. Mr Housing. The man who was building the city from scratch.

In 1938 Hugh became the Corporation Advisor on Building Contracts and Materials. He sat on the committees, a quiet king of the memorandum. And he kept a keen eye on the housing department's invoices. A professor of small details, and high ideals. He wanted the houses that money could buy.

More and more for less and less. And all was to come from the public purse. He impressed the Director of Housing with his youthful disdain. Young Hughie Bawn, just before the War, handsome and fast in his tartan tie.

There was one councillor, a moderate or a conservative, who was keen on the new private housing scheme at Garrowhill. This man believed that privately owned houses would, as he said . . .

'. . . counteract the spread of Communism *and* Fascism.'

He read these concluding words from a pamphlet. It was an airless day at the Trongate Rooms.

'. . . And it will establish democracy on the sound foundation of social enlightenment and individual freedom,' he said.

The committee room was thirsty. Hugh Bawn got to his feet. He took out a small piece of paper from his glasses case. He spoke very clearly. He was furious.

'Thank you for that interesting peroration, Mr Argyll. We might come to thank you for your efforts to restrain Mr Hitler, and will trust to your information that Mr Stalin is no better. It might do us well to admire a man so discriminating as yourself, and one, into the bargain, who upholds the highest standards of democracy. So all of this being the case, I wonder if I might ask you one or two questions related to your recent travelling expenses claim . . .'

Hugh met Margaret on the boat to Rothesay. It was a works outing. They sailed into the Clyde Firth on the *Glen Sannox*; they saw a dolphin in the water. The wind out there had a life of its own. But softly, softly it blew.

Rothesay had a salt-water swimming pool.

The crowd went there. All arms and legs and laughing faces, a flotsam of glee in the holiday soup. Margaret wore the most elegant costume: pink and blue, a short frilly skirt, a flower, a posy, sewn around her waist. Fats Waller called from the corner tannoys. At the shallow end, with their hair in caps, the girls from Typing did the jitterbug in twos.

It was 1939.

Hugh sat in the spectators' row reading a newspaper. Margaret says she saw him first. His nice clean hair over the paper. The whole crowd later went to a variety show at the Winter Gardens. Old Glasgow songs. Gangs of tartan clowns. Men dressed as women, and women dressed as Germans.

Margaret came and sat beside Hugh. A shy smile, she said later. A lovely smile, he said. Brilliant eyes and a talker to match, she said. A funny girl, he said, and the loveliest teeth he'd ever seen on anybody. And pure, he thought. And smells nice, she thought. They sneaked outside, and went for a walk along the promenade. Ice-creams. Lovely here, she said. Light going over the water. Down that day from a croft near the town of Muir of Ord, she said. A Highlander, he thought. She had come on the outing with a friend from the typing pool.

'What is your surname, Margaret?'

'Dargan,' she said, 'like the town of Ballydargan. But my folk have always lived in the Highlands.'

A Catholic, he thought.

'Did you go to school in Glasgow?' she said.

'St Mungo's,' he said.

She smiled at the water, green turning brown. He loved the way she spoke. It was singing. She was bold. He put his mouth in her hair and they leaned on the railings. He could see a light giving out on the mainland.

A nice kisser, she said. Noise coming down from the hotels. Let's go back to the boat early, he said, and sit up there on the deck, he said, and talk, he said, for a while.

And that was that.

Margaret told her mother she would marry a brilliant man. After Rothesay Hugh bombarded her with letters. He thought of her every day. She chewed her nails in Muir of Ord. But then one day she decided. She took her pictures down from the wall. She packed a suitcase. She came on the train to Glasgow. Her friend from the Corporation gave her a key.

Famie liked her. She helped her to a job at the Singer factory. And in six months' time Margaret and Hugh were married in St Andrew's Cathedral.

Rapid clouds of starlings flew over the seven bridges.

Margaret was different. Her family were gentle people. They liked to put pictures around their house, and the flowers of the field on the kitchen table. Her father read from novels when the plates were cleared. They had doctors in the family, and crofters; the sort of people, she said, who had followed Charles Edward Stuart to the water's edge. And she knew all the songs. She knew the songs like she knew herself.

Margaret told me once of her last days at Muir of Ord. She would go down the glen with her drawing book and her colours, beyond the fir trees and the water over stones, to the open spaces, with bell heather thick on the ground. And there she would bend and put an ear to the earth. She would listen, she said. She would listen for ages. And then she would try to paint what she heard. Rabbits and eagles and salmon and wind: the sound of her own blood turning.

She would paint the weather. She would paint other worlds, shoes.

The thought of the city.

She loved the women in Bunty Cadell's pictures: white-faced, harrowing. Their black hats. She had seen those pictures in postcards and prints. The women with shoes and low hats and necks, the women with pearls that go on for miles.

A Shambellie pug, a bather, a negro — a potted plant.

Cadell had shown her a world that was new. A new Scotland. She wanted those colours. As much as to say . . .

Change. She wanted to know about change.

Her father kept a scrapbook. He filled it up with the current day: Glasgow boxers, London princesses. Maggie looked at the pages with a kind of yearning. One of the scraps was a letter cut from a newspaper. The writer was a woman, Lady Constance Emmott; she hated all the recent Scottish painters. She called it the 'New Bolshevism in Colour'. She said they were not fit for public view. 'Screaming farces in scarlet, bismuth pink, Reckitt's blue . . .'

Maggie loved those paintings. They were everything to her. I can see my grandmother with those clippings, as me with mine. She wanted to know that world. She wanted to live in those colours.

When she met Hugh Bawn she was ready for life. Margaret looked for the place the world turned. She knew very little about her new husband. But she knew about herself. She wanted to be modern.

Hugh failed to get into the army. Something to do with his ears. He just made plans for after the war was over. And he spent his nights doing sums in the blackout. His cupboard in Shettleston; his collection of metal bells.

The day after the Japanese bombed Pearl Harbor he was called to Grace Drive. Famie was dying.

'What are the planes doing?' she asked as Hugh came into her room. She was in the bed.

'Don't worry, Ma. There's planes in every country now. You'll hear the siren.'

'Stupid pigs and bastards,' she said. Her eye was wild.

'Just settle, Ma,' Hugh said. 'You're going to be all right.' He tucked the blanket in around her. She opened and closed her mouth. Her hair was grey and loose on the pillow.

'We're in a guddle now,' she said. 'Time's it? Well and good, young man.'

'Shhh,' said Hugh.

'We marched to a drum and brought the wind into the

street. Did I tell ye, son? We know the laws of God, we know . . . we . . .'

'Take your time,' said Hugh. 'You're all right.' Famie wasn't old. Hugh couldn't believe she was as bad as she seemed. The doctor said she'd a fever. You felt her just slipping out to another place. Everything was jumbled.

'I can sew a curtain up the best you'll see,' she said. 'I ken the whitework, and the clean up your houses will you not? Now mind me. You can never expect the weans to breathe a clean them to the good soap and . . .'

Her eye was gone.

'. . . next to God the only scunner when the new windows in and . . . every man's the drinks the last to spend a good for Leuchars Station . . . better . . . and if your good houses for people . . . the trouble to a hundred thousand more in all St Michael and St Mungo rage and all the time . . . just us . . . just us . . . just us.'

She held Hugh's hand, he said, tight. She wouldn't let it go. There was a panic on Famie's face at the end no doubt. She had speeches, but they wouldn't come, and those who gathered heard only fragments. She repeated things. And then in the night she mumbled for God; she mumbled for God and the girl she once was. Famie's last voice was a voice going quickly. The words piled up to the ceiling at Grace Drive. And St Mungo looked down from the wall, a salmon bent across his hands.

'Who are as we forgive those in our day our day Our Father our day from every evil our bread on earth as hallowed be Father Our Father who in our day our daily bread in heaven our art our is in heaven our as it is in heaven.'

Hugh was beside her. He held up a blue bowl for her sickness. She let out a kind of sigh and then her breathing ended.

And that was her gone. Hugh sat with his head on her hand for an hour. There was a spit of rain outside; the waters of May.

Hugh asked the Society of St Vincent de Paul to take everything from Govan. They upped the clothes one day after the funeral, and the sticks of furniture. Hugh took away the tins of papers and all the photographs. They gave the map of Cork to an old woman on the next stair whose son played for Celtic. Margaret took two things to the Shettleston house: the washboard and a wicker carpet beater. 'If Effie had a coat of arms, these would be on it,' Margaret said.

Hugh gave no answer. For him the sight of the empty flat in Grace Drive was a vision of evermore. He felt like someone alone in the world. So much of their lives had taken place in these two rooms. He knew the very shadows on the walls like brothers. The talk of the waterpipes, the squeak of the boards, all his young years.

Hugh had become a powerful man. He was a councillor now, yet he stood alone in the kitchen on that last day, and he felt like nothing. He felt like nobody now that Famie had gone. Past conversations and laughter and radio noise burned through the air. The flowers on the wallpaper were fresh as today's. The taps dripped. Hugh switched off the light and stood there black. With both hands against the wall, he leaned in and kissed the plaster. He kissed it cold. He felt the years against his cheek. He turned to the door. Early in the new year half the street was bombed to the ground.

The war years made a tough politician of Hugh. The great housing speeches of his youth were now hardened with personal expertise. He wore rosettes for the Labour Party. He doted on National Health.

My father Robert was born in 1943. There are schools of

thought (my granny's, my mother's) that say Hugh never liked his son from the word go. The only thing the boy cared for was football. He had no interest in politics. He hated all talk of buildings and housing; he once said that the only house he'd like to live in was the one that overlooked Celtic Park. Hugh hated that talk, and held it against Robert for years. 'That boy has no vision,' he'd say. 'Maybe if we could roll up the future, make it into something he could kick, well maybe then . . .'

Labour was made from men like Hugh. They came into their own after the war. My granda used his connections to attract thousands of new workers to the building industry. The time had come. Glasgow would build. Hugh's plans seemed to embody all the lessons of the past: the gains of three decades, the losses of the war. He invented a motto for the City Housing Department: 'The maximum number of houses in the shortest possible time.'

As the great housing evangelist – the captain of modern living – Hugh became even more rigorous about his own person. He hardly ate. He lived off squares of luncheon meat and swills of tea. He swallowed sugar lumps. His mother's high standards in cleanliness and domestic order were often spoken of. Hugh came into his stride; he worked out costings and measurements on the reverse of every document in the house. On old bills, sweet wrappers. My father hardly saw him. Hugh came home late and worked in his cupboard for hours. He would often get up in the middle of the night. He'd stare out the window.

Hugh spent the 1950s clearing space for prefabs. For years the city vibrated to the sound of diggers and pneumatic drills. Old powdery tenements fell to the ground. Whole townships cleared away. It became part of the noise of Glasgow. To some folk the new music coming out of the wireless sounded like Hugh Bawn's drills. There were half-chewed buildings on every street. Dangling floorboards.

People would think: Jesus Christ.

Burst walls, the marks of picture frames, the shadow of a crucifix. Decades of wallpaper peeling under clouds of dust. An open fireplace mouth. You could see suddenly how close people's rooms had been, how thin were the floors and partitions. A sliver of wall. A bandage of plaster. You could see the remnants of hours now gone. The broken glass, the light-leavened panes. The shards of mirror: each one containing a memory of eyes.

Hugh finally found his machines for living in.

High-rises. Multi-storeys. Tower blocks.

Boyhood drawings of Wheatley's Scotland came back to his mind. Perfect streets, but up in the sky. For years he'd been trying to bring a clean breeze to the people of Glasgow. Now he had it. He'd bring them up to the breeze itself. The 1960s found Hugh at his clearest (and highest) aspiration. All his modern training, all his modern thought, had readied him for this: tower blocks.

For our nature must change, said Hugh to himself. That was his great feeling. He had grasped the politics, grasped the materials, but only now, with his advocacy of the high flats, did he come to grasp the central thing.

'We must make ourselves all over again.'

Rub out the past.

'And what are we here for if not for progress? If not for change!'

Join the air. High over Glasgow we can look down on who

we were before. Who our people were. And by climbing high we escape our troubles. We leave the past and its rubble below.

Open space. We need those houses. Thousands of them. Closer the moon, closer the warming sun.

'You can see the sea from Roystonhill.'

Closer to heaven, closer to God and his big blue hand. Tower blocks: nearer the saints who know our failings.

Hugh Bawn was put in charge of the high-buildings programme in Glasgow. A small group of them, architects and planners, engineers and tradesmen, were to oversee it, with Hugh the guiding light, the president laird. They met in yellow offices, behind blinds, and spoke of the coming wars. They knew a thing about leverage and bolts, but Hugh gave them philosophy. He gave them reason. Some of that group would laugh, years later, looking back: Hugh Bawn thought he was Napoleon.

The people called him Mr Housing. The paper called them *skyscrapers*.

Skyscrapers. Even the word made you feel part of a bigger universe. In the yellow room the Bawn group talked of Le Corbusier. 'We've been slow to catch on,' said Hugh. 'We've been working up to this.'

He would thrill the councillors with talk of Berlin and Chicago and Copenhagen.

'In Glasgow we have made a promise,' he said. Public housing. Made by the people for the people. The maximum number of houses in the shortest possible time! Let us move quickly in these months and years ahead. This modern housing will not only change the way we live; it will change who we are. Let us reach upward.'

And that was that. Glasgow was remade. A city of modern dreaming; Hugh Bawn's high-tech castles in the air.

The flat-roofed pub at the corner; all that was left of many a tenement street. Robert, my father, drank in them from a young age. He liked the company of older men. He hated all that roaring business of New. Margaret worked in a Candleriggs flower shop; she was proud of her famous husband. She worried though; he was so often lost in his plans. He was such a bad eater. She always worried about these things, even at the start of his high-rise crusade. But she loved him fair and square. They'd a secret world: history, flowers, meadows, streams. Surely one day their son would come round. Poor Robert. He was just silly for himself.

My father met my mother in a queue at the post office. She was looking for someone to be saved by. Hugh only met her a handful of times. Robert hated his father. He thought he was a dictator. 'A selfish, crazy bastard,' he said. When my parents got married they didn't even speak to Hugh. He was banned from the wedding. 'Fuck him,' said Robert. 'Fuck him to hell, the bastarding pest.'

My father found it easy to hate his own father; he had much more ease, in that sorry business, than his own son ever would have. But Robert and Hugh were a thing in themselves: they'd carry their angers into the grave.

They say it was quiet, my parents' wedding. Ten minutes in Martha Street, a drink in a hotel, and then they sloped off on a train down south. They never wanted to come back at all. And for years and years they never came near. They found a house by a Berwick pub. And two years on, the trouble: me.

In the rivermouth of Berwick he tumbled down, drinking

the waves. Northumberland's disputed waters. Thirteen times the town had changed hands: England, Scotland, England again. My voice cried out in the local hospice; a loud breach-baby in the English morning.

My granda used to pin his favourite tenant's letters to the wall of his cupboard. I have one of them here.

Dear Councillor Bawn,

You should go walking around the city more often and see the space that is being wasted on God knows. People have prefabs with big gardens. No need for big gardens with people desperate for new houses, and all with kids as well. You say you have looked high and low for new building sites but let me tell you there are some. Do we need the car parks? Bad planning is behind all the misery. Demolish all the prefabs and get on with the high flats. To hell with the gardens. Homes are all that matters here. Let us see action in 1968 and for God's sake let the mothers have peace of mind with a decent home. There would be less deaths and murders and mental patients.

Yours faithfully,
Mary McCandlish,
Castlemilk.

That was one of the first letters I ever saw. I remember reading it over and over. It was up on Hugh's wall when I first came to his house in Shettleston. I was little more than five. Hugh let me play with his rulers.

'There's a boy,' he said to Margaret.

I came from England on the train; my mother was keen for me to know my grandparents. She was smart that way. But she and Robert would never come along. Of course not. It was the middle of the dark ages. I would be put on the train at one end. Passing over the fields, fields like the ones I saw with Mrs

Drake. I changed in Edinburgh to a slower train. Hugh and Margaret would be standing on the platform when the train drew into Glasgow. The Central Station smelled of diesel and teas. The noise was exciting. A man's voice, like someone good and easy, the man's voice, coming out of the air saying places, the names of the places in Scotland.

'. . . stopping at Paisley Gilmour Street, Johnstone, Glengarnock, Dalry, Kilwinning, Irvine, Barassie, Troon, Prestwick, and Newton-on-Ayr. Arriving at Ayr . . .'

The sound of the man from somewhere above.

They'd swing me along the platform on my skinny arms. My head going back: the miles of glass on the station canopy; the starlings on the other side, a cloud of black smoke, this way and that, a cloud of smoke.

Hugh loved to show me the pictures of his new flats. In some of those pictures they looked like toys. Buildings all shining; up in the sky.

They made out their spare room like it was just for me. *Birds of Prey. The Life of Plants. Build, Build, Build. The Battle of Culloden.* A stack of books on an Ottoman basket. Margaret would sometimes read them beside me. 'William Augustus,' she would say, 'the Duke of Cumberland. He slaughtered our men in forty minutes. There's a flower named after him. Let's see if we can find it – Sour Billy.'

Hugh lit one cigarette off another. Embassy No. 6.

He had photographs all over his cupboard. Iodine-coloured photographs. Boys in muckle boots. Girls in soft bonnets. Crowds of people with banners and boards. Crowds to the distance, and under the banners their faces blurred, and the pavement wet, and all the suggestions of noise on that day. Crowds of unknowns. But a woman there at the core of one picture. A woman in skirts, a boy in her arms.

My granda was on the phone. He shouted down it like a man possessed. 'Get it done! Just get a fucking move on! There are people on waiting lists.'

Hugh was always a champion curser. Margaret always said he had a mouth on him, and he never hid it from animal or child. You would see Hugh in the most fantastic rages. Usually with his housing colleagues, or with pressure groups, people who had reasons to oppose the erection of this or that tower block.

'Tell me one good reason why this fucking city needs a bastarding golf course,' he would say.

'Leisure, Councillor Bawn. Leisure. I mean, you don't expect the people to just sit in your tall buildings all day, do you?'

'No, Mr McCafferty. They'll be at their fucking work. Or they should be. And when they're no at their work, they can sit on their arses and look out the fucking window. Look at the nice views we gave them to fucking look at. I mean: the view will be quite restful on the eye. There'll be no stupid fucking golf links for instance.'

I learned of these things only slowly. I was quite dazzled by who my granda was, and how he held to tradition with all his stories. To a child – and to many people whose childhoods were far gone – his vision seemed immaculate. He seemed so powerful at the time. He made an impression on everyone he met.

One morning outside the City Chambers – one of my holidays from Saltcoats – he took me by the hand. We were on our way to look at possible gap sites for new blocks. He liked to take me along to those sites. I think that my fascination fascinated him.

'Don't talk to me about fucking costs,' he said to a neat young man in a blazer. 'People are still living in slums here.

We promised new houses. Let's get them up. No delays. We must fucking move ahead with this.'

I remember the man said something under his breath. Something about 'standards'. My granda grabbed him by the throat and pushed him up against a stone lion.

'Listen here, snooty wee cunt. That boy there knows more about standards than you do. We are building good fucking flats. Great flats. For cheap if we can. I just want you to tell me how much we've spent once it's spent. Get it? They tell me you're a dab hand at the adding up.'

We walked to Hugh's car in silence.

Hugh knew nothing of my life at home. He never did know. And I had no interest in telling him anything. It felt like separate lives. I just wanted him to show me the new buildings. That day we got flowers from my granny's shop. Margaret counted out the stems. She giggled, and shrugged Hugh off, as he tried to plant a kiss, and nip her arms. I stood there laughing by a bin of lilies. Bus brakes were squealing out on the street. Hugh made us laugh. And as Maggie wrapped our flowers in brown paper my granda began to speak a poem. He did all that, looking at Maggie, a mocking smile about him, and her face flushing with pleasure and old surprise.

> Goodwill is in the blood, in you and me,
> And most in men of wealth and pedigree;
> So rich and poor, men, women, age and youth
> Imagined some ingredient of truth
> In Socialistic faith that there could be
> A common basis of equality.

'Oh don't, Hugh,' she said. 'It's terrible.'
'Terrible and true,' he said. 'The Bard of Barrhead.'
He took me to see the place where his mother had lived in

Govan. We put the flowers on a broken wall. A row of young houses with white verandas stood there in front of us. He told me about the ships that used to pass this way. Only once did he ask about our life down south.

'Do you follow the local history there?' he said.

'We live in Ayrshire now,' I said.

'Oh yes.'

He left all that to Maggie. 'Your father's a waster,' he said.

Some of those Glasgow blocks went up in months. Hugh basked in glory; he felt the flats were the great triumph of his life. He would cut the ribbon on many of the new towers. And down in the forecourt he would often speak of Wheatley and MacLean. He spoke of the rent strikes, and his mother, Effie Bawn. He would speak of the great Labour victory over Scotland's housing problems. And as he cut the ribbon there would sometimes be tears in his eyes. The flats were so personal to him. They grew right out of his private moments.

He took me to one of these openings in the Gorbals.

Bright sky, songs. The lobby was full of red balloons.

Hugh pressed a button sending the first electricity to the lifts. I stood in Florence Square.

The Maxton Block. Twenty floors. It seemed to me the most beautiful thing in the world. People took pictures. The great bank of windows. Yes his world was high and lovely. He lifted me up that day for one of the newspapers.

Councillor Hugh Bawn, 'Mr Housing', 62, with one of the local children.

We said goodbye that day for another year. And then one morning an envelope came to our house with my name on it. My granda's handwriting.

'Come to Glasgow, Jamesie. I don't know your number.'

The day I arrived he took me to see a new kind of earth-mover. I brought out some of my drawings.

'A young draughtsman and no mistake,' he said.

The new machine was something. I spent the day in a series of builder's huts. He drove me around his building sites. I was happy to sit in his car with a book. He did his thing with the workmen. He would often come back in a black rage.

At the end of the day we drove in his car to a field above Roystonhill. It was after dark; the last thing at night.

The lamps on the motorway glowed like flaming puffballs. Dozens of high flats with all their different curtains and radiator heat going through the rooms. There was a cold wind outside the car. We sat with the engine on. The radio whisper. The shipping news: moderate or good; warnings at Cromarty, Finisterre.

The complete dark beyond the yellow lights. Sea salt cracked the frost from the windows.

'We are coming to live in Ayrshire,' he said. 'I'm going to have a hand in some of the new housing at Irvine, the New Town. We'll be very close to you then.'

My breathing was heavy and quick. I was frightened. I should have been pleased. I would be pleased. But there I was . . . worried. 'I know it's not easy the way things are at home,' he said.

I tugged at my jersey. I looked at him; my lip was going. 'Don't say anything,' I said. 'I don't want . . . I don't want to talk about that place.'

A whisper of sea on the car radio. Water rolling on a shore somewhere.

'My job is done here, son. I'm getting older myself. Maggie and I would like to be nearer the countryside. Sometimes I wish . . .' And he never finished that sentence. He just stared up at the sultry flats.

From under the seat he lifted a bag of Caramac bars. Maybe a dozen in the bag. And we sat that night on Roystonhill and ate them all between us. We undid the wrappers, staring out to the flats and the lights and the darkness beyond. 'We have remade it, Jamesie,' he said. 'The world out there. And the future, the future will be fucking easy.'

He went on speaking in the car. Not to me, and not to anybody. Not even out loud. He just moved his lips as he stared out there. I could see the yellow lights reflected in his eyes. He just moved his lips. To no one, to nowhere.

The last of the chocolate went soft in his hands.

4

Old January

On the eighteenth floor I dreamed of the sea. Every night the sea. Mainly in the first two weeks. The walls of the room grew liquid in my half-sleep: small coughs passing on one side; shards of songs on the other. My grandparents were often awake in the dead of night.

The dream of water kept coming back. And every time the sea got colder, it came more slowly, the falling waves, the break on the shore. In the mornings I would wake early. The same gulls at the bedroom window. Since coming back to my gran and granda I'd hardly been out of the house. Just talking to Hugh when he felt like talking; helping my gran with her charity boxes.

Many a day I just sat in the box room. The bed covered in papers: old letters, plans, newspaper cuttings, legal reports, jotters. One day a letter came from my girlfriend Karen. It came in one of her blue envelopes; Liverpool postmark. Her handwriting was tiny. It was very legalistic. She wrote things down as if they could later be used in evidence. And that was

Karen's thing: she was a lawyer. The handwriting reminded me of why we were going out. We fell in love with each other's precision, or what we mistook for that. She had always seemed to me so ripe with the facts; Karen wanted the world to be rational, and to express itself in rules; she spoke of rights and responsibilities; she was very organised. And yet there was something romantic in her too. The way she laughed like the world was over. The fact that she danced and sang so easily. The way she kissed you. And the way she felt that the world could be better. But for all her training, for all her reason, she was lost in the drama of big changes happening; she wanted red flags waving, and shouts in the street, and good-minded people marching to a drum. She thought the new Labour Party was an embarrassment. Sometimes I thought it was my past she loved.

Karen was crazy about office stationery. She would drag me out of restaurants in the afternoon to go with her and find ring-binders. She would lose herself in Ryman's, wandering the aisles like a mental patient: staples, a hole-punch, some sticky notes, a brace of pads, a jumbo pack of elastic bands. And the letter she sent me was adorned with coloured paper clips and sticky notes. The date was clearly marked off. She liked to draw lines under things.

Dear James:

I miss you. I hope you haven't gone mad yet up there in Scotland. There's been a big postal strike here, so I hope this letter reaches you before the end of the millennium.

I don't know your grandparents, but I hope you will send them my best wishes. I'm sure it's just terrible, all this. I have spent these last few weeks thinking about things. I am sure going to Scotland for however long it takes is the best way to deal with it all.

Apart from missing you, I think it's where you should be right now.

It's not easy to write it down, because in a way I just want to run after you, and if I thought it would help you that's what I'd do. But on reflection I don't think I should come to Scotland, or that you should see much of me, until all this is over. You need to be away from everything, James — me, here, the office. I think this has been true for a while, and your grandfather's illness is only part of it. You need to sort things out. You know I'm here. But my honest opinion is you should take this time to yourself, and maybe think about everything, and what you want. I'm here all the time if you need me. Just know that everything's cool, and take your time.

Karen had judged the situation well. I missed her too. She knew me better than I knew myself. I had to go off on my own. Beginnings and endings were not to be confused: our love had to find its own level.

Margaret often wanted me to watch television with her. Every morning she stewed the tea and rolled the lid off a tin of meat. Four McKechnie's rolls, a half-inch of butter in the fluffy shells. The family meat. Pink as a week in Miami. Chopped ham and pork; a gelatine moustache. In every mouthful a toxic shock. That was all fine. We ate them with cheer in the grace of confinement. And even the tea began to feel good; its hazelnut languor suited the days.

My gran is the only person in Scotland who watches programmes for Gaelic viewers. She would insist that she is part of a community of telly-Gaels. She would often speak up (in English) for their virtual nationhood. But I suspected my gran was in fact the only viewer, besides me, a holidaymaker, an armchair tourist, in Angus and Mhairi's ghostly world of Celtic crosses. Every other morning we sat in front of the

TV in Maggie's bedroom, faces glowing from the phosphorescent breakfast, watching a scree of Arran-knitted hillwalkers tumbling through the mountain air.

My gran and I began to use this half-hour as a time to practise our laughs. Maggie would occasionally maintain the basic seriousness of the sessions, talking back to Angus, and she'd sometimes ruefully ignore my attempts to burnish the programme's absurdities. One of the days Mhairi was going on about fashion tips picked up from last summer's swim-suited holidaymakers on the Western Isles. I found myself unable to stay quiet.

'Swimming costumes?' I said, 'in *Uist*?'

'Oh aye, Jamie son. You wouldn't credit the things they have nowadays.'

'But swimming costumes. It's absolutely freezing up there. All the time.'

'Well they say it's getting warmer and warmer, Jamie. There's a hole in the O-zone layer. Have you no heard about it? And anyway, you know what the young ones are like nowadays. They cut about with nothing on.'

'You know something, Gran. I think it's the English that make this programme. I think Angus is actually called Timothy somebody.'

'Don't say that, Jamie. You're spoiling my programme. This is the best thing on.'

'No seriously. They make it in London with actors. I bet you. And they take those giant crosses all over the place. They're inflatable. I bet you any money.'

'Don't you believe that, Jamie son. That's your history there. It's all you've got at the end of the day. Come over and help me fold these pillowcases . . .'

We'd leave the television with its rolling credits, its tuneless Gaelic moan.

Hugh was not good at sleeping. But he was not always mad or outside himself. Odd noises would struggle free and rise from his discomfort, mostly at night; and old words, old phrases, would steer themselves from his burning throat. But for most of each day he just lay quietly in the bed. He was perfectly conscious, even chatty some days, and only now and then would he fall, in the daytime, into some far delirium.

Sometimes he would ask me to come through to his room, come through and hear tell of some glory or other. What he really wanted was a listener. A silent listener. One of the long gone boys. The glory days. That is why he called me back home. He never asked me a question. Never sought an opinion. He ignored my life as best he could. And who would blame him? It was all too late for that. Much too late for other people. He carefully let you know it. And yes it might have been so. For Hugh the world was almost chock-full of traitors and liars and fools. His grandson was all three. And some days he would just rage in his room. At hopeless builders, at phoney friends. At people more English than they should ever be. The smallness of the world. No-marks, he would call them. My presence in the flat at Annick Water gave him a final direction for all this fuss. A damp towel on the brow. It wasn't much fuss really. He was dying there, and he needed something. Somebody. Even if only to blame them for things going wrong.

Despite knowing all this, and caring about it, I would sometimes lose the rag with him. I came by his bedroom one morning looking for a box of tissues.

'Get the fuck out of there, soft lad,' he said.

I was carrying a toothbrush.

'They are *my* napkins,' he said. 'Go and buy some yourself, you tight bastard.'

And as I went to go he railed again. 'You know, Jamesie, I'll tell you something. You are a vain wanker.'

'And why is that, Grandad? Because I own a toothbrush?'

'Is that you getting smart?'

'Well. Tell the truth. You never owned a toothbrush in your life. Your cleanliness never stretched that far, did it?'

He went as if to get out of the bed. It was a horrible thing to say.

'No, stupid-appearance. All my teeth fell out worrying about you and your daft fucking family. Away you go. There's a mirror in there waiting for a date.'

'Okay, Grandad. That's me going into the bathroom now. I might even brush my teeth, just to break the family tradition you know.' I started walking away.

'Aye fuck off,' he shouted at my back. 'You learned all your selfish habits in there.'

And then half an hour later he would be shouting me through for a chin-wag. 'Come and listen to this story of how we managed to get the Springburn walk-ups balanced on two pillars.'

That sort of thing. And he did seem to have more colour in his face after an argument. The truth is that my granda, just like my father, really enjoyed a certain amount of aggro. It gave them a lift.

But then something happened. As the days wound on he seemed better. His body was full of shadows. We knew that. His head was unsettled. He was loaded with drugs. But in the last week of November he straightened up. He asked for coffee with milk. He wanted porridge. I remember how he specified Scots Porridge Oats:

'. . . The fucker on the box with the big arms.'

He asked me to bring him more milk. He was gruff and coughing and cursing as usual, but his eyes had a light in them. And then the swearing eased off. No mistake. The aggro decreased. And he grew easier with my clasped hands and my keenness to spell everything out, a keenness that left me day upon day.

'Shurrup,' he said, 'and find the record player. Bring it in. I want that pile of records.'

And when I sorted it up he handed me the Nat King Cole. 'Stick it on,' he said.

'Are you sure, Hughie, you . . .' Margaret started from the door.

'Give us peace, Maggie.'

> '. . . Jack Frost nipping at your nose,
> Yule-tide songs, being sung by a choir,
> Kids dressed up like Eskimos,
> Everybody knows . . .'

The Nat King Cole Family Christmas Album. Not an everyday occurrence. Not every day. Not in that building. But it was just like Hugh to rally and suffer in equal measures, and so brilliantly to manhandle our low expectations. To a fine point Hugh was unpredictable. Just when we began to think him strange and terrified — careering downwards — we'd discover him in bed with a tattered joke book and a bunch of songs. A toothless grin on him. A nerveless shrug. His power to surprise was the last thing to go.

Everybody has one day — just one diamond day — against which they are apt to judge many of the days of their lives. There will be other great days, warmer days, richer times, moments of love or of grief, but none of them will match the movement of life as lived on that one day.

A time when you most felt part of the world. A day where you somehow knew you were there in the company of all known things. Alive. Every bit alive. Angels high and the vermin below. All watching, all glory. And the great Scottish bridges making perfect sense in a shower of rain. The seasons at once reflected in your skin; the sky in your eyes; the noise through the trees like some sound in the groves inside you. Most days are lost in the decorum of trying, lost in the lanes of the almost known. And there you have it on that one day. You are in it. And with the slow-going afternoon the world all at once can make perfect sense. It will never last; you know that too. But you had it that time. You had it once.

Hugh lay in the bed with tears on his face. An old seventy-eight was turning on the deck. It was John McCormack, the Irish tenor. The voice sounded distant through a wall of crackles. A muffled wave of golden brass. The melody was slow. My granda's hands were shaking. He gripped the openings in his pyjamas. Squares of light coming past the curtains and dancing about the room. The singer's voice. My thin granda shook in the corner with all the years about his eyes. The water in his eyes. He looked up at me.

'Jamesie,' he said, 'I want you to go to the pub with me. Can you take me to Ayr?'

'Aye, Granda. I'll get us a car.'

'No,' he said. 'I like the bus. Can you no find a chair? We can go on the bus.'

I went through and told Margaret.

'You won't upset him will you, son?'

'Why would I do that, Gran?' I asked, hoking under the

phone stool for the Thomson Directory. 'I'm not here to upset him. Don't you think I know what needs to be done?'

'Good boy,' she said. 'You know his picture's been in the paper. There's a court-thing in Glasgow. They're trying to say he . . . misappropriated money. It's a load of rubbish. I don't want them near him. Help me will you, Jamie?'

I placed my hands on both her arms. 'I know,' I said. 'Don't worry.'

A look passed between my gran and me just then, a look that she had obviously been waiting for those past weeks. She almost swooned with relief. 'Gran,' I said. 'He asked me to come up here. I'd like to make things easier for him now. Do you understand that? Do you know what I'm saying?'

'Aye, son,' she said. 'I understand you fine. God help us.'

There was a British Legion club up in the New Town. They told me it would be fine to borrow one of the wheelchairs. Hugh wanted to walk up with me. He was sure he could make it there. Then we could take the bus. I was never going to argue with Hugh that day. He had to have whatever he wanted. Margaret put some light trousers on him. The shirt made his neck look scrawny, he said. She threaded his arms into a pullover.

'I want my good shoes,' he said. Maggie bent down to press on two wine-coloured brogues. She tied them double. With as light a touch as possible – he so hated this sort of fuss – I tied his tartan scarf around him. A fawn jacket over the top. And Margaret came in with a cap.

'Maggie,' he said, 'here a minute.'

He whispered to her as I put on my own jacket. Zipped up.

'Take it easy, you two,' my gran said. 'Mind, Hughie. Take your time.'

As I stepped to the door I saw her slip a bundle of notes into my granda's hand.

We made our way slowly. Down one flight to the seventeenth. Only the 'Odds' lift was working. 'These elevators are grand things when they get going,' he said.

His arm was linked to my own. Most of the buttons in the lift were painted over with pink nail-varnish. And the metal plate was scratched with names: ROSKO KOOL KILLA. SANTA AND LOVERBOYZ. INCA TEAM LOVES HASH. JULIE FUCKS NEDS. And up above them the usual drawings of breasts and cocks. GANG-BANGS PHONE THIS NUMBER. Hugh kept his eyes to the roof of the lift.

'Not as smooth going down,' he said. 'The pulleys feel worn. I must tell them to get the oilers in here.'

'Oh, Mr Bawn,' said an elderly lady on the ground floor, tight in her coat. 'You going out for a wee jaunt? Fine day. And you're looking that well, Mr Bawn.'

'Aye, Jean,' he said. 'I'm all of that.'

We walked down the hill and on to the towpath by the river. The brown water wrinkled. A calm wind was up, a slow breath, in all grace lifting the leaves, turning them twice, laying them lost on the water's top. The river poured into a small basin under the shopping arcade. The water settled there for a second, glimmering. Mud and roots circled in the soup; a swelling in the undertow. The basin like an earthenware bowl spun from the banks, containing plenty. We watched the river as it flowed and gathered, and watched as a wide lip opened at the other side, under the bridge, and tilted a gush from the edge of the bowl. The flood escaped, and more surged in, water over grass, grass over water. And all in the end went bending to the sea. All the way down the river a white light hung at the trees. The old moor rolled away in a fuss of hawk-weed. The churches were quiet. The stone faces on the churches were quiet. Hugh stared into the water; the Auld Kirk steeple was a shadow there.

'Jamesie,' he said. 'Did I ever tell ye it was churches I wanted to build?'

We crossed the Green Bridge over the water. Hugh decided he wanted some loose tobacco. I thought we might cut over for the wheelchair first.

'No,' he said, 'let's have a smoke. A walk.'

So up we went to the High Street. The newly pedestrianised High Street. Mr Haq was open for newspapers, for cigarette papers, for birthday cards and diet Cokes. A half-ounce of Golden Virginia. *The Racing Post.* Our walk past the shops was slow and stately. Out with my granda. Proud of him moving his legs that way; doing the job and no fuss. 'You okay, Hugh?'

'Aye, son. Brand new.'

His head was down all the way. He coughed under his cap. The kids going past us were high on winter bargains. A packed street. All the shop windows. Crimson lights burning at the core.

Boots Home Face Masseur. Boxes piled under one of Dr Jekyll's giant chemical jars. Green jars. Change your face. Make your day. Be a new person.

A gush of heat by the automatic doors.

Kestrel Lager. Your Festive Choice at Tesco's. A shock army in Adidas stripes were marching ahead of us with parcels of drink.

'Afore ye go.'

A good drink.

Afore ye go.

Mothers in leggings; a long queue at the photo shop.

The City Bakery's Own Strawberry Tarts.

I gave Hugh a roll-up.

'Fucking mental place the day,' he said, taking a light. He looked up and smirked at them all passing.

'Loony Tunes,' he said. He smoked his smoke.

Young girls came along arm-in-arm like us. Gold chains in their mouths. There are no prices on Cantor's furniture. Just terms. Nine months interest-free. A gust of wind blew up as two spiky-haireds went rollerblading past. More stripes on them. Both chewing gum. As we passed the Clydesdale Bank a young guy came towards us with a pile of *Big Issues*. A grizzled mongrel at his side. Steering Hugh round him I mouthed the word no.

'What was that?' he said.

'Oh just a collector.'

It was too nice a day for December. Real sun in the sky. All those mad festive tunes barging out the door of the cheap stores.

'I saw Mama kissin' . . .' Sound just fleeing out the doors, like shoplifters.

The guy at the door of the British Legion was eating a scotch pie. Not so much eating it, really, as making up to it. Licking it, and kissing it. His fat fingers danced around the edge of it. They pirouetted on the burnt crust. So he liked the pie. There was an action painting of grease across his chin. The man had an unbelievable drum of a stomach. A body in training for the Twelfth of July.

Corpulent homage to the dainty Dutch king . . .

'The sash my father wore.'

A Highland Fusiliers tie hung about his neck. The man sat with his pie on a Tennant's beer keg. 'By the Christ,' he says, departing his stool, 'if it's no Hughie Bawn. An elder statesman among us.'

'Hello, Davie. I see you're still at your dinner. The fat fucker that ye are. Jamesie . . .'

He touched my arm and pointed at the smiling bouncer.

'This one has six weans. Can you credit that? Six times that woman's put up with him. At least! And it looks as if he's the one having the weans. Yer a fat bastard right enough, Davie. It's good to see ye.'

All the while Davie Grimes just chuckled like a battery toy. He loved the abuse, you could tell. And my granda clearly loved dishing it out. As soon as we reached the door of the Legion his voice changed. He became one of his public selves. He was in among the boys now.

'And how is your suffering wife?' he said. 'The Maid Marion. You tell her from me the divorce courts are never far yonder. Tell her it's a good Catholic boy she's missing.'

Hugh winked at me. 'Come on in, son, before this one tries to tap us for money.'

As we walked through to the club we could still hear Grimes's broken chortles. Hugh stopped at the signing-in book – ballpoint on a string.

'Saddam and son' in the Name column. 'Free the Falklands. All property is theft' for the Address.

Davie Grimes came in with a low wooden stool. 'There ye go, Pops. Sit yourself down, and mind yer pockets. What can I get you?'

'We'll have two pints of yer best piss, and a wheelchair,' said Hugh.

Grimes went behind the bar to do the honours. He waved away the money. The club was empty. A large Union Jack was stretched across the far ceiling, over a narrow stage.

'You need to get the decorators in here, Davie,' Hugh said. 'Somebody's been drawing obscenities on yer Artex.' He placed his *Post* on the bar as he said this.

'Aye,' said Davie. 'Ye're some man. Did nobody tell ye the communists surrendered, Hughie? We'll all be under the one flag in a minute.'

'Right you are,' says Hugh, taking his pint.

He looked to me again. 'To think that boy had a good comprehensive education. And his da a miner too. All his days. Ye're a black-hearted Tory pig, Davie Grimes. Yer father will be birling in his grave. Next time we see you you'll be poncing votes for the New Labourers.'

Grimes handed me the second pint. 'Ye're no related to this auld commie are ye?'

'He's my granda,' I said.

'Yer sister still in that nice block in Ardrossan yonder?' asked Hugh. 'The one beside the library.'

Grimes was dragging a cloth over the bar top.

'Aye . . . well, she's still in there, Hughie.'

He lifted my beer mat and threw me a glance. Gently I shook my head. *Don't contradict him*, I thought. *Let him alone.*

'Aye, she's happy enough is Moira,' Grimes continued. His eye was still on me.

Hugh looked down his columns of horses. 'Beautiful towers they,' he said, almost to himself. 'I must have them looked at. See if they need a paint job.'

Grimes met my eyes again. For a second or two I just stared him out. *Say nothing.*

I could tell he was thinking about Hugh in the paper. *Say nothing. It's all a mistake. They don't understand how he was, how he is.*

'I mind,' he said to Hugh, 'years ago, when you came to our school to give a talk. Do you mind that? They were just building Broomlands at the time. Years ago. You came to the school and gave a talk. About the schemes. The talk was called "The Great Era of British Housing". In the school gym hall. I remember that, Hughie.'

'Wasn't me,' said Hugh.

'Aye, Hugh. Do ye no remember? You had lots of slides of the high-rises in Glasgow and that. In the gym hall.'

'I never gave a talk called that,' said Hugh.

'You did so.'

'Never in my life. "The Great" . . . what did you say? . . . "The Great Era of British Housing". No. You've been working in this bunker too long, Grimes. The talk was called "A Great Era in Scottish Housing".'

'Give's a fucking break, Hughie. It was a million years ago.'

'Nevertheless,' said Hugh, in his best mockery, 'an important distinction. When it comes to housing, England only followed the great innovations up here. They came at our heels. First with their praise, then with their awards, and then with their sticks of dynamite.'

Hugh paused.

'Is that no right, James?'

I passed him a roll-up.

A longer pause. We stared at each other.

'A stickler for detail is what you are, Hughie Bawn,' said Grimes. He lifted the bar hatch and disappeared around the back.

'That's what did for the Russians as well,' he was saying.

'Now where's that wheelchair? I know it's here; we used it to get somebody to their taxi on Saturday night.'

We stood in the plastic bus shelter by ourselves. The chair was still folded. Hugh said to wait with the chair till we left the town. The green bus to Ayr came to the stop in less than five minutes. I paid the driver, stowed the chair, and guided the old man to some seats up the back. Smokers.

Hugh sat in at the window. I remember him touching the glass. Just putting his hand on it. The whole of him vibrating with the bus as it moved along. His hand on the glass. On the edge of the town we began to climb. A good view of the factories and the housing schemes: The New Town. The many-coloured houses. Not so new any more. His eyes were lost in among them. He stroked his bottom lip with his tongue. He peered at the houses.

Under the sun. Coloured houses. Hugh with his hand on the glass, the housing estates below and beyond. It was something to watch, something to see, that open moor and the pine, the easy slant from the hills over there . . .

Down, and down again. The groups of houses and their washing lines. The white washing. The whiteness billowing out: Hugh was lost in his thoughts. And I was lost in his thoughts as well.

Where other kids lighted their imaginations with Buck Rogers and Outer Space, Hugh's was taken up with pictures of his own back yard, a place of well-oiled engines, and green belts, with rows of sharp modern houses, white sheets blowing on the line.

This was the future. Mr Wheatley had plans for humanity. He knew how people might live.

Even then, with Hugh in the world, I was thinking Hugh's

thoughts, trying to see the shape of his life, the shape and weave of all our lives. It was something to see. Old Hugh Bawn in the world that day.

From the Loans Road we could see the hills of Arran. The water looking silver. The Arran hills, the story of rocks their only secret. Over the years on that western coast, under the same sky, people like us must have looked out there, and wondered what those hills could remember, and would they remember anything of us.

Hugh and I looked at the silver shoals of water to Arran.

I was sure our good and our badness would stay there, all our desires, our disasters. All would remain on the face of those mountains of Arran, and one day others would see us there.

I thought I could hear voices in the air, see the marks of dead tribes on the slopes of Arran. And I knew I was only another one looking. On those beaches of Ayrshire they'd always imagined these things. They said it loud from their crannog forts. They spoke it from hay-thatched cottages, from broken castles, from fishing boats, and from miners' rows. And now I was saying it – Hugh at my side – from the back of the green bus into Ayr that day. But the Isle of Arran may never have known us, out there alone on the silver-looking sea. We imagined hard; we hoped out loud. But maybe the hills knew nothing of us. And they never would. We'd live our short hours, and pass as nothing.

'Did I tell you?' said Hugh. 'My own da, he died in a hole.'

'Yes,' I said. 'He died at Flanders didn't he?'

Hugh kept his eyes on the glass.

'Or somewhere,' he said. 'He should never have gone.'

Hugh had always looked on Ayrshire and Glasgow as the

great world. He had never wanted any other part of the planet. Never a thought of elsewhere. In a way he considered the rest of the world quite small by comparison. And Scotland to him was an entire globe. A full history. A complete geology. A true politics. A paradise of ballads and songs. There was some sort of fullness there for him. And even towards the end of his days, the force of his rejection, his late disappointments, served only to confirm his extravagant rootedness.

'No one has been where we have been,' he would say.

And he never meant that as anything but a statement of pride. He would never say it was perfect. He would say it was the one place that had existed in a perpetual age of improvement.

'Except in your time,' he sneered.

He really believed that. He was sure of it. At least on top he was sure of it. The world beyond Scotland was merely for him a point of distraction. A series of places where people dreamed secretly of the Firth of Clyde. As if they even knew where it was.

Yes. He would draw on the great cities of the world as examples. This disaster zone in Helsinki. That excellent housing estate in Madrid. The example of Brooklyn, the model of Denver. 'As illustrated by the northern suburbs of Tokyo.' In his high-housing days, he would mention these places as if they were theories, to be deemed useful, or else rejected. He used to excite his colleagues with the mention of such places, but he didn't quite grasp the nature of their excitement. He had no notion of them as places too with life and death, or the homes of people with dreams of their own. His father had died 'in a hole somewhere', not in Belgium, or the Continent, or any place with movements, and tears.

Hugh really wanted to bring the whole world home to Scotland. The best of its ideas. The core of its great lessons. Le Corbusier was an honorary Scot. Only in these glens of time, he seemed to imagine, where people stored their memories of loss, would the modern ethos serve to redeem the troubled years, and teach the people how to live. He liked Russia, a Russia of the mind.

Hugh was never on an airplane. Never once.

'Always too busy,' he'd say. 'Too busy with here.'

He was the sort of man who couldn't afford to feel diminished. This was his world. He was a great man here. He wanted no part of foreign soils. Let us water our own gardens he would say. All his waking life he pretended not to hear other voices. He had no ear for differences, no time for the opposing view, valiant in his deafness to contradiction. As I say, he pretended: I'd come to know he was obsessed with his detractors. But in his flurry of greatness and domestic pride, he imagined nothing could really be wrong with his country, nothing wrong that it made wrong itself. It was part of his great charm. All his life he remained alert to the faults of outsiders – outsiders like me.

'Look at that coast, Jamesie,' he said on the bus. 'The best days of yer life.'

The sale of council houses. Hugh would say it was all evil. And that would be an end to it. It was not what he taught me, not what he and his mother had fought for. And I learned in those months that it was too late to contradict Hugh. It was too late to argue. I came home thinking I might unteach my teacher. But no I would not: I'd offer my teacher his own best lessons. I'd bring his words back home.

He had given me his past. He had given me his tools. I would use them to piece together his life's end. And use them to explain something of my own life, separate now from his, but bound the same, by ideals and plans, and futures we could never know. Hugh and I had the same disease: we wanted the world to answer to us. But it wouldn't answer: we could only, in time, make peace with the land, and hope for love in this flurry of moments. We couldn't complete the world or ourselves. We could only live, and look for small graces, and learn to accept the munificence of change. Once upon a time, it was Hugh that had shown me, a young, saddened boy, how to grow up, how to make use of the past, and live with change. And now I was here: I would try to show him.

He wanted that. I knew he did. That was why he called me back. With Margaret to save him from an agony of doubts. He would never admit it. And he would never need to. I didn't want to convert Hugh: I wanted to let him die as himself.

I looked at Hugh. The bus took us forward. His hand on the glass.

'No one has been where we have been.'

A light came up, a glitter of sea.

We could only live, and look for small graces. Our dreams were neither true nor untrue: our dreams were out there, immersed in the self-renewing seas of the Clyde Firth.

'Troon,' Hugh said. 'The best-lit town in Ayrshire. Do you know it was one of they from around here that invented the gas lighting?'

That was pure Hugh. He always had stories about the Great Men. (His mother was a special case.) Most books had forgotten James Taylor, one of the men who first applied steam to the spurring of ships. 'Another local boy. He hardly had a thing to eat, bar the turnips out there.'

Whatever you were doing with Hugh, he could always

fashion a quick story on the wonders of human ingenuity, so long as the effort was local. 'Feel how good this bus is on the road,' he said. 'John Boyd Dunlop was the boy for this. Pneumatic tyres. Worked out of his wee shed in Dreghorn. Died when I was still a boy. We would be living in Govan by then.'

So every outing with my granda became a journey into the past, and into our own past now, and into Hugh's sense of his place in this line of great men. He loved memory. And people remembered his father.

Our bus bent around the golf course at Royal Troon. You could see Ailsa Craig beyond the fairway, out in the sea. A craggy pyramid. A sinking oil-rig. Paddy's Mile Stane. A lavender-tinted boulder in the slovenly-coloured sea.

'In every golfer you'll find a bastard,' said Hugh. 'They take up too much space.'

'I think that was probably your secret mission, Hugh,' I said. 'To rid the country of golfers.'

'Bastards,' he said. 'Pissing in the wind out there. Their stupid bonnets. Folk who think you need to hit a ball with a stick to earn a drink. Aye. I'd send them all back to America. We should get the boys from HMS *Gannet* to come and drop shells on them. Then they'd have a use for their bunkers. Arseholes.'

Hugh came back to Ayrshire as the famous housing consultant. He hated golf, though. He despised golfers. And he thought tourism was a plague on the nation.

'*Torpedo* the fuckers with shortbread!'

Hugh was never going to do well on the New Town Development Corporation. His hatred of golf and tourism made him a legendary curmudgeon.

'Did ye leave any golf links in the city?' I asked him.

'In Glasgow? Well, I tried to put a bulldozer through the

lot of them,' he said. 'But the thing about golfers, Jamesie — they always have their say. Masons. Coppers. The Chairman of IBM. Every one of them is at the golf. But ye know the flats in Sandyhills? The Balbeggie flats. The eight blocks. They were a golf course. And people screaming for new houses. I just took a plough over the whole field. Three weeks. And the blocks were up in the sky in three months. That was news for the golfers.'

We passed through Monkton. The fields around Prestwick Airport brought the smell of manure into the bus. We swallowed the gusts of sweet putrefaction. The tractors were busy at the December spreading. On the other side we could see them lifting the last of the season's potatoes. Clear skies overhead.

Hugh had picked a horse. Burmese Summer. The 2.45 at Ayr. We got off the bus and he sat down in the open wheelchair. Off to Ladbrokes in the Sandgate.

He twisted his cap on his knees. We waded through the mothers and prams; skateboarders in baggy jeans hung about the litter bins. We were in a hurry. Two-thirty. I pushed the chair faster and faster.

'Ride 'em, cowboy!' said Hugh, leaning back, laughing hoarse, as we cut up the town. The bookie's was the usual smoke cupboard. Clouds to the ceiling. Hugh smiled, breathed in, coughed, and asked for a fag. I sat him in front of one of the televisions. Ceefax dribbling down the screen. I found a pen. Betting slip. The guy beside us tore one of the pages off the wall and spat on it. He bounced it off the floor. His jacket was shiny like his face.

'Fuck it,' he said.

Hugh stared up at the screen: Burmese Summer, 6-1. The

room was red. The men all craning their necks or scribbling into cupped hands. Hugh handed me his slip with two pound notes. I tried to hand him back the notes. He nodded at the cashier. *On ye go.*

Guy in front with a can in his pocket. He kept lifting his finger as if to say something to the woman behind the glass. Nothing coming. A new slip on the desk. I scribbled 'Corncrake. £2. To Win. No tax.' The girl took the money and stamped the two slips without looking up. A scraggy English voice came at us from the sound system in the corner. I stood behind Hugh's chair. The heat in the room was up. Men closed in around the screen – the blue light flashing on their faces – sideburns and fingers bristling to know. When they opened their mouths to speak the smoke curled out, like shadows of words.

Whack!

'Off they go, and it's Lentil Broth making a good start . . . Up sides there with Gunga Din, and Gunga Din going steady on the inside . . .'

The heat was up. Blue light on the men's eyes, and into the deep behind them . . .

'The Earl of Stratford hanging back, and slowly picking up now, The Earl of Stratford, odds-on favourite, and a slow-burner, but coming up, coming up now . . . But it's Gunga Din, Gunga Din . . .'

The drunk with the can was pointing in the air, one leg anchored in front, the other tapping the floor at the back, his hands going here and there, reaching around the pole of himself.

'. . . and Lentil Broth now strong, and Corncrake just outside . . . Corncrake outside . . . Now Corncrake it is, coming up on the outside . . . Corncrake, and Gunga Din is losing ground. Gunga Din is . . . Lentil Broth is slipping . . . Corncrake . . .'

Hugh sat still in his chair. He smelled of medicine.

'Corncrake is now leading by a head. Lentil Broth and . . . Lentil Broth is fighting all the way. But Corncrake is . . . Corncrake pulling . . . into the final stretch . . . and yes . . . And it's Corncrake the winner. Corncrake, Lentil Broth, Gunga Din, The Earl of Stratford . . .'

Chorus of sighs. Betting slips ripped; tickertape to the floor.

I put my own slip into my pocket.

'No use to man nor beast,' Hugh said. 'Never a turn these days.'

'Never you mind, old boy,' I said, 'at least you're not a golfer.'

Toothless grin.

A trio of kids nearly crashed into us in the street. They beetled past; a game to top each other's sniggers. Towels rolled under their arms. There was a bus on the other side of the road with a yellow sign: BURNS COTTAGE.

'Let's go to Alloway,' I said.

'You're the driver,' Hugh said.

'We need this bus.'

Hugh eased up the bus steps, gripping the pole. The driver was a member of that club whose members like to use the fewest possible number of words.

'One-twenty,' he said. I paid him.

'There,' he said.

I put the folded chair in a gap at the back of his cabin.

He nodded. A jolly squire: disability was one of the daily bores.

We got off near the Brig o' Doon. Hugh wanted to pee. We went into a hotel, the Cottars' Arms, and I stood at the bar whilst the old man disappeared. The empty chair at my side. Deep amber glinting on the gantry. A man with a walrus-moustache craned round from his pint. Bleary-eyed. 'The legs buggered?' he asked, dropping his head to the chair.

I just smiled a tight smile. Times are you just feel tall and stupid and too much scrubbed in your ironed jeans. Hugh wanted a whisky. Two Glenlivets. Taste of peat I suppose.

'Tastes like shit,' said Hugh. 'But God I love it.'

Back in his chariot Hugh drained the glass. And another one.

'Okay,' he said.

He wanted me to take him down by the River Doon, the park there.

All by the road there were wild flowers. They nodded and shushed. We fell in with them, as the wheels turned, and we made our way to the river bank.

Margaret had given us the love of flowers. Her time working in the florist's shop was a time of eager smells and leaves. She had always loved them. She brought down to Ayrshire her old school jotters full of flower-pressings – the illuminated pages of her girlhood. All the wild blooms of the Highlands were there; the Latin names in a small hand. Hugh and I had grown together to love those books. They had everything of Maggie in them. And something between the faint blue lines of those jotters: the suggestion of a Maggie we never knew.

The love of flowers became one of the secrets between us. The three of us. Our shared notions of the beautiful and the just, the high and the mighty, the glorious, the very ancient, suggested in the thinly ordered leaves of the Yellow Mountain Saxifrage . . .

Her tiny letters: *Saxifraga aizoides.*

We were joined by a sense of ordinary grace. Or so we thought. And couldn't we see the shape of such a thing in the spreading petals of a Meadow Buttercup?

Ranunculus acris.

A promise of loss was held in the furry white pappus of the Northern Hawksbeard (*Crepis mollis*), or in the single flowerhead of the Milk Thistle (*Carduus marianus*).

Many of these wild plants we never saw in Ayrshire. We only knew them from Margaret's strange books. Margaret's books. How we had pored over them in our living room at Annick Water. The stories of soils; volumes of rain.

Plants are provincial and family-minded: they are made and are shaped by immediate conditions; ten miles up the coast and the air might kill them off, the soil soon enough might poison their stems. Plants only know their own ground. Their lives are encoded with local truths.

So many of Margaret's delicate flowers would never have made it in Ayrshire, and less likely still in any world beyond. But yes those flowerings were ones for the family. One-parent clones mostly staying near to home. But some of them made it away. Evolution tells us. Parts of each plant had travelled over water – a scrap of cells down a thousand streams. And others had seedlings, carried by insects, eaten by warblers, and blown from home on the changeable winds. And some had made new in their dying. Offshoots. Hybrids. Time making changes, again and again.

The plants of Scotland had mostly stayed in one place. But some had travelled. And some had changed.

'Negative geotropism,' her father had written. Bending away from the sun. But many of the old scents were upon those newly flowering perennials. A shade of hair. A bitter fruit. The ancient traits of the family name still there in the cells of the new-going shoots. The ancient traits. The unseeable roots. All those stories in Margaret's small hand.

The Mountain Pansy — *Viola lutea* — had gone to the hills, had lost its hair, grown large in its flowers; the Heartsease went off to rise tall and more purple, its runners now shrivelled to nothing. The Pale Heath Violet has a shortened spur, and is milky blue, and requires the lowland scrub for its life; and the Bastard Dog Violet with the heart-shaped leaf, its pointed sepals, and its upstart life in the wildest of places. All of them gone to the world with their memory of colours. Long since different, each one breathing in their respective grasses, singing their songs of independence. And yet we remember, as each of them does in its fragile veins, the deep-lying truth of their family relations. They know who they are. *Viola*.

Hugh was silent as we crossed the damp grass. The river smelt of rain. But with the quiet of Hugh in the meadow, and the coming grey of the meadow itself, there was nothing but riot in the branches overhead.

Twittering. Stratagem of twittering.

We could see the birds in their dark-stripped waistcoats. Their beady eyes, their semaphoring wings, black-beaking data from tree to tree, like a hall of stockbrokers at the close of the day. The sky was grey already.

From the Lindsay-style houses there came a sound, the refreshing sound of the ice-cream van. People would be out for cigarettes. The clink of empty bottles. Smokes and sugars: a gush of need at the edge of the park.

'Are you dreaming there?' said Hugh. He looked up.

'Mmm,' I said. 'I was just looking at the Lindsays.'

'Good enough houses in their day,' said Hugh. 'Sturdy. But they take up too much space. I mean, think of the block that could come out of there. You could get a hundred more families in that gap.'

I pushed Hugh to a garden wall and laid his back against it. The bricks were old and red. Dampened moss squeezing through the cracks.

Two cigarettes rolled.

'Ye know I'm right, Jamesie,' he said. 'High-rises: the only sensible thing. We never wrecked a garden that wasn't ugly. Now weren't we the ones for progress?'

I hardly missed a beat.

'Yes you were,' I said. The wall was cold at my back.

'Well you mind and remember it then,' he said. He drew a long time on the roll-up.

For an hour or so we kept to the park; along the river, around the trees. And all that time Hugh spoke of nothing else but his unfinished plans for the buildings. He said he would head a consortium, builders and planners and architects, one day soon. He said – if I might learn to *listen* – that I could come back and make myself useful as a technical assistant. I might know something about how to make the high-rises more durable.

'I've always been open to information of that kind,' he said.

He spoke of how his work wasn't yet finished. And slowly his story of the future melted into his story of the past. That had become his manner of speaking. He told me how the great John Wheatley had come one day to his office in the Glasgow City Chambers. The old gentleman had not gone to the office of the Housing Chairman. No. He came to the door of the true champion of the people's houses. The famous innovator. Mr Wheatley's face was gaunt.

'Like one of the old tenements,' said Hugh.

The old man's yellow eyes. Hugh said he wore a pressed white handkerchief in his breast pocket. He was one of Famie's Angels, said Hugh.

Mr Wheatley stepped down the long corridor like an emperor, his walking stick tapping the tiles, his head nodding gently to the typing girls. His thin bony hand going out to the young man Hugh Bawn.

My granda was absolutely certain about the words. They emerged from Mr Wheatley's lips in the very certain manner of a Scottish gentleman well used to the London parliament. A voice full of polished vigour, and lurking at the back, a faded Scots brogue. The power of his voice made Hugh iron out his vowels on the spot.

'It is a great pleasure,' said Mr Wheatley, 'to shake the hand of Mr Housing.'

'And a great many years have passed, Mr Wheatley. You were the father I never had. My mother adored you.'

He couldn't have said that.

'Ah, the kind Effie Bawn. Never see her like again. And how proud she would be you are finishing our job, Mr Bawn. We had hopes that you would. Mr MacLean had similar hopes of a career for you in what he called "national affairs". And I remember saying to the douce fellow, "John, this man will attend to the greatest of our national affairs. The great domestic issue of our poor century. Housing. You see his mother has passed him the torch. Mr Bawn is the sort of man who will have the *imagination* to follow through on our housing legislation. He is at the roots of our Labour Party." '

'Well,' replied Hugh. 'Your example, Mr Wheatley, and the

example of the Party, has always been a guiding light in this difficult business.'

'It is only to your credit that you have a memory for the struggles of before, Mr Bawn. Your new flats will provide the example for the whole of Great Britain.'

Hugh told me how they stood together, looking through the great window behind Hugh's desk, and all the tall cranes of Glasgow, as he recalled, were dipping to their task, north and south of the river.

'It is beautiful,' Mr Wheatley whispered. 'The people might see the sun at last.'

My granda ended the story there. And the words had sounded so strange to me.

The sun at last.

Hugh told me his story of Mr Wheatley as we moved across the park. The light was beginning to go from the sky; an orange glade stood around us. My voice was behind him as he told his story, and there I was, egging him on, asking for more of that perfect tale, adding my voice to Wheatley's grand encomiums. We spoke as if to silence the birds. Hugh in charge of the story; my voice that joined each phrase with a cheer.

God of mercy. Hugh was happy at our revived union. He appeared to float on his chariot seat. Happy to be outside. Happy to be telling. This was our day together. And for Hugh it seemed like a fine restoration. His grandson James was a child again, wheeling the General across the park.

I was happy that day too. The truth was not everything. Hugh had his story, and his story was good. A bank of winter heliotropes danced a jig at the park's end. They smelled of vanilla. There was no more talk of Mr Wheatley. The great

John Wheatley, who had died when Hugh was just a boy, and never saw the Glasgow tower blocks, closer the moon, closer the warming sun. Hugh had made it all up.

Cars went past in a fully leaded vapour. Raging colours. Vans and their puffs of diesel. It was just after five on the watch. Hugh wanted to see Auld Alloway Kirk before the light went out. We trundled there in minutes. The stones of the kirkyard looked bent and grey. We bumped up the steps. As usual the church was in ruins. Ferns poured out of a window; scurvy grass lay rotting by the wall. I crouched by one of the wheels as we looked at a stone in front of the yard. The stone was almost white. Chiselled, powdered. White as a page.

William Burnes. The grave of the poet's father.

'Look,' Hugh said. 'Robert Burns must have changed his name.'

'Yes,' I said. 'His father was Burnes, with an "e".'

'Wonder why he did that. It's a mystery.'

'I know he admired his father,' I said. 'He was a hard worker. A man for the Bible. He made sacrifices for the boys. Maybe Burns just thought it was a plainer poet's name.'

'Well,' said Hugh. 'He certainly knew his own mind.'

Hugh waited a minute, staring at the white stone, his eyes going all the way into the rock. 'You never really hear that old man's story. To have a son like that, a genius like. He must've been something himself.'

'Who can say?' I mumbled.

'The most beautiful words in all the language,' said Hugh. 'They really are. Famous the world over. That is what the poet does.'

He looked resolved.

'What?' I asked.

'Well,' said Hugh. 'The poets bring us in closer to ourselves, Jamesie. They make us better people. They help us to live our lives.'

His mood had changed for a second. He stared at the stone with frozen eyes. Then he tutted, and turned his head to the kirk.

'They make us celebrate this whole business,' he said.

'Or mourn it,' I wanted to say.

A fence stood around the kirk. We went up close and stopped on the grass. We were both thinking of 'Tam o' Shanter'. Hugh had learned the whole poem by heart as a boy. He began to shout it out with a giggle in his sore voice. The words went into the stone, that powdering stone, long-since beaten soft by Scotland's reforming hammers, and scoured by the local weather.

> When, glimmering thro' the groaning trees,
> Kirk-Alloway, seem'd in a bleeze;
> Thro' ilka bore the beams were glancing;
> And loud resounded mirth and dancing.
> Inspiring, bold John Barleycorn!
> What dangers thou canst make us scorn!
> Wi' tippeny, we fear nae evil;
> Wi' usquebae, we'll face the devil!

We smiled at each other: just for a second feeling the flames in the Auld Kirk. Lassies dancing in their short skirts. Blue darkness folding in about us.

There was heat in that yard. We felt the warmth, a burning spirit, a bit of hot song rolling time into nothing, we felt it strong in the listening yard, a wild flame, out of the ground to touch our cold bones that evening. We both smiled – smiled to the heart of a thing not there – and shivered into our own day, one man after the other, in that narrow field of the dead. In Alloway Kirk the cold felt warm.

'Bitter breeze,' said Hugh.

There must have been work going on at the church. Two bags of cement were parked behind the fence, and a stepladder there, leading to the top. Hugh knew a thing or two about bells. He would always tell me about the bells in a church, how old they were, which Dutch or French or Scottish man had made them, and in what way, in what year. When I was very young, and a lone visitor to his Glasgow house, he would point to a row of rusty old bells on the shelf in his work cupboard. He'd take my hand down the body of the bell.

The shoulder, the moulding wires, the inscription band, the argent, the ball of the clapper, the crown, the lip.

He sometimes stopped in the street and cupped his ear. Me at his side on the Glasgow pavement. 'Saint Mary's,' he'd say. 'Saint Aloysius.' 'Saint Alphonsus,' he'd say, or 'St Paul's.'

I couldn't hear what he could hear. My grandfather's look would be miles away. That was the thing: Hugh seemed to have an awesome sense of the world happening. No one else I knew could notice such things as bells ringing. But Hugh could. He also knew the tones of the bells, the numbers of them, the makers, the metals.

'It's easy to notice things when you're making it up,' my father once said. 'Half the churches he goes on about don't even have bells.'

Alloway Kirk (or the bold Tam) had made us thirst for a drink. We tarried, though; looking up at the kirk bell. There was a gap in the fence. Two bars removed. And the ladders now aglint in this coven of twilight. 'Dare ye, Jamesie,' said Hugh at my side. 'Up the ladder and check the bell.'

He was smiling something quite evil.

'On ye go. Up the ladder.'

Only a second's silence. I knew I would do it. A braver man would have said no. But the look in his eye, the dash of the moment.

Some way up the ladder I could see him below, snarling with pleasure, a mass of curved steel, his face as wan as Willie Burnes' tomb.

'Go on, Jamesie! Go on, son!' He shook his fist.

I climbed through the thick evening air. At the top I rested a second. You could see the muffled orange of the street lights for miles; the rows of houses over black fields. Headlamps going somewhere, people's voices. The stars beginning to show. And something happened at the top of the ladder. A feeling came over me: light-headed, awesome, a feeling of tender mercies. The sky was all eyes: peering down the millions of years; blessings of light from the cold, interminable distance.

Down, and down again.

I looked into the dark blueness above. The light coming down; it touched the pulse in my wrists, my hands gripping on, and it struck again, a second's glint on the silver bars, the two top rungs of the ladder. I felt like the first man in space: the earth below, the heavens above; and nothing could shame the universe we knew; nothing could take our minutes away, and say that we hadn't lived, and hadn't tried to live well on this smidgen of air. I took a deep breath. The light had seemed to know us. It had come from eternity to make that kirkyard blue.

Hugh was down in the trees.

'Go on, Jamesie boy! What does it say? Read off the bell.'

I put my shoulder against the gable wall, and reached in. I

held it by the flight of the clapper. It was hard to see. A note sounded out . . . It had struck the inside of the bell as I groped my way in.

'Yes!' shouted Hugh.

I couldn't see the inscription. But there was one. I could feel the raised letters.

'What of it, Jamesie?'

The voice below. I stroked the letters with my fingers. My feet were quite steady on the ladder. My fingers went lightly around the old bell. Over and over. 'A pattern border,' I shouted out.

'Yes!' came the reply. 'Good, Jamesie. And the words?' My fingers going over the cold coppery alloy.

'For. For the. The. For the Kirk. For the Kirk. Of A.l.l.o.u.a.y. For the Kirk of Allouay. 1659.' I shouted it down as my fingers inched over.

Hugh went quiet. When I came down the ladder he was standing up on the grass. The wheelchair was empty.

'A real beauty,' said Hugh. He took a step forward. 'That bell was hanging there a hundred years before Burns or his father ever saw this place. And the father now lying there for over two centuries. What do ye think of that?'

There was wonder in his voice as he said all this. And his hand went up to scratch at his ear.

'What do ye think?'

I couldn't say what I thought. I just looked across at Hugh's smiling face. His eyes as bright as the stars above.

'Yes,' I said.

Hugh allowed himself little peace. Towards the end he was ravenous for status. Sometimes that hunger would fade, as it did in the kirkyard, and he would stand exalted, as if he had come to a sense of himself, a sense of grandeur, something more than mere just deserts. But it couldn't last. His larger sense would always give in to something smaller. Or something else.

Rolling to the Cottars' Arms Hugh gloomed over. He began to diminish the moment just past. He said that bells were really no more durable than anything else. It was just a matter of luck. Bells had no place in the digital age. And anyhow bells could break. The bell in the kirk at Irvine had been cracked twice: after the joy that followed the passing of the Reform Bill, and during the mad clamour that attended Queen Victoria's Diamond Jubilee. It was just your luck.

'Many of them last,' I said.

'Not many,' he said.

There was a small crowd. We sat at one of the tables. The light from the fire danced in the glasses. The barmaid was operatic: Teutonic hair; lipstick rondo.

We drank whiskies and half lagers. Warming and cooling.

We put our hands on the copper-topped table. The fire gave our fingers a golden shadow on that surface. We could see the reflections: golden-fleshed, fire-haloed.

Four whiskies each, four lagers; a quickening in the blood. The drink knows its way. Down the grooves of the drinkers who made us, those deep-lying pipes, those holding cells, all of them built in the genes. Alcohol rushing to seize the heart. Even those who turn from the glass know that story.

Strong drink. A happy lament.

A sentimental fury.

An impotent passion.

A proud humiliation.

A violent tenderness.

A fondness for malice.

'Wine is a mocker. Strong drink is raging!'

A song was got up in the corner. The man's face was red. His eyes were all water. He pointed into the middle distance; his hand was numb on an empty glass.

'When will we seeeeeee . . . their likes agaiiiiiiin?'

The men at his table had similar faces. Red and watery-eyed. All the traces of former good looks upon them. Thick hair. Strong chins. And they too babbled in their heathen soup. Yellow-fingered like Hugh. The air was filled with their smoky laughter and the sound of the jukebox. Music, laughter, shadows of words.

In no time Hugh was in among them. He was the veteran in the wheelchair. They loved him instantly, like they loved themselves, with all the pity they could muster.

Hugh on the cross. The sponge wet with vinegar.

The fifth round. Then another. Hugh drunk and insistent with his tenner. He lectured the boys in all the great arguments of their town. Before they were born. All before they were born. His talk was just fuel on the fire. They all argued back with their loud nothings. Hugh nodded. All those men, their generosities fairly exploding over the table, their sadness building for the journey home. Hugh reeled off the jokes and the lessons of time. He had the whole corner in a roar. When he coughed they would pat his back.

'Ye're fucking right,' he said. He was dead drunk, and enjoying himself, his audience, and forgetting about me at the next table, the judging seat.

'When I was in Japan,' he said, 'in the war like, there were lassies that used to come to the camp. One squaddie after the other. In a line. The lassie's ears would be fucking stretched out, like an elephant's.'

Howls of laughter. A tray of drink. Hugh saying more. The story of how terrible life was before the war: black houses, bare feet, and all that.

'You don't know ye're living nowadays.'

He told them how people had fought for what they have. For their freedom, their nice houses. And then he would tell another vile joke; another lie. The assembly would crack.

'Are you a communist?' one of them said to Hugh.

Hugh looked over at me with his bleary eyes.

'Ye'd better ask him,' he said. 'Ye'd better ask him if we're allowed to use words like that nowadays.'

'Him sitting ower there?' said the guy with a grin. 'Who's he – yer da?'

'Aye,' said Hugh, 'he's the daddy now.'

They ordered food.

Lasagna; an avalanche of white sauce tearing down the glen.

Chips piled high as Stirling Castle.

A loch of baked beans.

Lumps of steak pie; livid red meat, clammy puff pastry.

Potatoes boiled down to silt.

Scampi chunks, breathless on kitchen roll, heaped in a buff-coloured basket, the breadcrumbs orange.

A puddle of peas. And a gammon steak that looked sore. It looked red and sore, like one of their faces, a half pine-apple-ring set in the middle, a yellow-toothed grin. The plate was a mirror: the man was eating his own Scots face.

Salt.

The one who was interested in Stalin sprinkled vinegar over

his lasagna. I was talking rubbish. I was drunk. I ate four jumbo sausages, a pile of water-logged mash.

I got the drinks in. The crowd dimmed. I wanted to use the phone. Hugh was busy telling the assembled how best to fiddle your electricity meter. I passed out the door unnoticed. The night was cold on the other side. Freezing. The pub blazed at my back as I walked off. The phones were further down the road. A square of light. I could see it. One of the road signs displayed an arrow: 'This way The Tam o' Shanter Experience'.

Two girls and a boy were crushed into the phone box. The boy wore a baseball cap and love bites. 'Phone's broke, mate,' he said.

'No,' said one of the girls. 'Let the guy use the phone.' She stubbed out the cigarette on the window pane. It burst into sparks. 'C'mon.'

I was alone in the box. And then the rain came on. Standing in the box with the rain's light drumming on the roof. Before I dialled the number, I began to think of what she would be doing there. In her front room. What was she doing right now? The phone on the kitchen table, waiting to ring. The newspapers piled up. The African bowl full of nectarines and leeks. She always turned round the bottles on the spice rack. She liked the labels to face the front. Was she standing at the cooker with an oven glove? Or eating yogurt from the fridge in her bare feet? Sitting on the carpet in a bathrobe, her back to the sofa, the television and the soaps, and a legal pad at her side, an open briefcase, a mug of tea. Was she thinking about me? Out of the window, over Dale Street, over Exchange Square, was she looking at the moving cars of Liverpool and thinking of me? Or was she looking into the sky;

the same sky above that phone box, filled with clouds and stars and distances?

Karen in the bath. Her bottles and potions on every side. Everything for softness; everything for moisture. Her 'everlasting freshness'. Her Body Shop. Long brown hair up like a palm. The smile on her lips tasting of cool lemon. And her smooth skin asking nothing. Only breathing in the perfumed water. At the base of her neck a shiny hollow. Wet like the mirrors. A place to kiss and hear her sigh those miles away. All her towels made for wrapping around twice. Made for comfort. Made for ease. And with the carpets clean they love and protect her.

Karen.

The clear-painted nails of her feet on the carpet.

Germolene rubbed in the lobes of her ears.

Her pristine vapours. Karen and her eyes not worried.

Frosted shadow, highlighter . . . lip-liners.

Her sober skin. All the cream and its promises of youth. With fingertips, with eyes closed, she draws the cotton-wool across her face, her neck; sodden with cleanser, stroking downward, downward.

Slow.

Toner. Moisturiser.

She licks the tip of a cotton bud and begins to comb her eyebrows. Karen's face. Asking me the names of flowers. Bunching them into her blue glass pots.

'How come you know these names, soft lad? Come here.'

Writing the words on sticky labels. Pushing the hair off my face. Smoothing her balm on my lips with a single finger. Kissing my eyes closed. I'm licking her finger; licking the palm of her hand. The taste of lemon.

Many a night we curled on the sofa like cats. Watching videos about people in France. Drinking red wine from giant tumblers. Arguing about why the women must always be punished or die. We would read the same paperback: I'd tear it down the middle and let her take the back half (she always reads quicker than I do). She would stand behind me as I was shaving. She would count my ribs and put her lips to my shoulders. Her hands spreading over my bare chest. Her hand running down and stroking my cock. Her lemon mouth going down my arm and biting my wrist. And I'd kiss her sniggers away; shaving foam on her face, in her hair.

We would go to bed. All the debris of our current lives on the living-room floor. The video unrewound. Things not said. The sheets in Karen's bed were as cool as a field of long grass. So cool I wanted to sleep there for ever. The cool sheets and all that calm for ever. The long grass. The Mersey nights at the patio windows. Karen's silencing world of clean cotton. She was always saying I whispered in my sleep. Quietly. No moans or groans but quiet words. Her hand in my hair.

Sleeping.

The smell of pines. The old smell of pine.

Every long minute of the night we would breathe our own in that flat of hers. We dreamed our dreams of oceans, and unborn babies, the windows like rigging, the wind against them, and both of us talking our strange words to nobody. There were words we couldn't say to each other; they were lost in the muddle of our separate pillows. Karen had wanted our baby. I shook my head a hundred times.

'Let's have no more of families.'

And still the night bore down on us. The night bore down, a blue returning of the city's breaths, the millions of souls asleep, our carbon dioxide, our flowers breathing, quiet there, alive in their pots. The North of England is radioactive. We slumber in gases: a red glow at the heart of every bed. The power stations run all night. Out on the motorways cars go into the fog. Acid rain at the rattling glass. We can hear the winds in our tangle of sheets.

Sleeping.

The all-night garages cold and wet in a gaggle of light. There are service stations to the North Pole, but inside our rooms there is no noise of baby. We slept all night; no gurgle to interrupt our privacies. No noise of baby. And that was the dead centre of our troubles. Karen and I had started a baby. By the sparkle in her eyes I knew she had wanted it.

Our baby.

'Please, Karen . . .'

Her sparkling eyes. I knew she wanted it.

'. . . let us have no more of families.'

She terminated it. We never spoke of babies again.

Our pregnancy. We caused it to come to nothing. I caused it. And in our clean lives, our dark sleeps, we are thinking about it. It is all my fault. We are thinking about that too. Mothers. Fathers.

The dead centre of our trouble. It lay heavy on us. Karen said I was stopping the future. My head was clouded with remorse.

The rain that drummed on the phone-box roof.

She answered the phone on the second ring. 'Karen, it's me.'

'James.'

'Are you okay, baby?' She waited a second.

'Not a hundred per cent, no. Are you drunk?'

'Baby, I miss you. I took him out today. My granda. We're in a pub. It's raining.'

'Is he well enough to be out like that? I thought he was dying.'

'He's up and down. I miss you. This is . . . this is terrible, Karen.'

I suddenly thought I might cry into the phone. I knew she could hear it.

'James. Do you want me to come up there?'

'No, don't come. Everything will be all right.'

She tried to lift me. 'You sound so Scottish, sweetheart. If you don't come home soon I might not be able to understand you.'

'It'll be a while yet, Karen. It's just so weird . . . all this.'

'Phone me more, James. Are they giving you a hard time?'

'No, no. It's not that. It's hard for everybody, you know?'

'I went round and checked your messages. Most of them boring. Phil from your office is looking for a number . . .'

'Tell him there isn't a number. I don't want anybody ringing . . .'

'You'll have to extend your leave. Do you want me to ring . . .'

'Tell them not to do that. There's no phone here, it's . . .'

'Okay, darling. It's fine.'

'Will you ring Phil? Tell him I have to stay on here. It's hard to know really.'

'All right. And a guy left a message, a guy . . . em, McCluskey. From Glasgow. He said you talked about a consultancy in Glasgow. They're doing some block. Do you want to ring him?'

'Can you give me the number?'

'Wait a second.'

I could hear her padding across the kitchen. The television music somewhere. In the bedroom. She came back with the number. I wrote it on the back of a betting slip.

'And that's it,' she said. 'Are you sure you miss me?'

'I do, Karen. I feel like a . . . I don't know what I feel. If I ever get away from here . . . If this is over . . . We'll go on holiday or something, you and me. I'll buy you a coat.'

She was laughing now. 'James, you're drunk. Don't say any more . . .'

'Better, Karen. I can make it better.'

She went very quiet. The hiss of the phone, the remote TV. I could hear her breathing.

'Better,' I said. 'You know we are good. You and me.'

The sound of our breathing.

'You take care up there,' she said. 'And if he improves just come back, and then go back when . . . you know . . . things get worse. I don't know why they need you there all this time. But anyway. I want you back here in one piece. All right? I love you, James.'

'Love you, Kaz.'

And then she put the phone down. But still in my head I could hear her padding across the carpet in Liverpool. 'Love you, Karen.

I.

I love you.'

The rainwater ran from my hair, down my face, into my mouth. There was a loch in the road. Water everywhere. I stopped at the edge of the path and was sick. I thought it would never stop. I held on to a low-hanging branch; the water ran down my arm. A revolt of the nerves, a violent breach. I stood for a while in the rain.

'Why did you leave me with all them fools?' Hugh said. His head was low.

'I thought you were having a good time,' I said.

'But I wanted you here,' he said. 'This is *us* having a good time.'

One of the crowd broke in.

'Your da here is some man,' he said. 'A great man.'

I just nodded.

Hugh studied me. It was an even look, a resigned stare. The other men got on with the business of each other.

'You think I'm corrupt, son, don't you?' Hugh said.

'What?' I looked at him funny.

He'd fallen under his own spell. He was speaking more to himself than me. The whisky was all the way through him. He was saying things he kept to himself.

'So we were for better railway stations and wage packets and clean houses and school milk,' he said.

Something long gone came into his eyes. 'Simple things. We wanted to better ourselves. The inside toilets. We knew the enemy in them days. We wanted milk for the weans and better teeth for them. And aye people made something out of it. I know that. They tell me people made something for themselves. Well, well. That's the way it is. There's always somebody making something out of progress. But I never did. As long as things got done. That was all I cared about.'

I said nothing. He turned with his heat.

'Don't stand over me, Jamesie, with your fucking regulations. I know who I am. And your crowd will rush over the Border with the big solution I take it?'

I thought to say nothing; my stomach fluttered. I looked at his eyes.

'Even progress changes, Hugh,' I said. 'Different notions. A new time that's all. It doesn't matter.'

'Different times?'

'A new time.'

'And you and your cronies are going to make something new out of this mess are you? This rubble you're creating? No, Jamesie. Tell you something for free, son. You will need much more than a couple of slogans and a big banner. You will need more than a demolition ball and dynamite sticks.'

I was too drunk to ignore him. I thought I knew better.

'It's a good place to start,' I said.

My resolve of the day, to protect him, was wavering now, as it wavered before, and would do again, before it was over. I should have just nodded, even in drink.

'When we blew things down it was a start,' he said. 'With your lot it's not the start of anything. It's the end.'

'We can change things,' I said.

'Good luck to you,' he said. 'Here's more for free. You're following the bad examples nowadays. Our example was good.'

'There are walls coming down all over the place,' I said.

He looked up, his eyes red-rimmed, and sick. He tapped his chest and pointed to the air. 'Our materials are stronger,' he said.

I came back to my senses then. I would say nothing.

He leaned back.

A taxi came for a girl at the next table. I asked her to get the driver to radio for another one. Hugh was ready to go home. His head was down, and he was no longer leading the board in their jokes and their songs, their high tales of world domination. He was content there; he wore a wearied smile. He had made his audience love him. He seemed to recede into a world of his own. His cigarette burned. And he smiled at me. My soaking hair.

Outside a pink firework burst over the distant houses. It was late in the month for fireworks; late in the day for the rites of treason.

Our car made its way through the circus of Ayr. Yards of water round the crooked trees; house lights dim behind a gauze of rain. And on the outskirts of town, with the roar of the sea, we passed by the Glengall House. To the everyday eye just another white building with its own sad business going on inside. A nursing home. The mute walls; the yellow rooms. But still the old madhouse where Hugh had been born. The ghost of his mother lying on a bed.

Knees and belly and head like the peaks of Arran.

We passed the building in a second. Both of us in the back seat. Those wraiths made of sea-salt in the asylum just past. A puddle of music. Hugh rolled his head from the window and stared at me with his sore mouth.

'Guy Fawkes,' he said.

I thought of fire blazing in the wards of Glengall. And women dancing: hornpipes, jigs, strathspeys, and reels. 'Weel done, Cutty-sark!'

It was pitch black. Hugh looked at me long. He was all of his years. Glengall behind us. And in minutes the old man was sound asleep. The driver was off on his own. My head went to the window on my own side. The front doors of houses just falling away. Those living rooms. All the houses just spinning back; a stream of fast-going brickwork. And a herd of ghosts coming after the car. I looked out the back window. There was nothing left but a whorl of mist.

We pulled away to the blackness of Ayrshire. My eyes wide open.

The child you have been will never desert you.

5

On Earth

Margaret said there was a Christmas tree in the hall cupboard. It was stuffed in a box, the wire branches bent out of shape, trapped in green tinsel. There were dozens of shiny baubles there too, and Santas and angels chipped with age. I put my hand right down to the bottom: a silver star, a home-made star, a thing I had made for them years ago.

The cupboard was heaped with old things like that. Boxes of books from Collins. The plastic bases of flower arrangements. A carton of iron bells. Knitting patterns. And while I was in there I noticed more of Hugh's old plans and time-sheets. I put them into a carrier bag, slipped them under the Christmas box, and lifted them together. The electricity meter caught my eye as I came up. The wheel wasn't moving. A length of twisted coat-hanger was threaded through the box, holding the wheel at a stop. I put out the light and closed the door.

Hugh seemed too weary to cough. He couldn't stand up. At times he seemed unsure if he was awake or asleep, and we'd hear him grumble at the coming and going.

'Fuck, fuck.' 'See us a fag.'

Some afternoons I just sat by the bed reading from Burns or Sven Hassel, or rolling the cigarettes. Now and then he'd throw his hand over to close the book. Or he'd pass a roll-up back to me. 'Too tight,' he'd say. 'I'll need a poultice . . . on the back of my . . . neck . . . to get a draw on that.'

And he seemed to know us well enough as the coughing returned. The two things came together. The sore cough and us. At times he could flame up with a moment's reason. 'D'ye hear my wife singing?' he said one of those times. 'D'ye hear her? She'll never forget, that woman.'

None of us was good at forgetting. That was a family ailment. But he was right about Margaret – she would never forget – and her memory could seem like something larger than all of us. Margaret lived out of her memory; the stories, and the keeping of stories, was what she felt the world was for. She held our lives to account. She wanted us all to remember what had happened here. When she lost her temper, with the women at the coffee mornings, the kids on the landing, the men on TV, the rogue members of the family, it was usually because they were 'ignorant'. That was the worst thing she could say about anybody alive. They were ignorant. They made an easy job of forgetting the rights and wrongs, and they were beyond care, and just ignorant.

Margaret used to be a great one for rote learning. My proper education began in her house. She would sit me down with her books of popular history, giving me the great names, and the final word on the holy terrors. I can still recall whole chunks of those books she made me learn by heart. A sense of betrayal lay deep in both Hugh and Margaret; it was an important part of who they were. Way behind both of them, or behind the words they spoke, lay thousands of acres of emptied land – bogs, glens – places filled with the sound of sheep and lost voices, where once their ancestors had thrived and raged. Margaret had taught me the names of her people, those men of the old Highlands, whose houses were burnt, whose land was cleared. They were men hanged on apple trees grown by their own fathers; they were women beaten with ash truncheons; they were starving children, sent under white sails to Canada, torn from the land they loved, their dark tartans turned into shrouds.

Over the months I had noticed how Margaret was without living friends. She saw the women at the coffee mornings, but she wasn't close to any of them. She lived her life in an element of ghosts. Death had long ago taken the people she felt close to, those friends and kinsmen she had never met, and just as far back it had silenced her foes, those lords and ladies who'd made the country a place of mourning. Margaret possessed a whole eternity of forgiveness, but only for the living; they may be ignorant, they may be wrong, and selfish on top of all that, but for living people she only felt sorry. She might, now and then, lose her temper, but really she only felt sorry. She had no inclination to blame people for their faults. She saved her fury for the ignoble dead. Them she hated. The people who betrayed her people. Them she hated with every shard of her being.

I dressed the Christmas tree in my granny's room. She sat in her favourite chair. An *Ayr Advertiser* was folded on her lap. A cup and saucer. Minute by minute she picked the fluff from the wrists of her jumper. It was a man's jumper. She often wore men's jumpers.

'I can still remember your history lessons,' I said.

'I'm sure that you can, Jamie son. And it will no be long until you're telling them to your own bairns.'

I didn't look up at this. I just stared at my face in a green

Christmas bauble. I had my father's eyes. A minute passed. I looked up then. 'I would like to have kids one day,' I said.

The words surprised me as they came out. They were true, and I just hadn't said them like that before. Something about the room, and the way I was stretched out on the carpet, and the Christmas tree, and my granny's white face; something about the radiator and the heat coming over, and the look of the light as it fell about her old photographs. I don't know why I said it to her then. Something made me want to say it. I suppose I wanted her to know something private about me, to see me just a moment in the glimmer of my own adulthood.

'We nearly had a baby once,' I said. 'But I don't think I'd be a very good father.'

'Ye mustn't think so,' she said. 'The days move on, Jamie. Nothing that's happened should make you afraid. You're a good man.'

'Not yet,' I said.

The words came out very quiet. She paused with them.

'Is Karen your girlfriend?' she asked.

'But who told you that?'

'You did,' she said. 'In the first days you were here, you were saying her name, just in your sleep. Is she nice?'

'Not bad for a Protestant,' I said.

We both smirked. My granny rolled her eyes.

'Well I'm saying nothing,' she said. 'You're the modern ones. Just don't waste yer life on worries, son. I want ye to be happy.'

She licked two fingers and smoothed away a drip on her skirt.

'I'm glad ye've held on to the wee bit history,' she said. And then she looked at me in a manner of trust. My granny had a look for everything. The last one had two meanings: I trust you have listened; I trust you will always be listening.

'George Granville Leveson-Gower,' I said.

Poor Margaret grew black-eyed.

She put both hands round her teacup, as if her body had sudden need of the warmth, and she hissed all her breath out at once. 'Evil,' she said. 'Pure evil.'

I rose on my knees and faced her. Those little acres of carpet between us. The Christmas ornaments were still in my hands as I started reciting. I smiled as the words came back. Margaret closed her eyes.

'George Granville Leveson-Gower. He was the Great Improver. Where there had been nothing in his opinion but wilderness and savagery, he built, or had built for him by the Government, thirty-four bridges and four hundred and fifty miles of road. The glens emptied by his commissioners, law-agents and ground-officers (with the prompt assistance of soldiers and police when necessary) were let or leased to Lowlanders who grazed 200,000 True Mountain Sheep upon them and sheared 415,000 pounds of wool every year.'

At this my granny opened her eyes: she raised her brow and sipped her tea. She thought I'd forgotten the next part. She put down the cup. 'He pulled . . .'

I raised a finger, smiled, continued.

'He pulled the shire of Sutherland out of the past for the trifling cost of two-thirds of one year's income. And because he was an Englishman, and spoke no Gaelic, he did not hear the bitter protests from the poets among his people.'

'And a fucking bastard he was as well,' said my granny.

'Maggie!' I said, laughing at the base of the tree, throwing a bauble up at her chair. 'That's no talk for a Christian woman.'

'Well,' she said, now deeply blushing, 'no wonder.'

A great light was up in her eyes. 'I'm so glad ye keep these things in yer head,' she said. And with that she switched on her television. When I finished the work and stood at the door she looked again.

'That's nice and Christmassy,' she said.

Her eyes went back to the screen, and she bit her nails. It seemed like she wasn't really watching the figures on telly though. Her gaze stopped a bit short of the screen. She was just staring at space. From her little twitches, her quicksome grins, I guessed she saw there some shapes of her own.

It was a younger Margaret who taught me those lines. She gave me a custard cream for every paragraph memorised. And afterwards she gave me indignant lectures about what it all meant. She would sometimes cry and sing in our kitchen seminars. It all meant so much to her.

Stitched between the lines of those lessons was a notion of how the horrors of the past might relate to Hugh's great enterprise. She would fix my grandfather – that other great improver – as the opposite of those long-named ravagers of old. She told me that Hugh understood the horrors of forced removal, and that he too came from people who fought against it. His mother, she said, had been a famous woman who beat back the landlords of another time. And Hugh's great experiments had grown out of those domestic trials. She was sure of that.

Hugh was a great man. He was the hero of her youth, and even in decline he embodied, for her, the higher things. He had made a difference; he had given the people betterment. She said she loved him for that and also for himself. That is the way she put it. And maybe no one ever got close enough to my granny to ask her just what she meant by that. Loving him for what he'd done, and what he was. Enfolded within all Margaret's certainties was a hard core of pride, and within all that, a smallholding, a cosmos, a kernel, of pity.

To say that Margaret was held back and stifled – trapped by a sense of duty to that pity – would be to say something against her wishes. She was not like my mother, who for years defended my father's actions for fear of the truth. Margaret was quite sure of her husband's gifts, and certain in the role she had sought and maintained, as his partner, his defender. She would be against any suggestion that Hugh's troubles had held her back, that the obsessions of Hugh's life had silenced her own cares. She didn't seem to feel that had happened to her. Hugh's cares and her cares lay side by side at the foundations of their marriage. If anyone said that Hugh had been too long distracted with the business of tower blocks, and changing the world, she would only say there were worse things to be distracted with. She didn't speak up. She didn't see any need to speak up. She would say that any worries she had were worries she had brought upon herself, and would add that Hugh had always a lot to contend with, that he had taken large tasks upon himself. In a worn moment – first light, last candle – she might confess that she had sometimes been unhappy. And no sooner would she have said such words than she'd take them back.

'It's my own fault,' she'd say. 'I never had any women friends, and I never went over the door.'

Privately I felt that Margaret was more than once a casualty of the great improvers. The first one burnt her houses and sent her people in ships to another world, the second kept her in exile from the truth of things, and made her a prop in the fantasy of his own spotlessness. By the end of his life Hugh had caused her to be more than a prop — she was a well-spring of propaganda, an everyday font of saving lies. I never intended to say a thing about it. Those months in Scotland, the days watching my grandfather die, were lived in opposition to any such saying. I too had become a prop and a well-spring. I too wanted him easy at the end. My granny kept her secrets to herself. She had always shown patience and self-denial when it came to the matter of other people's inventions. As Christmas came on, I grew more determined to follow that example, shadowing her measures to protect Hugh in his final distress, whilst all the time inventing new measures to protect her in hers. But I often failed to be as good as she was. I came late to these responsibilities. I sometimes got it very wrong.

One day we were washing Hugh in his bed. The morning had spread out badly. There was bedlam in the flats underneath. The sound of smashing glass. Kids were rattling the letter box every few minutes for hours. I went out to the landing. 'There's somebody sick in here,' I shouted. 'Keep away from the door.'

'Fuck up,' said a tiny boy, scampering to the stairs.

Both lifts were broken again. I wanted to go out and phone the Corporation.

'Don't phone them,' Margaret said, wringing out the cloths. 'The school holidays have started. They'll get the lifts going soon.'

Hugh's green eyes would open now and then. He looked at the wall.

Even with all this, the hollow cheeks, the scalp withered, you could still see how handsome Hugh had been. His face was like something out of marble. You couldn't tell if he was asleep; it had all gone quiet. It was very strange in that back bedroom: the holes punched out on the walls, our medicinal soap, the noise down below, that McCormack album sleeve pinned to the wall with a flightless dart.

I was washing Hugh's feet; Margaret worked at his head and chest. 'John McCormack sang,' Margaret said, 'and the things that came into his voice. You wouldn't believe it was possible. The Irish can sing. And yer granda here, his people freed themselves good and able. The people of Scotland and Ireland, they drink in the same water. And Ireland's its own country . . .'

The agitations of the morning got the better of me.

'Ireland's its own country no thanks to Scotland,' I said, catching my own breath. 'And Ireland never did you any favours either.'

Margaret looked like she'd just been slapped.

Hugh opened his eyes.

In a slow way, in a way very deliberate, and quite blank, I went on to say things grossly out of turn. I don't know why. Each word was a stab of something. Sickness, anger, frustration with lies. I just opened my stupid mouth.

'The brave Sutherland people we sing about, the great fencibles, helped the English defeat the Irish rebellion of 1798. Scotsmen had a hand in the spilling of blood on Vinegar Hill.'

'Shut up,' said Hugh, not moving.

'And then,' I said, my hands beginning to shake a little, 'later on, those Irishmen, those victims of famine and wars, they joined in the scramble over your fathers' glens.'

'Shut your face,' said Hugh, half-rising from the bed.

I stood up.

There was a flame in Margaret's eye.

'Those Irishmen we betrayed came on to betray us,' I said.

'Your books, Granny, are not the only ones I know. The evil English! It was some of your people that put swords into the heads of Hugh's men, and his men that burned your Highland cottages. They cleared the land you go on about. See? I've read other books. I know other things by heart, Granny.'

Hugh was coughing hard.

'Get fucking out!' he spluttered. 'He's a fucking liar. An English bastard. He's just his bastarding father all over. Get him out!'

And when I looked at Maggie she was pressing him down on the pillows. Her eyes were wet. I could have died. Hugh was whimpering oaths to himself. She looked up at me once he was settled.

'Would you leave us be, Jamie. I want to wash down the middle of your granda.'

She dipped her cloth then into the basin.

'I'm sorry,' I said. 'I'm so sorry.'

'Don't fash, son,' she said.

And just as I turned she spoke again. It was as if she were quoting from something long gone. A tablet of truths. I stood there ashamed.

'It wasn't just right what you said. Our people broke apart when they heard the drums of the Irish. There was no blood. We have it written down.'

No more was said about mistakes.

Our universe was full of unsaid things. And that was most helpful. That was best.

Fergus McCluskey was in charge of the blow-downs in Glasgow. He wanted me to come and supervise the demolition of a block in the Gorbals, at Florence Square. It was one of the show-towers designed by Marcus Booth. Hugh had commissioned them. I was with him the day it was opened.

McCluskey's number had been in my pocket since the day I went into Ayr with Hugh. More than once I had gone down to the phone outside the chip shop at Annick Water. I had stood there with the phone in my hand, the number on the betting slip, and a feeling I should go ahead, carry on with the job old Hugh had taught me to do. But I knew it wasn't the same job. Hugh had taught me to plan those houses. For five years now I'd been blowing them down. That was the new plan. And in Liverpool it all made sense. But there, at the foot of Annick Water, with the light all yellow on the eighteenth floor, I found it too hard to ring the number. Hugh's green eyes were somewhere above. My hand would return the phone to its cradle.

I phoned McCluskey too late to help him.

'Fergus,' I said, 'it's James Bawn here.'

'Where in Christ's name have you been?' he said. 'We've been needing a hand here.'

'I'm sorry, Fergie. Karen gave me the number. I couldn't get round to ringing until now. I just couldn't face it. I've been away from work this last while.'

'So your office said. But they wouldn't give us a number. Are you all right?'

'I'm fine,' I said. 'It's just that block. Florence Square. D'ye know, Fergie, that was one of Hugh's.'

'Of course,' he said, 'but I thought you never saw him any more.'

'Well he's dying in Ayrshire. I'm with him here. I just

couldn't think of it . . .' And then I stopped. I thought there was much I wouldn't say.

'I'm sorry,' said Fergus McCluskey. 'Nobody knew that here.'

'It's tomorrow morning, right? The blow. Ten in the morning?'

'Aye.'

'One thing, Fergie. Stick the stuff in the middle. Bang it right under the joists. There's a lot of steel in there, and it'll fold straight if you get under it. And keep the punters well back. More than usual. You know — the blunt force. Keep them out of there.'

'It's dense in those streets. That's why we needed the help. We can't have any flying metal. There's a lot of people in and out of there.'

'Just ring it,' I said. 'The whole area. Get the radio people to juice up the dangers.'

'Right ye are. All of it's in order.'

'See you before long,' I said.

'Hope so,' he said. 'And Jamesie. Send our best to the big man. We always talk about him.'

'No problem,' I said.

There were two things I knew outside the phone box. I knew I would set out the next morning to see the last of the Gorbals block. And I knew I would never be able to tell Hugh his apprentices were asking for him.

The early morning was cold on the bones. The air tasted of snow. Down in the housing scheme there was hardly a noise; the lamps fizzed quietly on the empty street. The lamps fizzed away out there, as if in conversation with each another, as if no one could be watching, no one awake. Places like this are deserted at night. Not a soul on the street. You hear the odd shout, the odd car, but mostly you hear nothing at that hour but the fizz of the lamps . . .

The sound of your own blood turning.

It was Saturday morning. I had stood at that window on Saturdays before. My good teenage years, freed from the Ferguson school and my mother and father, my eagerness then for days to begin; awake at the window in the early light, sandshoes on, and fishing rod, or looking way out for the milk-float, the first of my grand employers, the hush-hush whirr, the rattling glass, smoothing its way round the bend of our street.

I saw it again that morning: the milk-float, whirring into another day. That street and this block and the person watching, none of us new any more, none of us the first on the planet.

Hugh lay awake in a tangle of candlewick bedspread. The room was thick-breathed and vague; Hugh in the gloaming, a roomful of doubts.

'Morning,' I said.

'Aye,' he said. 'Bring me a bit cheese from the fridge, would you not.'

I came back in and cut it up on a plate. He pulped the cheese soft with his gums.

'My mouth is that fucking sore,' he said. The blanket smelt of old man's sweat.

'I know,' I said. 'Take it slow.'

I pressed some antiseptic cream on my finger and rubbed it round his mouth.

'Away,' he shrugged.

The bath was full of wet sheets. I shaved at the sink. The water was warm. I poured out some more, dragging handfuls over my shoulders, under my arms. My body had changed since coming back. No mornings at the gym. Eating funny. My arms seemed thinner. It was as if, in some strange way, my body was going back in time, becoming a child's body again. All the power had gone out of me: my chest and my arms felt weak; I hadn't thought of sex in a long while. My body was as secret as a boy's. I felt alone with it.

Margaret had ironed me some shirts and draped them over a clothes-horse in the hall. I put on a blue one; knotted a red-striped tie.

My face was thin in the mirror.

You can't be too smart as a Housing man.

John Wheatley and his walking cane. Down the corridor of the City Chambers. Tipping a wink at the typing pool. Tall and beloved, the great Housing man. Smart. A white hand-kerchief in the breast pocket. The cranes out the window. 'Aah, the kind Effie Bawn.'

Mr Wheatley so neat in Hugh's office. To shake the hand of Mr Housing.

I needed a haircut. I imagined hands mussing the hair on my forehead. The taste of lemon balm on my lips.

My head poked into the bedroom.

'I'm off now, Hugh.'

There was silence then; nothing there but a low, tranquil-lised breathing.

There was a story in that morning's *Scotsman*. It sat under a wide picture of the Gorbals: 'Booth's Tower Comes Down Today'.

An era will end in Glasgow this morning as high-rise flats in the troubled Gorbals area are blown to the ground. The unpopular Maxton Block at Florence Square, designed by Sir Marcus Booth, and built in 1972 at a cost of one million pounds, will finally be demolished in a controlled explosion at 10 a.m. The 'Maxie' block was viewed at the time as a work of architectural genius, held by the controversial former Chairman of the Public Works Committee, Mr Hugh Bawn, to be 'the saving of Glasgow'. The so-called 'streets in the sky', which were believed to be the answer to the City's notorious housing problems, were built at break-neck speed throughout the sixties and early seventies. But, in recent years, Bawn's blocks became better known as 'the blight of Glasgow' — dampness and vandalism making life a nightmare for the nearly 500 residents in Florence Square.

Mrs Moira McPhail, 42, who lived in the block for six years before moving to Carntyne last year, is glad to see them go. 'It's good riddance to bad rubbish,' she said. 'They were a misery, and they should never have been built in the first place. They're nothing but an eyesore.' Mrs McPhail said her eldest son Ewen's asthma got much worse while they were living at the flats.

But not everyone will be so happy to see Maxie go. Pensioner Jim Ainsley, a Gorbals resident all his life, said yesterday how much you got used to them. 'I'll miss them,' he said, 'they were nice on a summer's day, and much better than the slums that were there before.' Ex-Chairman Hugh Bawn, who is among those under investigation in the City Council's corruption hearings, was not available for comment. He lives in Irvine New Town, and is said to be in bad health.

A spokesman for the Housing Department would only

say that the tower blocks had seemed a good idea at the time. He warned that the area would be out of bounds this morning, and that spectators should stay well behind the perimeter fences.

End of an Era? Opinion, page 16.

Two kestrels hovered at the railway siding. I had never seen two. One higher up, pinned to its spot of clear air, wings beating, its eye on something small in the grass. The second one hung much lower. It was just about to dive as the train ran on. I put the newspaper back on the seat.

Ayrshire out there, and all its purple leaves. On a hill just ahead, the last of a broken Franciscan monastery, its dome of low cloud smeared in grey. There was something of a window remaining. A shower of rain came through the window the second we passed. A schoolboy across from me fussed about with a calculator. He wore a green blazer. 'Going home?' I asked.

'Aye,' he said. We crossed the edge of Glengarnock Loch. The boy pointed.

'Could you show me that on a map?'

I said it was easy if he had the right one.

Out of a rucksack he drew a pile of Ordnance Surveys, more than a few, held together with an elastic band.

'Let's see,' I said.

The second one down in the pile was the one for North-West Ayrshire. I unfolded it, laid it out flat beneath the window, there in the space between the boy's legs and mine. 'Here we are,' I said. 'You can see the line we're on. Here. Between Kilbirnie and Milliken Park. You can run your finger all the way to Glasgow. And that's the Loch there. The patch of blue.'

He twisted the map round to himself. And he looked at it quietly, his finger running up and down the lines, over the hills and their forests of birch, up and down the sands of the coast. 'And this is all sea?'

'Yes,' I said. 'All the way to the islands.'

After a while he folded it up and went back to the mind of his calculator.

'I like maps,' I said.

The boy looked up like I'd just said nothing. He made a frowning smile with his lips and his chin. Far away, unfazed, his eyes said that he liked them too; there is nothing the matter with maps.

I found an Avis car in Paisley. A swipe of a card made it mine for two weeks. I hadn't wanted a car until that day. I wanted to walk everywhere, or sit on buses, mope on trains, face the future in the backs of taxis, but now it seemed easier to have a car. The one I hired was made for the serious smoker. It had two lighters. A place to stand up a packet of fags. The car was a Turkish bath in minutes.

A guy on the radio — sour-voiced, bone idle — was talking tripe to a legion of teenage phone-ins. He spoke like a drunk impersonating a drunk. 'It's time now to burn the St Andrew's flag,' he was saying. 'Scotland the brave, it is Scotland the bollocks and no mistaking the fact. Okay. Here we have wee Regina from the Garngad. Gina, is that you?'

'Hello, Lou. I love the show. I'm glad you got rid of they bampots were on a minute ago. Lou, tell me this. Tell me. If Scotland's that brave, how come we've never won the World Cup? All they idiots on your show going on about the football. Good talk. Tell you, Lou. It's all just balls — tell them that out there. Show us your World Cup if you're that smart.'

'Go'n yourself, Regina. That was wee Regina from up the

road. Great stuff. You tell them, hen. The problem with this country is there's too few people with brains. That is the problem. Now, heavenly bodies. Phone in and give us the benefit of your view. This morning's topic is The Scottish Nation: Why Have We Made Such an Arse of It? Stay beside your phones. Okay. Jim from Foxbar, give us your view.'

'Aye, Lou. That lassie was on there. What she's needing is a right good . . .'

'Well done, son. That's the brainy stuff we like. It's dunderheads like you that's got the country in the grubber. Next — line two, Angela from East Kilbride. Angela?'

'Morning, Lou.'

'Turn down your radio, hen. That's a helluva racket.'

'Okay, Lou. Is that it? Right. The reason, Lou, the reason this country's in a mess, right, is the way men talk to women. Like that idiot just there. There's, there's no respect for the female. If my father had spoken to my mother the way these boys speak to us . . .'

'I wouldn't like to bring in a broken pay packet to the likes of you,' said Lou.

'Right you are,' said Angela, laughing away. 'And another thing. These condoms. They're too available now. It's encouraging them all to bloody well abuse the system so it is. Women don't need condoms, it's work they need. And men can learn to talk right.'

'Okey-dokey . . . Line three . . .'

I turned it off.

The old Labour men just loved to talk housing. I can hear it still. It was waiting lists, it was good, clean air, preserving community, the back-to-backs condemned. It was land being scarcer than money. It was packed with amenities. It was creating a taste for the ambience of the suburbs. It was clearing the slums. It was improving quality. Aesthetically pleasing.

'The saving of Glasgow.'

One of my granda's oldest chums was an architect, a pipe-smoking man full in love with those phrases. And he believed every one of them. He spoke of the blocks as social saviours, artistic wonders, a triumph of this over that. He once described some of the creations he fashioned on the slopes of Sheffield as looking like Tuscan hill villages in the half-light. To the Housing Committee he passed out postcards of St Mark's Square in Venice. 'This is our example of a mixed style,' he said.

They wanted so much. And their wanting so much made us want so much less. The ones still alive send me hate mail in Liverpool. McCluskey gets it too. Letters still written in the old Corporation style. Commas in the date. Reference being made. Typewritten. And to every one it's a personal matter. I always want to say sorry. I want to say thank you and sorry. We just don't agree any more.

Sorry. Thank you.

And yes, I know. They say there was nothing of aerosols then. Nothing of satellite telly and dining rooms. People wanted to be like other people. And now they want to be themselves. They want garages and trips abroad and a different-coloured door.

I want to say yes. I know. Sorry.

Those letters made me sad because of Hugh. But not only because of Hugh. Every time we blow a block I feel it for those who built it. The old men are always in our minds. We want to say sorry. Thank you. And we live like you with our plans and our words in the dark. Their names on those plaques at the front of the blocks. Those newspaper clippings. A day out for the Committee. Women in hats. Men in dark coats. Eyes raised up.

I parked the car at the Argos Superstore. I walked past a wedding boutique: 'Kilts and veils on special offer.' And then the woo of the public bars, the everyday magic of Stockwell Street, the stumpy haunts of lovers and fiddlers and scribes. A blackboard was there with its chalk half-gone: 'Mary MacDonald of The Songs.'

Last night's laughs. The smell of old drink in the street. People milling around. And up at the bridge they were gathered in thousands. Down by the river. All the eyes looking past the weather-scarred wall. All the eyes. Over the River Clyde they looked. And tall over there, shading the Gorbals, the clouds up above them, the Florence Square towers, and grey they were, and grey the windows, and overhead a school of starlings moved as one.

I thought of long-ago crowds by those banks. Women in bonnets with placards aloft. The Green all mud. The rumble of feet. The leaves in some past autumn spinning in circles in the public parks. Up on the streets they marched to a drum. A bad day for images of Gladstone and St George. The rumble of feet growing louder and louder. Down among the citadels of St Enoch's the procession passed, the clamour rose, brushing the fronts of those ornate buildings with their clocks insensible. *We are Fighting Landlord Huns.*

A tarpaulin sign lay over the roof of the condemned block, tied on the head, a knotted hankie:

DALE CONSTRUCTION — DEMOLITION.

The women beside me at the railing were tearing sandwiches for kids. 'Keep your eyes open or you'll miss it,' said one of the women. There was buzz and Saturday chatter all the way down. 'It's ten past ten,' said the woman again. 'If they don't hurry up we'll miss Donna at the majorettes. She'll be standing at the door.'

'Aw she'll wait for us,' said her friend, chewing a cake, then bringing the top of an orangeade bottle up to her lips. She held it there like a trumpet. All the way along the north bank of the Clyde, the noises of children, the clapping and crying, and mothers in leggings, wiping and catering, boyfriends and fathers staring ahead.

Bottles like trumpets; the Saturday hoopla.

My eyes were steeped in the brown river water. There was hardly a movement there. Just water; calm and slick and oblivious. In the middle of the stream you could see reflected the swooning towers of the Gorbals. The tall buildings. A glint of the windows coming out the water; a dazzle of glass. And calm the water. Calm and slick and oblivious.

Just then a foghorn sounded right clear. For half a minute it went. When it stopped there was silence. No one spoke; the children looked up. And still the water was calm to my eyes. A bang went up like a noise from the core of the earth. It was a good blast: you could feel the tremor up through your shoes. People gasped.

I looked up from the Clyde: the block just dropped right down. Out of the sky and into the river, the tower disappeared, and dust and smoke rose up in its place. In a minute the water was calm again; the rumbling had gone.

Everything was quiet.

The sadness you feel when a house comes down. You feel for the people who lived there. All those sitting rooms and painted walls, gone in an instant, as if the hours that passed inside meant nothing much, as if they never happened. The shape of those rooms will always remain in the minds of those who lived there. People will grow up with a memory of their high view over Glasgow. They'll remember the sound of the elevators, the lights down below; the cupboards, the bathroom, the smell of the carpets. They'll know that they once lived high in the Gorbals. The thought of the rooms will bring back conversations, the theme-tunes of television shows; they'll remind them of parties and arguments and pain. And above all that they will bring back innocence: a memory of the day-to-day; a time when the rooms felt modern and good, when no one imagined their obliteration. The people went into those towers with hope: life will always be like this, they thought. But what they thought came down with the rubble too. They lived in those rooms, but will never see them again. They are gone.

Over the Gorbals the smoke climbing up from the wreckage was met with the everyday spew of the Polmadie furnace, the ascending fumes twisting there, a double helix, and drifting out to the nothing above.

The laughter and chatter came back again. Children shouting. The mother beside me wiped her eyes.

'Well,' she said, 'that's that.' And she led her children away from the wall.

Down below, in the river water, the Gorbals reflected was thinner than before.

Alice my mother was married again. It was ten years ago. And for most of that time we had not felt badly: we'd agreed to get on with our lives. I saw her one time at an hotel in Blackpool. It was the Labour Party Conference. I came in with a colleague; we were carrying boxes. My mother was sat in the bar with her pal. They had come down to Blackpool on holiday.

'Hello, stranger,' she said with a smile.

'Hello, Mum,' I said.

And that was the way it was with us. We liked each other in a simple way, but we saw no reason for cards and cuddles, for monthly rehearsals of what went wrong. This was something my mother had done for me. She didn't demand that we grow up together to better times; she let me move away, and she sensed, in a harsh but dependable way, that better times would mean losing the past. She had trained me well at our fresh-air breakfasts, standing years ago in the cow fields at Saltcoats.

The cows seemed to watch us with their big brown eyes.

'Tatty-bye,' she said. 'Sure and see you get good marks in the class. We don't want any dunces about the place.'

Two hot rolls; a carton of milk.

'Never you mind . . . you're just passing through here, Jamie.'

And in a way that I'd got used to – to other folk, quite mad – she had meant I was passing through her life too. People have thought it abnormal of her, and abnormal of me to accept it. But we have known better. There was nothing to do but wish each other well. She said years ago I was different. 'You're different,' she said, 'and that will bring its own troubles. Let your gran Margaret have time with you now.'

She didn't argue with me the day at the hospital. The day I said I wasn't coming back. She cried on her way down the corridor. But she knew it was right. She had set me to do this leaving. Alice knew then that my father would haunt her for years to come. She was good at knowing these things. She wanted peace for me; she wanted her marriage to sink if it must, but not to take me down with it. That was the thing about Alice: she saw my life before I did. And no one saw hers. None of us thought of the power she possessed.

The cold, blue morning she fell in the road, she knew it then: our family was dead. At the snowy window she knew it: the time had come to separate our lives. And meeting her in Blackpool I saw there were signs it had worked for her too. She had never looked so healthy to me. Never so blonde. And so we eyed each other proudly among strangers. We knew the sore facts we had both escaped. I slipped two twenties under her glass.

'You look lovely, Mum,' I said.

And after some jokes, and a pint of beer, we stood up as we remembered. We said goodbye. A solid goodbye, and phone if you need me.

But the day of the demolition I felt that something had changed. The river was calm and slick and oblivious. Losing the past had run its course. I wanted to see my mother. I wanted to speak to Alice, see how she felt. I wanted to know about her life now and her husband's job. I wanted to say something . . .

Stop running. I wanted to say, 'Stop running.'

Let's stand on the same ground and notice the weather. To show her pictures of Karen. To say stop running we are all right now. She would make a good mother. Like you are. Here in your garden. Please stop running. We're okay now. My granda is dying there and what's the use? I saw his favourite block come down today. Who are all these new folk in your life, my mother? Is he good to you? And all these towns have changed so much. Nothing can last for ever. Even the tide goes somewhere in the end.

Stand still. Listen here to your only son. It's all calm now: calm and slick and oblivious. Let us drink the cool water. I imagined saying that to her. 'Let us go down to the water now, and paddle and laugh, like a family.'

I was sleeping at the wheel in Auchentiber. Lulled by the roll of the uniform hedgerows. Two seconds at most. But that was enough to make me stop. I pulled the car over at a farmhouse pub. A wagonwheel filled with winter plants. My breath was chill as I pulled the hand-brake. I looked in the mirror. My hair was damp. My face was white. My lips were red as blood on snow. I'd not felt right all day.

And that change was more than a change of mood. I felt different. Something I'd known I no longer knew; something was altered; a lasting shift had come about.

But every such shift that occurred in my life had tended in one direction: changes as stiffenings of the basic will; terse new advances, never reversals. The changes I had known about were changes of degree; usually they were changes in the ways I felt apart from family matters, untouched by all that old chaos. They were times of fresh resolve, novel encroachments of the selfish gene. They were hardly changes: they were surprise confirmations. And over the years those increments of certitude had made me the perfect foreigner. I had no original home. No old belongings. Nothing but the certainty of where I was now. I'd no doubts, no switherings, no turnings-back. And no sense of what it is to be one thing and another. No half-heart. No struggle. No evolving self-pity. There was only me, and now, and other people themselves. The rest was just history.

Yet none of that seemed true any more. All my defences were down. What happened that morning made me different from myself, and strange in my skin. It wasn't about mood, or depression, or emotions running high. It wasn't nostalgia or

Yuletide regrets. I don't think it was any of that. It was a fresh upwelling, a notion of death, a sense of expiry in the broad afternoon. And I wasn't disheartened. I wasn't scared. I just wanted to speak to my mother, that's all. I wanted to tell her I'd a girl called Karen. To take her aside and to say this and that; to look at her, and say here we are, and what have we got, and hold me a minute I'm not always right. I wanted to say a few words about Karen. That I thought I loved her. That we nearly had a baby. That I thought I might die in my car one day.

For years I'd been walking out the door. Walking away. And being always certain I knew the way forward. But now I wanted to walk in. To sit right down at the kitchen table. To say make me a cup of tea will you not? And tell me about years ago. And listen: this is how I felt as my grandad's block came crashing into the ground. This is what I felt. And maybe our plans are only our plans. Maybe my work's not the only truth. Maybe it's not the truth at all.

I phoned 192 from the pub telephone. Her name was the same. Her house was still her house.

'I gather she and what's-his-name were living there in sin. It was a good thing they jumped the broom last year. Living it up at their age.'

This was the gospel according to Gran Margaret. The woman on the line fed me the number. It felt like a pattern I knew somehow. I rang it. What's-his-name answered. 'Hello,' I said, 'we've never actually met before. I'm Jamie, Alice's son.'

'O hello there, son,' he said, with a nice person's effort. 'I've never had the chance to meet you yet.'

'No,' I said, 'but I hope so before long.'

'Aye, that would be grand. Alice is not here at the minute.

She went up to the Railway Club. Do you want the number there?'

'No,' I said, 'there's no emergency. I'm not far from Saltcoats. I thought I would just come in and see her.'

'She'd be delighted with that, son. You'll get her at the club. And maybe I'll catch sight of you later myself. I'm not sure if I'm going up there yet. I'm supposed to be on the night shift the night.'

'Okay,' I said, 'see you one way or another. Bye for now.'

'Nice talking to you, son,' he said.

And down went the phone. It came as no surprise to me that my mother had found someone who spoke carefully. The first half of her life was nothing but bastard language. I would bet it was a priority: find a man who will speak gently amongst women and strangers. If nothing else, it would make her feel that her circumstances had changed; her new life was made of better sounds. And that in itself would be something to her.

The seafront at Saltcoats was dead for the winter. The coast lay strangled in a beige silk gown. No children threaded through the metal of the play park. Beer cans were afloat in the paddling pools. A mound of mussel-shells useless by the road. And every tea-room a sanctuary for one. Sometimes two. A double-wafer out of season. The jinkle of a spoon in a cup.

Music and lights – a fruit-machine's nervous breakdown.

A candy-floss booth was Windolened on every side. The fun was abandoned; only strays went up and down the front. A man, a dog, a packet of chips. Nothing going on but the weather. The art deco cinema was closed; a round pile of elegance put off for good. The seagulls bored on the castle wall. It's blowy out there. The pensioners came down to the small hotels; they were keen for the cheap high tea.

Scampi-in-a-basket. Scones. More tea. A mad sherry.

'Nothing to stop you at your age, Helen. Drink it while you can . . .'

Not so long to the summer now. Warmer soon. Better days for the Arran boat.

'Tell the wee lassie it's McEwens Export.'

The town had grown much since my days at the Ferguson school. All the fields now were filled with streets. Barratt houses, oval-shaped windows. Triangular gardens, the different doors. All the running burns were culverted and walk-safe. For hundreds of acres now you didn't see chimneys. No cooling towers, no real coal fires. Even the parts that had seemed to me so modern in my youth — the black-and-white factories, the council dwellings, the streets named for heroes — much of it now seemed grey and diminished, or fading somehow. The white houses had worn badly. I found it hard that day to imagine the boy who was spurred by the sight of those buildings, the thought of their builders. None of it seemed so modern any more.

The school was demolished. It was taken down. Most of the staff and inmates had been taken to a secure young offenders' home near Ayr. Mulligan's Pool was now under the road, the drowned man a bother no more. I drove through the town with no trouble in my chest. I was glad to see it. The place you grow up in is not an option. Not like your adult places, argued over, decided on, paid for, one day left behind. Your childhood homes existed in dreams; they had seemed to exist for nobody but you; a bundle of shapes, some shadows on a wall, beyond our reckoning, above our powers to say yes or no. A mythic address, not chosen by you. A church spire rising at the centre of town. A bank of trees on the brow of the hill. The trees' fingers. The way to the sea.

The Railway Club is a blue-glossed cabin that stands well up on a rock. Its windows look out to the islands. There are serpentine steps leading up from the road. I left the car at the bottom, and climbed, the wind all around, the steps pure green, and oily. There used to be a coal-mine above the town. Ardrossan Mains. Halfway up the steps there's a standing wall, the remains of an engine room.

Tufts of grass at every nook. Ashlar stone.

Once upon a time the gas exploded underground. Twenty men died. Four of one family. There was nothing of mercy on the wind that day. The wind came again. Salt and spray at the top of the rock.

The Firth of Clyde – an iriscope.

The sea is black glass. The wind breathes over. As the wind breathes over it seems to find colours: yellows and browns and greens out there. The wind moves on. The colours disappear. The sea again is a pane of black glass. Dark water: a half-second's peace. The sea is black glass, and the wind comes again. Yellows and browns and greens out there.

A fishing trawler floated in the sea's dark middle, outriding the waves and the EEC, the rocks, the Ministry of Defence. The spray ran white on the beach below me. Up at the door, with the sign above it, and pale ale logos here and there, I stopped to remember my lines. But nothing was there. Just the wind and me, the curve of the rock. The dram-drinking noises, the song inside.

An elderly man with smiling jowls asked me to sign the book. His tie flopped out of a V-neck jumper.

'Wee Alice is in the corner,' he said, 'with all the girls.'

He laughed to himself, enjoying his role.

'Now you watch yourself with that lot,' he said. 'A parcel of rogues the lot of them.'

He continued to laugh as he turned the book, and dropped my two coins in the cash tin. A card school was busy just past the doors. Headless pints and a smattering of loose tobacco. Folding tables and plastic chairs. The men at the bar were talking about football. Hair pomaded, beer-bellied, loud and restless in their three-button shirts, each seemed ready for anger and joy, high on a boast, or a promise of fun. Every one had a hardened look; their features said something familiar.

I thought I knew them. Each one looked like someone I knew.

My eye stayed there for a second too long. I just nodded. I didn't know them. My shirt and tie made a small fellow nervous.

'It's not me, it's him,' he said, pointing to one of the card-players. 'He's the poll-tax dodger.'

The circle laughed. And I did too. One of those smiles that's a frown of the lips and the chin.

The women were cheery, each one festooned with gold chains. They all wore a variation of the same blouse. My mother looked up from the table as I came across the dance floor. The girls all hushed.

'Is somebody dead?' my mother asked right away.

'No,' I said. 'We're still alive. I'm here to buy you a drink.'

She smiled and bit her lip. The girls looked nowhere, or inspected their nails, waiting for Alice to open. They knew something large was happening. This stranger, this dark suit. And Alice stood up, a spark in her eye.

'Lassies,' she said, 'this is my boy Jamie. He lives in England.'

And each fell in with smiles about them, hands to my mother's wrists.

'What a lovely big fella,' said the one I liked. 'Bonny like you, Alice. Oh my. The big blond.' Cackles came down, a jackpot of coins.

'You can sit beside me any time you like, son,' said a ruby-faced one.

Easy laughter.

'Hey, moaners,' she shouted to the men at the bar, 'you can all go home now. That's the talent in.'

'I hope his suspension's in good nick,' said a man who sounded like her husband, 'if he's to take you anywhere, that is.'

'Cheeky bastard,' said the woman, and all the girls laughed, and lifted a glass.

I went round the table and sat with Alice.

'A nice big boy,' said her friend at my side, and then, with all the others, she fell away to allow us a notion of privacy.

It was as if this group was used to trouble. I don't know if Alice had ever mentioned her son in England. But there was no embarrassment, no shy looks. Everyone played it just right for Alice. No wrong questions, no mock surprise. It was something to talk about for later, I'm sure. But just then, with my mother still flushed, and worry in her eye, they all turned their backs, new jokes rising, cigarettes burning, Alice and me just a moment to ourselves.

'You look a bit thin,' she said. 'Your hair's down over your ears.'

'It's your Scottish water,' I said. 'Never did a poor soul any good.'

'Hey, watch what you're saying. We sell it now in fancy bottles. Your smart people down the road can't get enough of it.'

We laughed into the table. When the girl came past I lifted

the list from the kitty tumbler and handed it over, with money. 'Bring us a round, would you please,' I said, 'and add on a pint of Export.'

'You don't need to be buying rounds,' said Alice.

'Never mind us, son,' said the woman nearest, with a cough.

'Not at all. No problem. It's fine.'

My mother and the women exchanged looks and smiles. Alice was great; she seemed so alive and well tuned. She looked like she knew her way around herself. And here was the person she wanted to be. Her hair all layered and tinted in a shop. Her make-up light and carefully done. I took in everything about her then. Her perfume upgraded from the Avon vapours of yore.

She once had the scent of weekly instalments. The new smell was hers: softly it spoke of her affluent days.

I had never seen her with painted nails. Light brown and smooth, even-cuticled.

I never thought my mother could have such nails. And everything about her seemed just like that. Mature and stylish and kept in check. Her look spoke of time to herself, and few money worries, and no constant back shift. She looked like a woman with charge cards. A person with views, opinions, and shocking things to say. A woman of silences and thoughts. And most of all, I could see it there, and see it there as I never had. My mother looked like a woman who was having sex. She was not the object I'd long made her into: the desireless wonder, the queen of endurance. This was not the woman I saw. The woman I saw was having sex. And it struck me. It struck me as something new and important.

The oddness of thinking these things of my mother, of seeing so much in the wave of her hair, the hand on her glass;

of finding so much in the tone of her voice, the depth of her laugh, the way her scarf was knotted and tucked; the oddness of this, of grasping these things, was wiped clean away, just by the force of who she was now. I didn't recognise her. She was different from the woman her first life allowed her to be. So different. And not the person in my imagination. She was suddenly herself, and so very real, and living out nobody's version but her own. I thought in those seconds that perhaps none of us had ever known her at all. We had no idea but our own idea of her. And that idea was dead. She had her own life now. And it was new. Sitting beside her in the Railway Club I suddenly saw her for the first time. She wasn't just a child's lost mother, or a victim trapped in time. She was something else. She had not just lived her life as an absence. She was here, and was much, much more than the bare, abandoned thing that lived alone in my head.

I saw her that one time in Blackpool. But I didn't see that she was so much herself.

'You're so like your father in some ways, Jamie,' she said, 'wanting us all to live in the kitchenette.'

'No,' I said. 'I was just wondering. I mean. When did you start coming to the social clubs? The pubs. I mean how did you meet the ones who come?'

'Let me tell you something, Jamie. You'll remember it yourself. All the singing and dancing was knocked out of me years ago. When you were a baby, you know? But I had a life before then — a good life. My mother was a singing-and-dancing person, and I used to go with all the girls then to the Scarborough. I had a life before your father, and I've had a life since . . . since that all ended. I wasn't going to just lie down and die. These are my friends here. They've been good to me. And so has Bob. But, you know, that's fair enough. I've been good to him.'

'When I saw you that time in Blackpool,' I said. 'I was happy for you. You seemed like you had . . . you seemed like you'd survived all that rubbish years ago.'

'We've never spoken of anything, Jamie.'

'I know.'

And just as she spoke it occurred to me that I wouldn't say those things I had thought about all day. The tower block, the demolition, and Hugh bad now and dying in his bed. The fact that I sometimes had panics in my car. None of that. The long-term plan. The getting back together. My Karen and the baby that wasn't born. None of it. I was happy to just be there with Alice, talking a little, one thing or another, and just watching her there in the middle of her own life. Everything could wait for another day, or could wait for all time for that matter. What I'd come to find was here quite differently. The sight of Alice was an answer in itself.

One time my mother allowed me to go free, to learn about houses and history and flowers, and to lose my cares in an act of becoming, and now it was her turn, and she wanted to be free to lose her cares, and not be silenced by the forces of before. The fact was clear in her every aspect. I mustn't confuse her with my own confusions. And nor did I want to. I was all the man I would ever be.

Steady enough, and made up for her. Contemplating Alice.

She was happy and free on the rock over Saltcoats. And when my mother said that – 'We've never spoken of anything, Jamie' – I knew she just wanted us to stay friends, and not the people who make big claims, and who make or break each other. She wasn't cut out for family routines. She said it herself in so many words: 'Let's be as we've been, my Jamie boy. Only more so, and with more sense of what is good in us; more days like these.'

'. . . And your mammy came in,' said Ella, the one with the ruby face. 'And she gave each one of us a miniature of vodka. (You know the wee vodkas.) We're sitting there in our rollers right, drunk — four in the one room in a bed-and-breakfast — and the wee baldy guy's ready to pap us out if we don't shut up. Yer mammy and the vodka. Next minute, the bold one. Muggins here. I'm out on the landing there looking for the toilet. I sees a door. No problem — in I goes. Feels around the wall. A basin. That'll do nicely says me. (Puggled as a monkey.) Messing about with the night dress. The light comes on. Big Malcolm! I'd walked right into his room. Well. The look on him. Mental he went. Your mammy here had to go in there in the morning and speak nice to him. Right out of order. What a laugh.'

The women at the table were screaming with laughter. All the tales from a weekend in Rothesay. My mother was chuckling away to herself.

'Characters,' she'd say, just under her breath, at the end of every story.

'A bit of order over there,' shouted one of the husbands at the bar. 'The pensioners here are having to turn down their hearing-aids. Shut it.'

But the women just went on as before. Alice was right about them. They knew how to enjoy themselves. They knew they wouldn't have to wait around for tragedy. In years still to come there'd be cancers and cures, failures of the heart, trouble with nerves. Husbands would wander; a car would appear out of nowhere. The women in this group would one day have police at their doors. Drugs and failed marriages; loneliness, depressions. And grandchildren too; the troubles ahead.

All would know tragedy, and each their own. My mother's friends and my mother too. But this day they were laughing for all the world. Cruising along on a second wind. They laughed at each other and poured out drinks. No time to think of a world not here. Alice was right about these women. They could enjoy themselves.

'You're good company,' my mother said to me. She had noticed my giggling and jokings-back, my silly-arsed flirting with Ella and Joan. 'And you take a drink,' she said.

'Well,' I said, 'did you think I was boring and plain, my mother?'

'Well no,' she said, 'you were a funny kid. Always a bit of a shadow-mouth. You were always thinking. Always making plans. And you had the harsh eye. I hadn't cut you out as a raver.'

'Oh I'm mad, me,' I said, with a blush and a grin. We laughed at the beer-mats again.

'Bob,' she said.

And there at the table was silver-haired Bob, easy-going, false-toothed, and tall.

'Pleased to meet you, Jamie,' he said.

He shook my hand like to shake it off. But his eagerness was just like mine. It seemed so civilised to be liking Bob. My mother's husband. And it wasn't hard. In his grey flannels and blue blazer – his full sovereign ring – Bob was the opposite of my father. He looked at you when he spoke. He'd a feminine manner of patience about him. He drank half-pints. He carried his things in a wallet. He seemed to like listening to Alice.

And he touched her more in ten minutes — a pat, a nip, a squeeze, a kiss — than my father had done in ten years in my presence.

There was an air of instant generosity about Bob. He was a stretch of clear water.

'Come up to the bar,' he said. 'You must be just about exhausted with these women.'

The men at the bar were all plastered. They laughed at nothing and spilled their drinks. 'You better watch your time,' said one, 'if that suit's to be back today.'

'You're a daft cunt, Jimmy,' said the easy-going Bob.

And that was no surprise either. It was said in a certain manner, in a way that was harmless and private. All the men in that part of the world have a voice they preserve for these moments. It always comes out with men along bars, so long as the women are distant: a knowing, all-men-together, Masonistic thing, a deft orchestration of 'pricks' and 'dicks' and filthy jokes. Even the gentlest of husbands are prone. They like the inclusion, and recognise the code; they join in the banter, to show themselves worldly, to show themselves open to the commonness of things. And young boys grin over their first pint of cider. The church of men. The sense of connection.

A greasy-faced Sammy pressed in between us. 'What do you call a woman with three jugs?' he said.

'Don't know,' said Bob, unpeeling a ten-pound note.

'A godsend,' said Sammy. He spluttered into a brown pint. I grinned like an idiot, with one side of my face. Bob chuckled.

'Very good,' he said. 'Now piss off.'

The guy went away and pressed himself in further up.

Once or twice we tried to speak at the same time. Eventually Bob broke through.

'She's a smashing lassie, your mother,' he said. 'She's been the making of me.'

'Well,' I said, a bit weaker than I meant, 'she's never looked better.'

'Happier,' Bob said. And then he corrected that. 'I mean. It's always a struggle to be happy with yourself.'

Always a struggle. I didn't ask him what he meant by that.

'You know, my mother and me, we haven't seen a lot of each other. Not in recent years.'

'Aye I know,' said Bob. 'I mean, this being the first time we've met, and all that.'

Bob was speaking nervously. Everything he said was vague, as if it would be out of order for him to be too definite now, too certain, and to seem to be making judgements, on this our first meeting. But he did make judgements. He was too organised a person not to say the thing he thought would be most helpful.

'You know,' he said, 'I don't know much about Alice's earlier life. I don't think it's my place . . . but, anyway, I know that Alice has strong feelings about you, and want you to know you're welcome in my house. Any time.'

'Thank you,' I said.

But I suddenly wanted to walk away. Or just leave. I was overcome with a sudden feeling that I just wasn't part of this world. Maybe I never had been. I was glad to see Alice; her husband was a nice man. But what had this to do with me now?

What had this . . . why was I here?

I tried to swallow my inconsistency with a gulp of beer.

A stretch of water. *Calm and slick and oblivious.*

Bob continued to talk about the good life he wanted for him and Alice. A caravan near Pitlochry. Plane tickets to the Via Dolorosa. And nice meals on patios in wide hats and shorts. An abundance of sun creams. All cares behind them. He told me he had been married twice before. Three daughters. One son. Never sees the son.

'We all just have to live with our mistakes,' he said.

'Yes,' I said.

The karaoke had started, and Ella was up there. 'I'll take the blanket from the bedroo-em,' she sang, 'and that means we can't stick ar-ound. We'll go walking in the moonlight, where our true love hmm-hm-hm. *I can't see the fucking words.*'

'They women know how to enjoy themselves,' said Bob.

I was starting to feel the drink. The barman put another two whiskies down in front of us. I got us two more half-beers as well. I lifted a whisky. We stood with our backs to the bar.

'Well, Bob,' I said, 'you're a good man. I'm glad you're nice to my mother.'

And I chinked my glass against his on the counter. Bob lifted his beer. 'Steady, son,' he said. And then he let himself smile. 'She's a great lassie.'

Alice was looking over. I lifted my glass in greeting. She just looked at us. She looked almost through us. The look on her face said nothing in particular. And yet it did somehow. The men boozing and clinking their glasses. She seemed to see us more clearly than we saw her. That was her look. A soft and a fleeting contempt, across the airless dance floor.

A guy emerged from the corner's thicket of bar-stools. He had one of those poor beards, the kind that camouflage a slack jaw. Another Sammy. His handshake was cold and liquid. He exhibited the customary interest of one shirt-and-tie in another. Rheumy-eyed and bored, Sammy was a reporter on the local paper.

'I'll need to leave that beer,' said Bob. 'I've my work to get away to. You watch yourself.'

'Okay, Bob,' I said. 'It was . . .'

'Great,' said Bob. 'Great to meet you.'

'That's right. Great,' I said. 'And sooner than later I hope.'

'I hope so too,' he said. 'It's good to keep in touch with your mother.'

And with a lightsome air of paternal authority, Bob winked, squeezed my arm, and moved with busy intention towards the far corner, and his heart's desire.

The man from the paper moved closer. His breath smelt of scampi fries.

'You don't like me, do you?' he said.

'I don't know you, mate,' I said.

But he was right. I didn't like him; I thought I knew his kind. It was pretty straightforward really. He looked like someone who had something unhelpful to say. He staggered up like someone with information. Someone with news. The sort of guy who's keen to tell you much more than you'd care to know about yourself. And I could see from his face that he meant to let me know. He dived with unpiloted fury; the hapless wrath of the truly disappointed professional.

'You must be one of the great Hugh Bawn's long-lost tribe,' he said.

I lit a cigarette and blew smoke at the floor.

'I hear he's in deep shit. Some lectures the old boy used to dole out. Seems the old fingers were in the till.'

'Get lost,' I said.

And I wanted him to walk off. I didn't want a fight. But I wasn't moving. I wasn't for running to my mother.

'No, it's very interesting,' he said, a grin smeared over his face. 'Very interesting. I mean, it would appear that your old man, the big socialist, was never shy of a wee chance here and there.'

'Shut it,' I said.

'No, it's interesting. Him being such a saviour and everything. People desperate for the new flats. It seems he riddled those flats with cheap asbestos, just to get them up. Just to win an argument. Cheap materials. Never safe. Soaked up water like a sponge. It seems your old man was doing deals on the fly. A wee deal here, a backhander there, a wee . . .'

'Shut your fucking face,' I said, putting my glass on the bar.

He moved in closer.

'Now, now, big man. Don't get upset here. I'm just saying, you know, it's interesting. Mr Bawn, he was never by saying this and that, you know, about progress and the future and all that. They say now he might have been skimming a wee bit profit for himself. Would that be possible at all?'

'Never,' I said.

'It's interesting what you hear. I mean . . .'

I could see my mother in the corner. She was looking down at a song-sheet. I made a grab for the guy's throat.

'If you put anything in your poxy paper I'll break your fucking jaw,' I said.

A few of the men at the bar had turned, sensing an incident.

'You and whose fucking army?' said the guy.

His face spun back in a whirlpool of anger. He was scarlet. He was shouting now. 'Your cunt of a granda took the people for a ride. Progress and progress and progress, my arse! Don't blame the people in here. We're the ones that had to live in his fucking hovels. Get your fucking hand off me, the English prick that you are.'

I let go of him. I was much taller than he was. My anger meant more. But his awful words had dazed me somehow. I could see he was ready for anything. I let him go and just stood there glaring.

'You're disgusting,' I said.

'Eh? Go to fuck, you middle-class prick,' he said. 'Coming in here . . .'

I felt I could have crushed him into the floor. For having that face, for saying those things, for writing the stories I knew he would write. For making a show of us. For seeing Hugh's misjudgements as something cheap and low.

He would never know how much he was wrong.

'Leave it, Sammy,' said one of the men, pulling him over.

Our crusader for truth.

Words marched out of my mouth and dropped dead to the floor.

'Hugh Bawn was an idealist,' I said. 'And who are you? What are you to Hugh Bawn? He gave his life to things. He believed in them. And he made other people believe in them. What are you to him? He is a fucking god compared to you.'

People were really looking now. The reporter spat at my feet. 'I'll tell you something,' I said. 'Even his greatest mistakes came from a better place than your truths. My grandfather has worked all his life. He never had a penny he didn't earn. He priced his blocks too cheap. He built more houses with what they saved. His mistakes were better than your truths. You fucking pig.'

Alice was beside me. She tugged at my hand.

'Come on, Jamie,' she said. 'Sit down now. Come on.'

The reporter struggled against the arms that held him back. 'Aye fuck off, son,' he said. 'Away back to where you came from.'

'That's right,' I said. 'New ways to kill your fathers. Crucify them for their mistakes.'

I was drunk but my voice was quieter now. A man stepped from behind the reporter. 'There's a different idea of progress now,' he said. 'This corruption. They want it to stop. You know that, pal.'

I looked at him. I looked at my mother.

We have to live with our mistakes.

'The city fathers are taking a tumble,' he said. 'You know the way it is. A different idea of progress. The old way didn't work.'

I looked at him. My blood seemed to retreat in its veins.

'So they tell me,' I said.

The women sat like nothing had happened. We tried to forget it. The club lit up in a flurry of songs.

Karaoke sunset.

I stopped drinking. The women went up one after the other.

I'm Gonna Sit Right Down and Write Myself a Letter.

Sometimes a man with a serious eye. Lifting the microphone wire with the notes.

Lochnagar.

The waitresses know the song-numbers by heart. They warble and bop their breaks away.

'Alice,' I said, 'old Hugh is at his last. He is going to die.'

'I know,' she said. 'I heard that. It's sad, Jamie. And you're closer to him than any of us were. But he's an old man, you know? You should try and not let it get to you so much. Hugh's had a good life.'

I looked at her a second.

'Yes, you're right,' I said.

And I didn't say any more. She didn't ask me if I was staying in the flat at Annick Water. She didn't ask me anything like that. She looked back up at the singers. And what she said she almost whispered.

'Poor Margaret has had it for years. It's no been easy. But God knows how she'll live without him.'

'She has her memory,' I said.

My voice had faded inside itself.

'Aye well,' said my mother, 'there's always that.'

I touched her hand when her turn came to sing. I'd heard it said: she's a lovely singer. She'd the full attention of all her friends, her making-the-most-of-it pals. I inched away from the table unnoticed. Ella and Joan were mouthing the words to my mother's song. Eyes all water. Enjoying themselves.

Stardust.

I looked up at Alice. She was a lovely singer. She knew how to put it over too. I raised the fingers of one hand, and slowly I folded them into the palm. Berry's wave, in the Ferguson darkness, all those years ago.

'Bye, Mum,' my mouth said.

And she blew down a kiss. A kiss and a smile from my mother up there, so easy now, and so free.

> Beside a garden wall, when stars are bright,
> You are in my arms.
> The nightingale tells a fairytale
> Of paradise where roses bloom.

The door snapped shut at my back. The wind again. The breath on the black glass sea.

When I dream in vain. In my heart it will remain.

I could hear my mother's good singing voice as I stood at the head of the serpentine steps.

A stardust melody . . .

On top of the miners' ruin four magpies pecked at the broken stone, and over the green steps the sea-salt spray was fresh and welcome. The spray was welcome over the rock. My face was cold and new with that spray. I stopped in the middle of all those steps and felt for a second just salt and sea. Nothing was left inside my clothes, nothing of me, just salt and the sea, and the roar of the sea-lap rising.

6

As It Is in Heaven

Half-owre, half-owre to Aberdour,
'Tis fifty fathoms deep,
And there lies good Sir Patrick Spens,
Wi' the Scots lords at his feet!

Hugh died on St Stephen's Day. It being low water, he went out with the tide. There was no noise at the end of his life. Everything was quiet. He died by himself, four feet high on a hospital bed, on every side a screen of green nylon. Somehow his breath grew supple in the final hours, and cleaner, as if he were back in one of his cool meadows, and lifting up his chest and his nose as he used to do, and purely breathing, as if to take possession of the whole of nature. When we had gone for the evening he just lay open-eyed. His breathing climbed down from its high place of trees. The nurse said he just stopped. His last breath gave out to the emerald curtains; the long day was over in the Martin Luther Ward.

The day before had been slow. Margaret cooked a small Christmas dinner. She laid the table in her own room, dressing it with crêpe paper, a doily under a Dundee cake. A battalion of condiments was grouped in the table's middle. Malt vinegar, a jar of beetroot, a bottle of brown sauce, some ketchup in a plastic tomato, a pot of pickled onions, a salt and pepper. She'd made some soup from a knuckly ham bone. She put out steak pie and peas. We ate it without saying much.

Her electric fire burned its bars. All her pictures stood hot on the wooden surround. And here and there the gifts from Spain: a leather-clad bottle of sangria; a flamenco doll; an ashtray shaped like Ibiza; a lush table lighter, 'Welcome to Santa Ponsa'. Margaret had never gone to those places. Hugh's old friends, people in the Housing Department at Glasgow, or related to the construction business, they had gone, and they had brought these things back, along with their stories of sunstroke and wine on the beach, and always they brought them 'with many thanks'. Margaret thought they were terrible objects, but she liked to remember the people.

When she spoke it was almost a whisper.

'I see you've your granda's papers by the bed,' she said. 'So you know all the carry-on. The hearings in Glasgow?'

'Yes,' I said. 'We spoke of it before. You said he was under investigation. Did they know he was ill?'

'Aye,' she said. 'They called him in to speak. A letter. I sent it right back. I said he couldn't speak.'

'They don't understand, Granny. He may have cut corners. But only for the good. He wanted more flats for the people. And he wanted them quicker. Is that not right?'

'That's right, Jamie,' she said. 'Only for the good. And I know you don't think these houses are great. But we thought they were great then. We thought they were everything they wanted. And you're all tearing them down. But they can't tear him down. He's going down anyhow in his own way. He always meant to do the best. It carried him away. He made deals with the builders; he got them to deliver cheaper materials, so he got more stuff for the same money. And he sometimes paid them in cash, to speed things up. He only wanted to build more and more. But the high-rises were never as good as they should have been. They were built too cheap. They were too damp. That was his mistake. He was too keen.'

'I'll stick up for him wherever I can,' I said. 'They're lumping him in with those other people, who took money and things. Hugh was just . . .' I couldn't find the word.

'You're a good one, Jamie,' she said.

Her hand pulled at the loose skin about her neck.

'They used to call your granda a moderniser. That's what you are now. But you're not trying to pull him down, sure you're not? Coming back was good. It has been like years ago – the three of us years ago.'

'I'll do everything,' I said.

'Let's say no more,' she said. 'The Queen is coming on. Let's hear what she's saying this year.'

And that was one of the few times we made reference to Hugh's troubles. One of the few times we actually said it. And although it was for ever on our minds – I had first heard word of it in Liverpool – there was no point in making a show. It was just something large that was happening in public, a bad and involving noise from Hugh's great profession, and mine too, the one he had given to me. My granda's bold decisions, his long obsession with new housing, his wayward manner with figures and budgets, his bending the rules, had come forward to hurt him, and to throw our deepest devotions into relief. He had made mistakes. At first he saw me as part of the mob – those forgetters of past necessities, those rectifiers of big mistakes. He thought that he saw me coming: the man with the killing truth.

But in those last months, as Hugh lay dying, I think he, like me, began to ignore the public noise. We swam that while in private concerns. The tower blocks stood around us — we were wrapped in one too — and they joined us up. But as he raged and moaned and stared at the wall, and as he travelled with me through the lanes of Ayrshire, I think Hugh began to leave behind those public problems, those matters to do with immense futurity. It was all just behind him one day.

Hugh trusted that Margaret and I saw the good in him. We were on his side. That is what I had come to hope for anyhow. We were all lost in the past he cared for. And I'll always say it: being lost in his time made my own time clearer. I wanted my own day, but not at the expense of every day that preceded my own. Hugh's gains and losses were mine too. I watched the last of his anger and sadness. I saw his end. And though there was nothing especially brave about Hugh, he had tried to make changes, and live with his lies, and that showed a sort of courage too. I came home to Ayrshire thinking I would take a stand against Hugh's delusions. But that is not what happened. I stood beside him, and listened to his life, and I held his hand, and I finally grew up.

Margaret and Hugh would tell me my life was just at the beginning. And maybe it was so. But all their stories and their ancient songs, their history, their ambitions, their troubles and decay, had brought me to feel, in that season back home, as if I too was part of some great and personal reckoning with the past. They gave me that feeling. And I gave it to myself. I imagined some world I had known and loved was dying with Hugh and Margaret. There was a fading light I had never quite seen. And seeing it changed me. My mother and father rose up in my mind. And so did the children I had yet to have. I had learned that our fathers were made for grief: I was grieving myself before my time.

On Christmas Night my granda wet the bed. He lay looking up at the low ceiling. We tried to feed him crumbs of pie and cake. He cowered from us. It seemed that he and Margaret had come to some pact: they wanted him to die at home. But his mind went wandering out of the room. Margaret said he had grown like his mother. His eyes like the ends of his fingers were yellow. I took hold of his hand.

'Don't speak,' I said. With my other hand I stroked his head, the side of his face. His eyes were scared. He kept them on me.

'I love you very much, Granda,' I said.

And at that my own breath shortened. There were tears on me. My hands seemed too big, like hands against a baby's face. Too big for such a small person as this. His scared face.

'You are one of the greats,' I said. His yellow eyes were all water. He rounded his mouth with the effort to breathe, and to speak.

'I owe you my life,' I said.

His voice broke through at last.

'We were good, Jamie,' he said.

'Very good,' I said. 'And none better.' I held both his hands.

'Good, son,' he said. His eyes half-dipped with the effort. He lifted them back up.

'Maggie,' he said. And my granny stood there covering her face.

'Aye,' she said, and ran her hands along his legs. 'I'm here, Hugh.'

I wanted to leave them to silence. Or to each other's eyes. I went along the hall and into my room. It all felt like something that was happening outside of time: Hugh dying. The books and pictures stood out on the shelves. The piles of papers too. Monuments there, or stops on the road. Keir Hardie's face, a mocking tea-brown complexion.

This imperfect room. This crumbling tower.

I had grown angry with weeping. I put pillowcases over the pictures.

Lying on the bed as Margaret's voice came through. She was singing Hugh down to calmness. I have wondered since then if he asked her to sing. She never told me, and so I'll never know if he asked for Robert Burns. Nevertheless her voice passed clearly through the wall. Hugh fell unconscious an hour after the song ended. He would never come back.

> John Anderson my jo, John,
> When we were first aquent,
> Your locks were like the raven,
> Your bonny brow was brent,
> But now your brow is bald, John,
> Your locks are like the snow,
> But blessings on yer frosty pow,
> John Anderson my jo.

> John Anderson my jo, John,
> We clamb the hill thegither,
> And mony a canty day, John,
> We've had wi' ane anither,
> Now we maun totter down, John,
> But hand in hand we'll go,
> And sleep thegither at the foot,
> John Anderson my jo.

The morning of his death I phoned Riccarton, the doctor. During the night the fear had come into me. I didn't want him to die. Not like that. Not there. He lay splayed, unconscious, on his single bed, a frozen Annick Water morning, the winter light coming into the room the colour of milk.

The radio said that all the boats to the islands were off. A weather-plane had come to grief on the Tarron Rocks. Flood-water was rushing through the council estates of Paisley. The Black Cart had broken its banks. And none of this news was for Hugh; deep in his bed he heard nothing. There was nei-ther blink nor sigh for the goings-on of the world. Only the thinnest breath came from him now. A smile lay over his peace-seeking lips. It was nearly finished.

Riccarton was a sly old bird. Small and contemptuous, he moved at one pace, filled with certainties and cold warnings, neat with advice, and all the while he stroked at the carnap-tious whiskers of his beard. He was an Ayrshire doctor to the very bone. A drinking man, a Masonic general. His hair was a prosperous confection: dark brown and sprayed to a fix. And there was something hopeful in what he was wearing: a three-piece tweed, a pair of white trainers. He was one of the New Town's old-time retainers. He knew everything about every-body. He knew about livers and breast-lumps and mid-life depressions. He knew about unwanted pregnancies and impo-tent fathers. He knew about heart trouble. He gave Valium to teenagers who'd unsettled themselves at raves. And with all this knowing came a sense of authority. People sensed it, and paid respect to him, a respect that Riccarton came to demand, having himself, over the years, gained an ever-deepening sense of his own importance. This was true of Riccarton when I was a boy. I could see it was even truer now. Margaret had told me the doctor now lived in a Victorian mansion in Ayr. He was married to a woman who taught the piano. They had a girl at the University of St Andrew's. Riccarton drove around the town in one of those jeeps. He would go, said Margaret, 'with the windows down, playing concertos at full pelt.'

'Hello, Doctor,' I found myself saying. 'It was good of you to come here so quickly.'

'I'm rather content to be here,' he said, 'the cold being what it is. And you, James. Where on earth have you been hiding? I have it on the best authority that you're something of a blaze in the southern parts.'

Margaret sniffed.

'Actually,' he said. 'My Jennifer is one of your kind. She is bent on going ahead to Bristol, to carry on her research, you see.'

'And Mrs Riccarton?' I said.

'Oh much as ever,' he said. 'In love with the back room and the garden. I'm afraid it's more than I can manage to tear her away. We have girls in to do the cleaning, and I'm afraid it only adds to Sylvia's load. She spends a great deal of her time now cleaning after them, you see.'

Margaret soon brought him some tea, with biscuits on a plate.

'Very kind, Margaret,' he said.

He stood in the hall. He dipped one of the biscuits into the tea and ate it in one. Then he drank the whole cup down.

'You'll remember how very pretty our town used to be,' he said to me. 'Very lovely, with the old shops, and fields, and so on. But now! I swear it. There are incomers – not yourselves, of course – but incomers, the Glasgow overspill, good Jesus, they've played the bigger part in turning us into a jungle. It's all the drugs and so on. Do you know, James? Gone are the days when I could carry a prescription pad. Now it is only one prescription at a time. The addicts were robbing us. Three times I was mugged in my car. For the pad. Now it's just one at a time. Then back to the surgery. You wouldn't believe that now, would you? Of this town? I don't dare to guess at where it will all end.'

I looked over at Margaret. Something in her face told me she had suffered this many times before. I felt my back stiffening.

'Doctor Riccarton,' I said, 'could you go into the room and see my grandfather?'

He lifted another biscuit off the plate.

'Now tell me, James,' he said, 'has he been showing signs of anxiety? You know. His name in the paper and so on. I, for one, can't believe . . .'

I took the biscuit out of his hand and chucked it at the table.

'He's fucking unconscious in there,' I said. 'Go and look at him.'

The expression on Riccarton's face suggested a suspicion had been confirmed. He stroked at his beard for a second. Then he lifted his case and went down the hall. We followed him. We could see him looking up at the holes in the walls as he lifted my grandfather's wrist. He put a stethoscope to his chest. Then he turned to face us.

'I'm sure you will object to this,' he said, 'but in my opinion this is not a fit place for Mr Bawn to die. And he will die soon. If you know anything about this building, you will know that the lifts are not always working. There is one lift working now. I can't guarantee it will be working tomorrow. You might find the prospect of having your grandfather carried down these stairs in a chair bearable. I am bound to tell you I do not. Mr Bawn, I need hardly tell you, is a man of considerable dignity, and I would not leave him here. In any case he has long been in need of oxygen. I leave it to you.'

And with that — with a look of complete regret on his face — he packed his things away and moved to the door.

'I'm sorry,' I said to him.

'We are all sorry, James.'

When he had closed the front door I took Margaret in my arms. 'It's what he wanted,' she whispered.

'But it's not what we want,' I said.

Riccarton was right. One of the faults of the high flats was the lifts. They couldn't be relied upon; and, even when they were working, you couldn't fit a coffin in them. It was a design fault: you couldn't fit a coffin. Of all the people to go down the stairs in a chair! No. I wouldn't allow it.

Margaret nodded with her eyes closed and her head down. I went out to the landing. Riccarton was waiting for the lift to come. Our eyes locked in that dismal space.

'Doctor,' I said, 'would you send us someone to take him.'

I could hear the bleep as the lift door closed. He was using his phone to call the ambulance.

The Bawns had things in common. Each of us was a good liar. Each could inspire love, and yet feel unloved. Each of us ran away. We never found ourselves comfortably at home. Home was a problem for all of us. We spoke too much to ourselves, and not enough to other people. The only friends Hugh's father ever had were the ones he died beside at Ypres. Hugh had heroes in place of friends. He had been easy to like but difficult to know. No one had ever been allowed to help him. We were all a bit like that. I would later be shocked to find how lonely my father was inside his own life. It was years since anyone had shared a meal with him.

The men in our family had tired hearts. And they all had them young. I would often hope that the similarities had come to an end with me. I had broken the mould. What if my spirit could be large, like theirs, but not imprisoned, not lying poisoned at the centre of my days? I thought of how I might be different.

You're different, Jamie, and that will bring its own troubles.

I'd believed in that too much. I thought I could move in the world of all possible lights, and breathe, breathe, breathe.

I went out to college to be smarter than them. I went to the gym to be stronger. I was not much different from Dr Riccarton. And, all in all, from moment to moment, I was not much different from the Bawns before me. I saw it most in our native duplicity.

Thomas Bawn
An angel of the fields, a man of fathomless serenity.
But he guzzled from bottles and broke his own heart.
He died for a country he didn't understand.

Hugh Bawn
A master builder: one of the higher citizens,
who worked like a Trojan,
who gave life to people's hopes, a social engineer,
a man who carried on his mother's good work,
who knew the names of trees, the history of bells,
who altered the landscape of the place that he loved.
Lost himself in a welter of ambitions, unsafe buildings,
cheaper materials; he cooked the books to make more blocks.

Robert Bawn
An alcoholic, the kind that rages and mourns.
He never meant well, and he never did well.
And yet he found himself trying.

Hugh lay there dead in the hospital ward. Screens around us. His whole life passed in front of me; the lives of his fathers, his sons.

The hands moved slowly on the clock.

Hugh's great second self, the one we had tried to protect him from: a truth-maker who turned his back on the truth; a high-minded pioneer who degraded his vision for the sake of expedience. He died without too much honour on his side. But he was peaceful now. And we knew more of him than that; we knew better.

Hugh travelled across my mind as I watched him lying dead. What would become of us all? I thought of my father lost in the wilderness. I thought of me. And Margaret sat on the other side. She laid down her head on her husband's chest, and wept for mercy in the cup of his hand.

From the hour of his death Margaret became like the wife in one of her songs. She was almost mad with grief. She was soundless for all that. But her thoughts were racing mad. Confronted at last with that unyielding corpse, the electrical hum of the Luther Ward, my granny Margaret was gone from the world to a better place we know. She grasped at the only comfort she could trust, a comfort that lasted like a dwam for weeks, and she was lost for a time, at the funeral, and after. It was the comfort of her childhood; the solace of the ballads. I knew all the signs and the talk of them. And I knew Margaret better than she knew. Those old words had seen her through a year or two of pain. They would do for some time yet. And there was nothing for me to say then. I had just to watch over her. We had passed all need of ordinary speaking.

Meanwhile she consorted with the saints. Her white lips moved in holy supplication. There was a soft murmur to her voice, as a hush through the trees on Mount Olives. The clock on the wall kept firm. We could hear the seconds going off. And long hours she sat with her dampened beads. Her face flushed with its need of angels. And Hugh's cold blood sank low in its vessels.

The priest had come and gone. Margaret sent for him in the afternoon. As my granny made ready with verses and prayers, with the time-dark customs she needed to live, an ordained man, a man I once knew, went round about my granda with oils and beliefs. Into the late hours we sat with our dead idol. The ward was dim. They let us be with him much of the night. We sat there in shadows. Old men slept around us. Margaret's eyes glistened on in the dark. We had come to rest with our final feelings. Time grew still: a hope of salvation passed into the air, and out to the wards that smelled of soap.

Margaret went to sleep on his hands. The thought came back of the two as young lovers. Sailing up the Clyde with that smell in her hair. Her face coloured up like one of Cadell's. The laughter of the typing pool. The boys and their beers. Some long-ago kiss on the promenade at Rothesay. And the immense future out in front. Hugh's lovable plans for the way of the world. His modern ideas. The homes they would build together. The homes they would build.

And still I could see my grandparents, their arms entangled by a rock-pool, enjoying my knowledge of this or that shell, finding a plate in my small, green book. Up among the Carrick Hills I could see them too, holding hands, the grass full of stories, and the druid forts that told us stories. That was the sort of love they had: it drew out the history in one another; it made a pact with the land. They wanted to know about the world they loved in. They had wanted to see themselves clearly there. And knowing what they did, and being who they were, they wanted to break the mirror they held. They followed the seasons with avid eyes. They believed in renewal and progress. It was all of a piece with them. History and nature had offered its lessons: make it all new; bring on the future; revolve the world again and again. Feel the rain in the hills over Galston.

All of this grew from their love of each other.

My heart felt sorry for them. The two young people they had been.

I placed my hand among the grey curlicues of Hugh's fallen chest. Nothing lived there now. An empty house. The pulse had gone from his small chambers. Yet I couldn't believe it was so. Not just yet. The power that had lived there. It was not easy to deal with Hugh's sudden absence. He had been too much in the world for that. His body was grave to a hundred notions. What could remain of his long life's burning?

He lay motionless.

There was nothing of life any more. His face was strange. He'd gone into the dark with a look of dispute.

He's an old man . . . You should try and not let it get to you so much. Hugh's had a good life . . .

The corpse was a shadow of Hugh Bawn; it left us with none of him. And so, as the night wore on, the person in the bed grew to seem like someone never here, and never loud, or moved to action, and never loved by anyone. It seemed like a strange new collection of bones. No signature marks on this pointless cadaver. No record. The clock came louder. The story in the bed was well past the telling.

The night takes over your thoughts.

Hugh became an animal on his deathbed. A cold dead

animal. A bird in the road with its feathers raised in shock. A liquid frog in its bed of long grass. A mouse. I once saw a tortoise dead on its back. He looked like that. Something sinister had come of his flesh. He was ominous. Like some small vertebrate that lived outside. I knew he would never speak words again. But in the early hours I had thought he might scratch at the air, or bristle, or scamper, or mew from the depths of his faraway pain. I thought he might hiss. Or bray.

Nothing happened. He lay soundless. A skinful of animal fibres, a dead-eyed old mule, or the last of some mortified rabbit, poor fleshly creatures now just like him.

Everything goes to nothing in the end. And just like this, under the moon.

I dreamed with my eyes open in the black. I dreamed I could hear his blood curdle. The noises of retreat. Every fluid of the old man was seeping away. Or going mineral-hard again. His tears dried up. His semen atrophied. The saliva in his mouth grew thick and congealed. His stomach shrank to a stone. The cowl of his brain was a small arid bag. He was dead.

What was it about that room, making me think I could hear those noises?

Outside the curtains, oxygen oozed through sterilised tubes, sore men coughed and snored, the elevators shinned up their metal ropes, the nurses giggled on their lighted island. And here lay Hugh's stiffening corpse. The geology of death asserting itself. Time and pressure having their day.

Carbon fruit. Mineral-hard.

I put my head on the blanket and felt him gone. This was no one now that I could know. He was dead.

I pictured his soul going out in the country. Over the rivers. Around the towers. Sloshing through puddles and pools of algae; ringing the bell of Alloway Kirk.

His rapid feet on the frozen soil; the fields in Mauchline and Ochiltree. He strolled in the harbours of Troon and Saltcoats.

I saw him over the Irish Sea, a smile about him; and then stopped for a second, or stopped for all time, with whisky and bread, on the graves of the people who gave him his name. I saw him bow to an ugly Virgin. All dispute gone from his face. I saw him raining bricks and mortar on the people of Clydebank. I saw him running up the Necropolis hill with a tattered flag of Scotland. His young hair and this old flag tearing away at the back of him. I saw him lying in the grass with a set-square and pencil. He had boy's legs. He had child's eyes. And sat there beside him was good Mr Wheatley. I saw them both. They looked on the city. They sat on these piles of books. The land was all shapes. The man and the boy were there. I saw them there, and they sat on the grass, and the day was white, and they disappeared.

The sky in the morning was warning-red.

I stood at the sliding doors of Crosshouse Hospital, my arm around my grandmother. The hedges and sky went on for miles. The Kilmarnock bus came through the trees with its tiers of golden light. We watched the people getting off. Quiet young men in plasters. Upset girls.

Margaret linked her arm through mine and we walked to the zebra-crossing. The car park was acres long. Hundreds of cars there, under the open sky.

'All these cars look the same,' said Margaret.

Hugh's body was laid out in the old-fashioned way. The woman came with candles and incense and cloths. My granny presided, her antique words sounding grave and absurd. To me Hugh lay in his coffin. To my granny, and to the strange woman with the mortician's eyes, my granda was 'chested in the death hamper'.

Margaret protected the old woman's ways. She didn't let the undertakers involve themselves in this intimate business. We bought their carpentry. We hired their cars. She asked that the carrying men be there on the day. But she refused to have his body in the undertaker's parlour. It hurt her not to have it at home. But that couldn't be. She begged that the body remain in the hospital mortuary, which it did, and she came to and fro on the bus, with her lady friend, her prayer book, her weeds.

Hugh had a pile of penny policies; he had never been rightly insured. They lay in a tin: *Empire Exhibition Scotland, 1938.*

I collected four hundred pounds from Friends Provident in Kilwinning. I drove to Saltcoats, then Prestwick, a hundred pounds here, forty there. The books Margaret gave me had columns of figures, written in different inks. Each book had been abandoned years before. I put the money under the clock in Margaret's room. I wrote some cheques. I put an advert in the *Evening Times*:

Hugh Thomas Bawn
'Mr Housing'
Beloved husband of Margaret, father of Robert,
grandfather of James
Died, at Crosshouse Hospital, on 26th December 1995
Eleven o'clock Mass at St Joseph's Church, Affleck,
on 30th December
No flowers
Ecclesiastes: "One generation passeth away, and another
generation cometh: but the earth abideth for ever."

St Joseph's was not as I remembered it. The church sat different in my mind. But here it was, aslant at the head of the har-

bour; the green shutters of the church-house fading now, and
ready to drop to the sea. The pews used to run in rows from
the altar to the door. Now the altar was to one side. The pews
curved around in the new style. There were children's drawings at the stations of the cross. But the same old angular
Marys were there. The wooden apostles with their agonised
faces, the pointing fingers, the open mouths. The Roman soldiers with oversized feet. And new stained glass in the windows. Indigo glass.

Hosannas above; fish below.

The names of local boys who died in the wars out there: in
Gallipoli, Normandy, the bogs at Goose Green.

Up by the altar hung a painted board; the names of St
Joseph's parish priests were picked out in red.

Father Seamus Brady, 1948–62
Father Dominic Savio, 1962–66
Father Martin Healy, 1966–79
Father Ian Timothy, 1979–

The chapel was half full. The air was heavy with hymns and
incense. My granda's coffin was there. Father Timothy came
up as we stood at the back. His hair was still lush – but lushly
grey. He put his arms around Margaret. He took her hands.
He whispered a word.

'Faith,' he said.

She gripped at the front of his jade-coloured robe. And
then he turned to me. The smell of after-shave was there
about him. It roamed in the air just between us. I thought I
could see that his years had been hard.

'It's good to see you, Father,' I said.

'James.'

We hugged each other. It was not as easy as it used to be.

Standing together after all those years. He felt like a boy in my arms.

'I am sorry,' he said.

'We are all sorry.'

I stroked at his arm just a second. It seemed to be me that was comforting him.

The father went back to the sacristy.

Margaret and I walked down to the front. On the way past the coffin Margaret bowed and kissed the lid. It was covered in cards.

Words took over, and music too, and a slow-stepped liturgical dance, a standing and sitting and kneeling and bowing, a run of steps too dreadfully known.

God the Father, God the Son, and God the Holy Ghost.

There was purple light coming down from the roof. A thousand tiny rags again, falling as dust on the father's hands, on the empty pews, on the water font. And down it came, with nothing of pity, nothing of shame, on the small-looking coffin of Hugh Thomas Bawn.

'The most sacred of our Seven Corporal Works of Mercy,' said the priest, 'is to bury the dead.'

Eternal rest give to him, O Lord, and let perpetual light shine upon him . . .

The children's drawings sang yellow and red in their clip-frames. There was something very happy in their mixture of small and big letters. Four were pinned like a window above the baptismal font. The Four Cardinal Virtues:

Prudence (a smiling man in a suit holds a few gold coins); Justice (a woman in a long wig with her hand on a gate, an arrow saying 'freedom'); Fortitude (a cowboy stands on a small hill surrounded by crimson Indians); and Temperance (an old man with folded arms; he looks at a bottle labelled 'Vodca').

A larger drawing took up the back wall. The work of several crayon-happy children; the work of a class, P4. It was filled up with mountains and lightning, a long-bearded Abraham, a frightened Isaac. Their eyes were wide to the world. Abraham's dagger hung in the air. The son saying no to his father.

No.

. . . grant to the souls of thy servants departed the remission of all their sins . . .

Father Timothy turned up his hands.

'Through Christ our Lord,' he said, 'in whom there hath shone forth upon us the hope of a blessed resurrection: that those who are saddened by the certain event of death may be consoled by the promise of future immortality. For to thy faithful, O Lord, life is changed, not taken away; and when the earthly house of this our habitation is dissolved, an eternal dwelling is made for us in heaven.'

The chapel was like a great shell: the sound of the sea.

Hugh lying dead in his box. I wondered: would Hugh be as a vengeful ghost? Would he storm about the country? Would he haunt us in our own infirmity? The words of the mass lapped out. The sound dimmed in my ears; familiar faces, lips moving. The way of the cross showing out on the walls. Jesus meeting his afflicted mother. The cross being laid upon Simon of Cyrene. Jesus falling the third time. Jesus being nailed to the wood. His mouth saying no.

No.

Up in the choir a woman was standing. She held a black book. She wore a black coat. Her lips moved out of time with the rest. The church cleaner. I had known her all my life. She was up in the choir. Her lips moving.

'Confiteor Deo omnipotenti . . .'

I confess to almighty God, to blessed Mary ever Virgin, to blessed Michael the archangel, to blessed John Baptist, to the holy apostles Peter and Paul, to all the saints, and to you, Father, that I have sinned exceedingly in thought, word, and deed, through my fault, through my fault, through my most griev-ous fault . . .

The words came back in a roar. And still it was out of sync. People were saying different masses. They were using differ-ent words. There was a babble of voices, separate streams of prayer, eddies of litany, coming together, falling away. Some-times only Father Timothy's voice would be left in the air. His voice was the central one: everything else, a clash of whispers.

'It started with Father Brady,' a woman said at my back. 'They still say mass in the old way. They've had hassle about it. They use the old words. The Bishop's been hauled in on it, but they seem to get away with it still. Other out-of-the-way churches do it too. They use the old words, and some use the Latin.'

The priest read from John's Gospel. Then he nodded down. Margaret made a space to let me out. My legs were weak as I took the steps. The red carpet seemed to glare at me. There was something mocking in its brightness. I felt sud-denly tall as I swayed at the pulpit. My suit felt short. I wiped the hair from my eyes. And I looked up. A few seconds seeped like a century of minutes. There were all those faces. My granny in her overcoat and black scarf. My mother a few rows back, with Bob in his tie, his white shirt, and ring. There were people there whose faces I knew. A half-dozen rows from the Corporation. Fergus McCluskey and my granda's apprentices.

The local MP and his surly wife. The barman from the British Legion. A bank of young men who meant nothing to me. My teacher Mr Buie. He stood on his own. His eyes seemed narrower now; he held himself low. My keen enemy from the local paper was there. Also Riccarton the doctor. And several young women stood with babies by the door. I wondered if they were mass-goers, or if they knew Hugh, and just liked him as he walked in the street, or spoke of large things in the pub. Maybe they had lived in one of his tower blocks. I had never seen any of them before. Maybe they just felt sorry.

Some of the men's faces were marred with booze. And their expressions showed respect for life's public duties; there was something deeply broken-in about their black ties; they carried themselves like men for whom things had gone wrong. There was a quality of few words about them. They stood to attention. They had seen the world change. You could see all that. All their confidence and hot contempt had grown cold; they stood there like invalids.

At the very back was a man in a leather jacket. His head was bald; red at the sides. His mouth was still. The sort of man who radiates a vast separateness. His hands held for care to the pew in front. His face was pale. My father.

I cleared my throat.

'The Responsorial Psalm,' I said. 'The Lord is my shepherd, therefore can I lack nothing.'

The Lord is my shepherd, therefore can I lack nothing.

'The Lord is my shepherd, therefore can I lack nothing.
He shall feed me in a green pasture,
And lead me forth beside the waters of comfort.

He shall convert my soul:
And bring me forth in the paths of righteousness.
For his name's sake.
The Lord is my shepherd, therefore can I lack nothing.
Yea so I walk through the valley of the shadow of death:
I will fear no evil;
For thou art with me,
Thy rod and staff comfort me.
The Lord is my shepherd, therefore can I lack nothing.
Thou shalt prepare a table before me,
Against them that trouble me,
Thou hast anointed my head with oil,
And my cup shall be full.
The Lord is my shepherd, therefore can I lack nothing.
But thy loving kindness and mercy shall follow me,
All the days of my life:
And I will dwell in the house of the Lord for ever.
The Lord is my shepherd, therefore can I lack nothing.

Margaret was weeping in her hands. I went back to my place and held her. The chapel spun before me, a chasm of memory and unbelieving. I held poor Margaret for all I was worth. I wanted to weep for her broken heart. I wanted to say something, to raise up a voice in that holy place, and make our losses plain, and not let my grandmother's sore weeping pass into nothing. I wanted to break the secrecy of her trials. Just for a minute, just for a day, to cheat the devil of all indifference, to make the saints stand up and listen, and in one vast moment of truth, to make the people in that chapel know of our lives, and know of their own, and let Hugh Bawn's burial day be a time of gentle recognitions, a longed-for day of the open heart.

Shivering there, with Margaret undone, I wanted to silence our exotic muttering. There had to be a word. We had need of a word to unsay ourselves. But we hadn't that. Not in that chapel, in that country, on that day. All we had was our clash of whispers.

I turned and looked at Mr Buie. My old teacher had his head down in prayer. We hadn't a word between us. Not between any of us. Margaret was alone with her faith. Others behind us were speaking to gods. The rest of us roamed in our heads for comfort.

Father Timothy went to the pulpit with a square of paper. He unfolded it there and raised his head.

'This has been a century of very great challenges,' he said. 'I think of wars, diseases, famine, new technologies, visits to the moon. But for most of us, for men and women like you and me, the greatest of all the challenges were here, on our own soil. They were challenges about how we lived. Our time has been one of improvements — not in morals, perhaps, or in church attendance, or in our ability to break those unchristian habits which daily tempt us. But it has been an age which set high goals for itself, especially in the area of social reform. Even in a small place like this, in Ayrshire, in Glasgow, or in Scotland as a whole: this has been a century of progress. Hugh Bawn was a man who believed in that progress. It is often said of him that he stood alone. But what he stood for was good and plain: clean, affordable modern houses. More than any other person of his generation, he saw to it that this goal was achieved. One does not have to look far into the history of our parishes to see evidence of the terrible slums. Since the end of the last war Hugh made it his task to drive ahead one of the biggest social revolutions ever to take place in this country — the building of high-rise flats, or tower blocks, as he called them himself.

'The job of cleaning up after the war, and building again, could not have fallen to better men than Hugh Bawn and his kind. His mother was the famous suffragette and rent-strike organiser Effie Bawn. She called herself a socialist. She taught him what it meant to be a citizen, to be a visionary, and to be a Catholic. And as well as these things Hugh was a patriot. He loved this country, and all his life he seemed to yearn to make it better.

'Fashion is wont to cast a shadow over them whose moment is past. Hugh Bawn's buildings, like the man himself, like all of us indeed, were deemed, in more recent times, to be imperfect. Hugh himself remained philosophical about this. He saw that another generation must have its day. He was a man of some passion, and again, in recent times, he was to be drawn into one dispute and another. But as he begins his journey towards God's everlasting protection, in a dwelling-place built for eternity, we can only be sure that Hugh has left all earthly concerns behind. But we can also hope, with Our Father's heavenly grace, that something of Hugh Bawn's pioneering spirit will remain here with us, and that his consideration for his fellow man will serve as a guide and example to all. It has been said that this is a country without many modern heroes. Hugh Bawn was such a thing. He bound tradition and the future like no one else I can think of. For his life we must always be grateful.'

He folded the paper.

We sat in silence.

It seemed that one large pulse had entered the room. This was not the truth for which I'd stirred. It wasn't a story some would recognise. But it bound the people in that chapel like no words spoken hitherto. I was rooted with shock that the priest had managed it. He had spoken with all the strength he had. He had given a shape to the terrible mess of our feelings that day. He had spoken up. He'd shown courage – the courage to believe that the truth is not everything. When he returned to the centre of the altar I looked at his eyes. They were fixed on Margaret. He had done it for her.

'Take this, all of you, and drink from it: this is the cup of my blood, the blood of the new and eternal testament; the mystery of faith, which shall be shed for you, and for many, to the remission of sins.'

The father held up the cup.

An altar-boy in sandshoes rang the bell. He yawned and bit his lip. His face gave no notion of why he was there. He just yawned. He rang the bell. The sound sparkled down the air, as if that moment was all there was, and all there ever would be. The boy stood beside the priest. He held a bowl of Communion hosts. I joined the line for Margaret's sake. They all took Communion in their hands now. I stepped up to the priest and put out my tongue.

'Body of Christ,' he said.

He placed the bread on my tongue.

'Amen.'

I did what I did as a child: I made the rice-wafer soft on my tongue, and then I pressed it up to the roof of my mouth. It stuck there, as it always had; I spent the end of the mass, a boy again, straining my tongue, scraping an age at the sickly-sweet plaster.

Father Timothy put his hand on an open book.

'Instructed,' he said, 'by thy saving precepts, and following thy divine institution, we presume to say . . .'

And then he looked up, paused, and he nodded.

They said the Lord's Prayer. Everyone said it — relieved, no doubt, that this was something they all could say. And so the volume grew in that church. I thought of the sea outside, taking these voices away from the west coast of Scotland, making the words of this common worship heard in another place, in another time. And yet I was too much myself not to doubt it. I could feel the prayer rising from their throats — something of the life of each mourner rising with it, and tears — but falling like nothing in the sea out there, going nowhere, and washing back as vapour on the frozen rocks. Who can say of a particular sea that it is old? Distilled by the sun, kneaded by the moon, it is renewed in a year, in a day, or in an hour.

. . . thy kingdom come: thy will be done on earth as it is in heaven. Give us this day our daily bread . . .

And by then it was almost at an end. The dark lady up in the choir folded her book. The priest and the altar-boy conferred. Out of nowhere came a gold incense cradle. It swung on the end of a chain. The boy and the man were busy with eyes and hands. Eventually the smell came to us. The acrid burn at an ended life. Quills of blue smoke rose out of the swinging ball. It was the smell of ancientness; the smell of Rome. With that expense of scent in our nostrils — the embalming scent, the swing of hypnotic gold — we dreamed that we breathed as a mighty civilisation. Father Timothy swung the ornament around Hugh's coffin.

Out of the depths I have cried to thee, O Lord; Lord hear my voice. Let thine ears be attentive to the voice of my supplication. If thou, O Lord, shalt observe iniquities, Lord, who shall endure it . . . ?

I asked McCluskey and four of his men to join me in carrying the coffin out. Margaret said nothing. They came to the front with sombre lips. We lifted the coffin with ease from the sticks. Margaret walked at our backs. The woman in the choir started a hymn as we paced to the door with the last of Hugh. McCluskey's arm came under the coffin and on to my shoulder. He steadied me there with his draughtsman's hand. The woman's voice went over St Joseph's.

Hosannas above; fish below.

Faith of our fathers living still, we will be true to you till death. We will be true to you till death.

We wanted Hugh to be with his mother. The dark cars followed his hearse to the Royston Cemetery in Glasgow; 30 miles of tree-spattered Ayrshire, the villages here and there, inhaling the white afternoon. We crossed the fields, each field tight with frost. Outside Lugton a farmer stood, transfixed in the meagre grass, his cold cows lolling around him. He took off his cap as the cortège passed. Margaret turned in a daze from the window.

'It was a good turnout,' she said.

Glasgow now: a gaseous plaid of one-way roads.

We passed the old municipal Post Office. It was closed down. A saltire banner flapped up there, over George Square, the castle of Fletton brick. Margaret swallowed hard. Her speech was slow. 'The flag that fans our people cold.'

She turned to me. 'I want you to know that your granda made mistakes,' she said. 'He wasn't always lovable to people, though I always loved him. And he made mistakes. Let it be clear in your mind, Jamie. He got above himself as a housing man, and he spread the money a bit thin, and the houses suffered, but he never took a penny out for himself. You must realise that. I think you said you knew that was true.'

'Yes I do,' I said.

'The idea that he had money,' she said. 'He barely had a pension at the end. He never bothered about money.' Her eye glinted beneath the net of her veil. 'And don't think I don't know you're paying for most of this.'

'Shhh, Granny,' I said, and took her hand. 'We're going to be all right.'

'They will never believe that he was only trying . . .' she said.

'Shh,' I said. 'They will believe. They will.'

Someone had taken care of the grave. The gravestones on either side were covered in moss, but not Famie's. You could see the words clearly:

Euphemia Bawn
Born 2nd March 1893. Died 19th May 1941.
Councillor and Reformer
Beloved wife of Thomas Mangan Bawn
who died at Ypres on 6th January 1918
whilst serving his country.
'In my end is my beginning.'

I had never known so much silence. A small wind, the strands of grass vibrating like strings. And our few dozen breaths showing thick on the air thereabouts. The men mostly stood with their hands clasped in front. The women's were stuffed into pockets, or trapped in handkerchiefs. Father Timothy started his words. Much of what he said I couldn't hear; his voice went over the houses; my eye was absorbed in high windows. One thing came over:

'. . . the inevitable courses of Nature in reclaiming what she has lent to us.'

Margaret had entered on other proceedings. She wasn't with us. Her lips moved slowly. She ignored the priest. I placed my arm over her. She made no movement. She was out somewhere in her salt-seas of comfort; she spoke with her national ghosts.

'He should be buried in swansdown,' she said, her voice just a murmur under the priest. 'He's only asleep.'

The people put their eyes to the coffin lying over the grave.

'He'll step out of that chest on the high day,' said Margaret.

I looked for a time at the sorry ground. Some of the people whispered words in response to the priest's holy things. One or two of the women put a hand on Margaret, but she was lost to us then. She seemed like an aged tribeswoman, a rune-reading witch, strange and erotic with her fingers. She began to whimper. 'Our Lady wept for Darnley in a white cloot,' she said.

'Granny, I'm here still. Hold my hand.'

She held it tight.

'My very own,' she said with tears coming down. She was now ignoring the presence of everyone else. She had come to look frightened. 'Jamie my own,' she said, 'I'll be the last in that grave. I'll be the watchman, sure I will?'

Out of dust we came, and unto dust we shall return . . .

'I'll take in water for they're a' thirsty,' said Margaret.

'Shh,' I said. 'I'm here. I'm here, Granny.'

There was nothing more to say. Margaret shook cold in my arms. I could see a silver helium airship over the city centre. It glinted there in the distance. It flew high on a string from the City Chambers. I don't know what it was doing up there. It was the sort of thing they did now. The sort of thing many of us did. I suppose it was meant to make people feel they were living in a good place. Or maybe it was just for the new year tomorrow. A Hogmanay balloon. It turned slowly in the air over George Square. It turned very slowly.

'Put in the mirror and put in the bell,' said Margaret. 'He'll come out of there with a rage forenoon.'

Her voice was loud and plain now.

'Shh,' I said.

I held her straining arm. I thought she might throw herself into the pit, so glazed was her eye with fear and sorrow; to hurt herself to prove Hugh's honour, an act of suttee in the heather-touched lanes of the Royston Cemetery, under the cloud-shade of Glasgow. She seemed to melt into common tears as the coffin went into the ground. She came to quietness then. Father Timothy lifted a handful of soil. I stepped up to him. I took his hand in both of mine. I took the soil. I held my hand over the grave; the cold clay took seconds to slide away, falling at last to the coffin below.

'Goodbye,' I said.

I went back to Margaret. The people had left the grave. She leaned over with a small twist of violets. She kissed them and dropped them in. She spoke seven words in the great stillness.

'I won't be long at your back,' she said.

I held her hand as we walked to the car. Lines of graves going down the hill, and just at the foot there, a spread of houses. The light was beginning to go from the sky.

7

Jamie, Come Try Me

The Bruce Hotel,
12 Market Square,
Dumfries.
3 January 1996

Dear Karen,
This is the place where the man who wrote Peter Pan spent his boy-hood. You would like it here. There are lots of old communists, and frock shops.

I've come down here to find my father. I just want to see him that's all. Dumfries feels like what it is — a country's end. The Galloway hills and trees are amazing. The hedges are all Protestant. It's all very tidy. You would like it. Maybe we can come and see it some day.

What a time this has been. I used to think that only old houses could be haunted, and old people. But that is all over now. I'm coming home.
Love Jamie.

I sent that letter from the hotel desk on my second day in Dumfries. The letter carried all my love of Karen. But also, as

255

I wrote it out, a feeling came over me, a red-eyed conviction, a sense of things that would never leave me, and of things now slipping away. I felt in a moment my strength, my weakness. I knew that the world was less certain now, and I'm sure I saw it for the first time, how changes come about, and that some were for good, and some for bad, and that in one day's closing lies the opening of the next. As the pen went across the paper I knew I had changed. I could only love where I could. I could only hope to be happy, and find comfort in the hope, as people do, wherever they are.

I see that letter in front of me now. If it contains something of the gathered obsessions of my life so far, then let that be so, for it also contains a promise of them one day being dissolved, and of the future coming into its own, and blowing medicinal wind into the rooms of all those hours gone by. The days to come might be days like these; Karen and me, and the life we could make between us. I had always thought I would turn to salt if I ever looked back: but I was all right now. I would soon go home.

The hotel wallpaper was tea-time flock. The curtains were Terleys-white. I sat on the bed — back on the headboard, sachet of coffee in soft-boiled water — and there I saw blocks of Dumfries light meandering through the bay window's glass. It had something to do with cars and clouds, the way the light-blocks went round and round; like fireworks on snow they burst into shadows at the door. The light came into the room, shifting along the walls, as if time were no object, as if time itself were impervious to all that happens under its passing. All you could do was watch it going, the shadows a pretty companion, the broken marks of a thousand sun-dials, running away from time, and me.

I posted the letter. Then I sat on the bed and watched

the light for an hour. I think it was an hour. I closed my eyes and dreamed of young men singing songs from open windows. They sang in their pyjamas. I came down to hear them. They stood at the windows with big smiles at night time. And then we all went out to the sea. The boat was dry. Red fish swam on either side of the boat. We all sailed ahead thinking nothing could be wrong. And nothing was wrong.

The boat we sailed on was big and dry.

When I woke, dark fingers of shadow swayed on the wall. Trees outside. The light had moved to the trees now. The new shadows played on the wall. They danced in a ring. A movie of children on the far wall.

As a boy I ran out on my parents. I never came back.

Dumfries became a place in my head. I thought of it now and then. Hugh told me it was red-stone. They never wanted any blocks like his. It was a blush-spot on the map below Ayrshire. We thought not to like it was good. When I left my parents to their final disasters — pain and mind-loss, the eventual split — the last places in Scotland were my father's ports of call. My grandfather always had the word on him. He'd be pickled in Ecclefechan, sozzled to hell in Gretna Green, or lost to himself in Langholm or Canonbie. The last places in Scotland: the beginning of England.

My father was nothing but mad on the drink. I was afraid of him. The look in his blood-dimmed eyes that day, the day he said he would end me for good, those years ago in the Ferguson home, the damp walls encircling us. That was the picture of him I carried in my head. His gaunt face. His collapsed cheeks.

My life-blood, my enemy.

In my last year at school this picture was replaced once more. I went down to Dumfries to see him. It was summer. Hugh and I had inspected the roses at Culzean Castle on the way down. I know the sea there sparkled in a fair tumbling of blue. Only the rocks seemed asleep that day; down on the beaches they lay about, in ghostly spray of sea-salt and softness, those glacial ruins, their hard memories, and all around them the full-blooms and bickerings of summer.

The rocks stood still. Auld Wives rocks, in threes: hurled from a mythical Ireland out there, launched in the days before Christian boats, by infamous women in their heathen cloth, who had nothing of beauty, but hurled these rocks to show they had strength in its place. That was the story of the rocks at Culzean. Hugh told it again. He loved to tell it. The Auld Wives stood on the beach below the castle wall. Some phosphorous bombs were washed up; they fizzled and split at the tide's edge, those mini-worlds of lava. Yesterday's sewage was held in a gluttony of blue.

Dead crabs. American voices.

The sand was slick with an inkling of coming oil.

They had found my father's car on the edge of the Solway Firth. It was up on the grass with the doors wide open. He'd abandoned it there. The back seat was piled with drained bottles. Lanlakes, Eldorados.

A string of keys dangled beneath the wheel. The floor was all Woodbines. The roof was bashed. It seems he had found his way back to a local pub. He leaned on the bar and began to scream. He just screamed. No words. He took a water jug off the bar. He continued the screaming. He broke the jug and tore at his wrist. He ripped again and again at the flesh of his arm.

Gouts of blood, on the bar towels, the ice bucket.

All the time he screamed. He hurt himself. The police came.

The peat-moss water of the River Nith; its glimmer down to the Blackshaw Bank. A mineral souse over hills and dales; the waters of thirst and oblivion. The Burgh of Dumfries. A civic neatness; a well-fitting collar round the tie of the Nith. A place of ease and worship. Long queues at the post office; satellite dishes on every street. But quiet Dumfries. A place of cakes.

They put my father in a nut-house. Eskdale Brattles. It was a posh place with high fencing; some kind of old baronial hall. It had once been a place for nervous gents. They taught them to spoon their soup in peace. It was so much of an orderly world about there. They had Wellington boots stacked by the door with people's initials marked on them. The consultants wore watch-chains. There were birds of all kinds making noise in the gardens. I will never forget those lawns. Every colour under the sun. And the day I came there were bees outside, bees that buzzed, or were crooked in thistles. The bushes were heavy with sweet-smelling bells. My grandfather sat on a bench in the garden. I went into the ward by myself.

'You're very thin,' I said to my father.

'Porridge they feed you,' my father said, 'and kippers.'

His hair seemed redder than it ever had. The light in the ward was grey. He raised his hand. 'You don't look a fucking bit like me, so you don't.'

'Suppose not,' I said.

'No way. My family were all good at the football. You could never kick a fucking ball. A bastard's no strength in his ankle.'

'Not much. But you can play can't you?'

'I'll put my boot to your arse,' he said. 'The fucking right way. No problem. No fucking problemo.'

A stack of cardboard sick-trays was beside his bed. And something odd: a small, painted, alabaster statue of St Joseph.

'It's all a load of shite. Stories of things that never happened. Cunts waving their arms about the place. Big noises. Bampots the fucking lot. Everybody wants to give you their big fucking story. God this and God that. God the fucking lot of them. Bampots. A load of piss.'

'And what . . .'

'What's your name?' he said.

'My name?'

'Your name. Your fucking name. What's it to be?'

'Jamie,' I said.

'Oh Jamie is it? Jamie. Wee Jamie. O Jamie fuck off.'

'Dad.'

'Don't dad me. Don't fucking dad me. I'm no your fucking dad. You must be fucking joking. Away you go and fuck. Wee Jamie. Big fucking head and wee fucking shoulders. Can he kick a ball? Can he fucking kick a ball? Go and take a fuck to yourself, son. What a fucking laugh eh? We are all daft in here. Don't tell me they away and said nothing about it. Go and fuck yourself!'

'Are you needing anything?'

'Peace perfect fucking peace. No messing.'

He wiped his mouth and stared at the blankets.

'I want you to go away.'

'I don't think I deserve this,' I said.

'Don't give me what you deserve. What wee Jamie deserves. What does wee Jamie deserve? A kick in the arse. A good doing. A good kick in the bastarding arse. And he can go and blame some other cunt. Go on, my friend. Saint this and saint fucking that. Build them big, build them strong! On you go, wee man. Make us all sick. Into the valley of death rode the six hundred . . . gone yourself!'

I stood up. I felt a dangerous quickening about me.

'You're the fucking bampot,' I said. 'Your only son comes to see you . . .'

'Fuck, fuck, fuck, fuck you. Fuck you! Fuck up! Fuck up! Dickslapper!'

'You make me sick,' I said.

'Nurse, nurse, get this sick bastard out of here! Nurse! He's evil. He's a bad wee bastard. He just offered me a drink! Nurse.'

The nurses came running.

'Mr Bawn, come on now. This is no way to behave.'

'Honest, nurse,' he shouted. 'He's a bad person. He keeps tempting me with whisky. He said he would bring me in a dram. A big fucking tumbler of Grouse. He said it just there.'

I nodded to the nurses.

'It's all right,' I said. 'I'm on my way. The best of luck to you. He's disgusting.'

'Fuck him!' shouted my father. 'He thinks he is something. Can't even kick a ball. Never could. Hopeless fucking wanker. Charge! Charge! Comes in here and offers me a drink! Bastard doesn't know what a drink looks like. Pure wanker. Fucking hopeless cunt of a boy. See he doesn't steal your flowers by the way. The pansy likes flowers so he does. Comes in here with his fucking lies. Liar!'

I was outside before his voice drifted away. My grandfather was sleeping on the bench. He woke up and looked into my face. His eyes turned to the garden. He patted me about the head.

'You know,' he said, 'there's a Franciscan monastery up the road. Do you know it? The place where Robert the Bruce stabbed the Red Comyn. The beginning of the wars. Scotland's independence. Happened just up there. It's a lovely day.'

And we passed out of those high gates in silence. But soon we spoke of the local stone, and things that happened a long time ago. He didn't ask me about his son. But he linked my arm as we walked up the road. We fell quiet as we turned the corner at the road's end. The old monastery was now a super-market.

'Well well,' Hugh said. 'Life must go on. It comes for us all in the end.'

My father had gone quietly from the funeral mass. He didn't come to the grave. The look of him standing at the back – lips unmoved to prayer – had stayed with me over the days. He had seemed so altered, a man of the parish, nicely filled out in his leather jacket. He was just like a person I had never known. He seemed all of a sudden a smaller thing: a spent force, a man of quite ordinary bias. There was nothing very tragic about him. He was like a lot of men who'd never known themselves: he'd made a life out of small and distinct realisa-tions. And here he was. He was living with himself. Maybe he'd grown tired of his confusions, and now he was just their final sum, a character formed out of resignation, and the set-tled notion that this was all the life he could ever know.

I sensed he had come to this. There he was, depleted in his fawn-coloured scarf. I wasn't happy and I wasn't sad. The look of him stayed, that's all, and it passed along my veins, as ice-water to the heart.

They told me he now drove a taxi in Dumfries. I walked down the steps of the white hotel and was quickly lost in the crowd of English Street. The January sales had started. Every window was loud with a string of red words: BARGAINS. MUST END SOON.

The charity shops had moth-eaten toys in their windows. Over-lashed mannequins in yesterday's dresses. African baskets and chutney from Annan. A team of boys came riding past on their souped-up bikes: a great rush of air; a rail of stripes. They each wore a mask against pollution.

Lead poison, bumble bees, sea salt, asbestos?

They slid towards the countryside. As they made their way they looked like one people; their slim ankles, their gossamer hair. One people: a club for surviving, a tribe on the move. There was something optimistic in their bright-eyed passing. Something modern. The street was bored without them.

A lot of the shops were old dwellings. Victorian blocks with the lower brickwork ripped out for glass. There was silver chrome over many doors, plastic wording everywhere. The winter light seemed absorbed in the chrome and the plastic.

Outside Woolworths, a man who couldn't lick his stamp.

I came to a stop.

The man leaned on a zimmer frame – leaning forward on his elbows, as if he were somewhere else, propped at the fence on a football terrace, or hung at the bar of a boozy saloon. He was trying to lick the stamp. His tongue was too deep in his mouth. It seemed to exhaust him, lifting his arm to his face, and the gum-paper would barely reach his lips before he'd to take it down again. He tried it over and over. I stopped beside him.

'Can I put that on for you?' I said.

He unhunched a bit. There was uncertainty in his face.

'I'll just put it on for you,' I said. 'These things can be buggers to stick down.'

'Grand,' he said.

I just licked the stamp and pressed it down. It was a postcard. My eye caught some words: 'Dearest May.'

I handed it back to the man.

'Can you post it all right?'

'Aye, son,' he said, 'thanking you. The pillar box is just up the road there.'

And with that he took a grip of his frame and I passed on.

I drifted away on the thought of him, of who he was, and why he was here, of who his family were, and did he have children? I thought of what his days might be like. I wondered what his teeth had been like in the days when he had them. Did he have black hair? Was he a man in the army or navy? Was he a digger for coal? I thought of the old man's memory. I wondered was it good to him, or bad. He seemed to know his way in the town. I thought of his wide shoes, his pension, his 'Dearest May'.

I stopped. I had found one of the roads I was looking for.

My grandfather had taught me to notice the builtness of things. He would say that nothing comes from nowhere, that even stones have stories. The smallest thing had a purpose. It was an offence to his affections, to take the life of things for granted. He always saw the work – man's work, God's work – behind every last thing he looked at.

The street was exactly like one of those forties drawings, the ones dreamed up in war-fog, and put to paper the morning after Victory. Lines of white bungalows, paved and simple, with rounded doorways, yards of garden. Those drawings had once had a space-age feel, a heat-resistance; their cleanness a promise of mica. I used to look at them with awe. The lines so very pure. The sense of open air and ever-decreasing gravity.

Some people had lived for houses such as these. The advertisements in the newspapers. The drawings of pencil-thin women in their glad-rags. Children beaming at the immaculate pavements. Husbands in suits with their dazzling mouths. The whiteness. The even-spaced trees; the kitchenette. And binding the streets together: a drainage system that would flush away the worst of the Scottish weather.

The Houses of Tomorrow
A Reality Today!
Enjoy the cheerful, healthy conditions, which only proper planning can ensure.
The modern home is the focus of the new Scottish family. The Maxwell Estate, Dumfries. Waiting for You.

Walking along I began to feel the street under me. It held little of the blank optimism of old advertisements. A monument to the dreams of dead people, but now it stretched away. It was a living place.

The houses of tomorrow, a reality today!

And tomorrow was here. The futuristic glare was now dulled to a matt commonness. It now belonged to others. It was their experience now. Much of the whiteness had gone. Down that road there were no dreamers and builders with their arguments for the world – just little houses, and people living there, and no big dispute at the core of the bricks. There was none of the breath of past ideas. The houses were only houses now. The bricks were only bricks. The street was quite filled with its own ongoing day.

I came to a grey bungalow. There was a garage built like a big wooden shed. The notice on the door said: Arrow Cars. Someone had put soapy water on the grass. The earthworms were out. And overhead the sun was white. The clouds all charred. No god came down to help us. Not me, not the worms. I stood by the grass for a good five minutes. The windows were mirrors of vertical light. My eyes had nothing to gain from heaven: they looked at those windows, purple and yellow and red for a second, a column of yellow that hailed from God only knows. The light moved, the window cleared. The colour went out to another place. A woman's face was looking right at me.

In a matter of seconds she opened the door.

'Are you looking for something?'

I walked up to her.

'Yes, sorry,' I said. 'I'm looking for one of your drivers.'

'They're all out on hires,' she said. 'Which one is it?'

'Robert Bawn,' I said.

She looked at me, guessing. Her voice was mellow. 'Who are you?'

'I'm a friend of Robert's,' I said. 'My name is Jamie.'

There was some kind of movement in her eye. Her coolness seemed to go. Her movements suggested a wish to make things easy. 'Right you are,' she said, 'come in here just now. I'll try to get Robert on the radio. Would you like a wee cup of tea?'

'Some water would be nice,' I said.

'Good for you,' she said, bringing the glass from the kitchen.

'Does Robert live here?'

'No no,' she said. 'He drives for my husband's firm. We run the taxis from the house here. Robert has his own place.'

She took a long cigarette from a purse. She lit it while she spoke.

'It's a right cold day the day,' she said.

And with that she moved to the back of the room. She spoke into the radio. The phone rang at the same time. I saw someone pass beyond the glass door of the living room; it looked like a boy with a fishing rod.

I sat on the sofa with my wrists on my knees. The glass was empty. It was one of those rooms that was all sofa; a TV pressed between upholstered arms. On top there were medals for bowling and darts. A silver cup for Scottish Curling. On the walls were pictures in cardboard frames: a boy and a girl in school ties and jumpers. A picture of a cairn terrier had something written underneath.

'Bonny. Rest in Peace.'

A row of football videos ran the length of the window.

The woman was muffling her voice.

'I don't know,' she said.

Crackling.

'I can go out if you want,' she said. 'I have messages to get.'

Crackling again.

'All right then . . . that's okay. See you later. Cheery-bye.'

She answered the phone again.

'Picking up from?' . . . 'Your number?' . . . 'He'll be there in about five minutes, darling.'

She then went back to the radio. She called to the men in their cars.

Nothing.

She called again.

Nothing.

Then another burst of crackles.

'All right, Jamie,' she said, standing over me. 'That was Robert. He said to meet him at the Monument. That's right at the end of the street and turn left. It's in the middle of the road. Is that okay for you?'

'Great,' I said, putting the glass on the carpet. 'Thanks for doing that.'

'No problem,' she said. 'I hope you . . . find it all right.'

The boy with the fishing rod was bent over the grass. He lifted worms into a tin. He was a longer-haired version of the boy in the school photograph. As I walked to the road I could see his mother out the corner of my eye. She was behind the window. The window was coming over blue.

The Monument stone was softened with rain. The years had made it red powder. The man at the top looked mild with his rifle; his helmet a metal boater, good for Henley and a drop of hail, but no use against German shells, or the corroding shite of Lowland blackbirds, who know no song but their own song, and no time but this. Our soldier stared ahead with a beatific smile. The people he'd fought for went round him in cars. His valediction was engraved on a frozen plaque.

'They shall not grow old . . .'

I looked up at the copper man. I tried to imagine a body like mine in his war clothes. Under his helmet, my own hair. My blood-rush blown to a stop. The Argyll and Sutherland

Highlanders. There was something yellow in the ring of poppies' nylon. The wreaths around British war monuments: rings of synthetic flowers which start out red, and fade with the rain, the passing of days, until all their redness bleeds away, and they rest on the stone these remnants of thread, a forgetful yellow.

My father was there in minutes. He parked the car over the road. I had never seen him in jeans before. He was wearing jeans. He'd a smile on him. He came over to the Monument and put out his hand.

'Well, son,' he said, 'you've a head of blond hair on you.'

His handshake was weak, but the skin was hard; his hand was warm and arthritic. He had always had freckles, never young, never sunny, but now they looked raw in their folds of skin. He had watery eyes. The sort of eyes that grow greener with feeling. He looked like his father standing there. He'd the similar look of toil just abandoned. His face was large like his. The same idle sniff of embarrassment. The same smoker's primrose thumb. He was purposeful-looking, a jack of all trades; a plumber, a painter, a builder's mate. I remembered the cook in the school for bad boys. I remembered his face in the boiler room. The hate and the pride in his mouth back then. His long night's derangement in the bush with a knife. But the eyes now before me were plaintive for peace: he was somebody else now. I shook his hand and said hello.

'I saw you at the funeral. You left.'

'I know, aye. I couldn't have gone to the coffin and that.'

'No.'

'No.'

'I wasn't certain you were here. I don't know what your life is like.'

'There but for the grace of God go I.'

'Sorry?'

'I'm lucky to be alive. It's a wonder I'm not dead, Jamie. There but for the grace of God. And into the fucking bargain I was tired. The drink was killing me.'

'You're better now.'

'One day at a time.'

'I thought we would never meet like this.'

'I always did my best for you, Jamie.'

'No you didn't.'

'I tried . . .'

'No you didn't.'

'We were . . .'

'Robert. They were horrible times. We won't talk about them any more. I don't want to listen to you saying it was all fine. Just . . .'

'Fucking hell, Jamie, we were young.'

'I know.'

'We were *young*.'

'I know.'

I thought I might walk away from him then. Just walk away and never turn. I had wanted a moment of grace between us. The world would go on without us, I knew. But this one day I had wanted him to listen. I hoped he might stop for a second and hear me. But he wanted to speak. He had always wanted to speak. And somehow I couldn't blame him for that. He was pathetic, and so was I. Walls of self-pity had risen up between us. We each of us wanted to mend our ways. We wanted freedom. We wanted futures. We looked at each other; two men stood in a drizzle of silences. He touched the arm of my jacket.

'I don't even know who you are,' he said.

'I'm not a child any more.'

'No. You're not a child. You were never much like a child.'

'But I was one, Robert. I was one.'

'It's an illness, Jamie. I was sick. I was sick then. And I was sick long after. Call me all the names. Call me a bastard. But all I know is I'm fucking trying now. It's a terrible thing to be hated . . .'

'You hated your father long enough.'

He was upset now. Years of sorrow came into his eyes.

'I didn't hate him,' he said. 'I was never the son my da wanted. He wanted somebody he could mould – he wanted you. Your granda was a dreaming man. He needed people that could believe in his goals. I was no good for that. Maybe not good for much. But I didn't hate the man. You'd be better to say I hated myself. My God, Jamie: your mother and me made our own judge and jury when we made you.'

I heard myself say the word sorry.

'No. It's me that's sorry,' he said.

We closed our mouths. Each of us held back a century of troubles. We just let them sink to the graves we knew. There was nothing much we could say. We had wanted to talk our lives out loud, but neither, in the end, was fit for that. We looked at the copper soldier. We looked at each other and almost smiled. Our battles had been so domestic. They were fought in kitchens. They were fought in bedrooms. The Great War. We fought it in our sleep. To make lives as good as the houses they built for us. To make ourselves modern. To think of ourselves as a family on the move.

The sea whispered somewhere. Our mothers watered it with their tears. The tears went to nowhere, whilst sons and lovers stood watching the waves.

I thought of Margaret's battle. Robert's battle. The battle of Hugh Bawn. My mother's long war. Each of them marching to a different drum. I could see it then as I looked at my father. He had not been a part of Hugh's great campaign, and never a part of mine. But he had fought for himself. He had fought and won. He was off the drink. He was sober now. I was there and then charged with a sense of Robert. The nights had been long and slow for him.

Drowned and washed up, drowned and washed up.

A never-ending chaos, a spew of losses, the sad and perpetual ruin of his life. And now he was here, a sober person on a winter day, a man in jeans, and touching the arm of a son he barely knew. A new thought came over the air: nothing had ever been easy for him. In a way I would never forgive him for that. He had no ease; but there in the road I knew something else. He was here now. There was feeling in his eye. Something had removed him from the person he was. He'd survived himself. He'd survived his father. My will to speak had sunk with the recognition of something good in Robert. He was trying to live his life, as we all were.

'I'm fucked if I know what to say,' he said.

I liked the silence between us. All words slipped away. I had waited all my life to say nothing to my father. I wanted quiet now, and in time we could just forget the old words, and look up straight, and say one thing: 'We are fine.'

'I could drive you to my place,' he said. 'We could go and have a cup of tea.'

'Yes,' I said. 'That would be good.'

From my father's car the hills looked black. The trees up there were forked and bare; nothing moved. The car's ashtray was empty. A St Christopher medal hung on a chain. The car smelled of sweets.

Magic Tree. Vanillarama.

My father stared right forward. He spoke about driving. He spoke about Queen of the South. He gave me his view on the system of parking in Dumfries. His temper flared at the manners of other drivers. He talked of the spring fair; he said there were tourists who came there now. And while he talked, his eyes were deep in the road. They followed the lines; his eyes were glass.

We stopped by a field on the road to Cummertrees.

'This is where I live,' he said.

There in the field was my father's home: a blue caravan.

He walked among the gas bottles in the wee bit yard. He proudly showed me this and that – the washing line, a radish bed – and he showed them off like a timorous child, a boy with a castle of sand.

He made the tea and we sat inside.

There was a fold-down formica table. It had pickle jars in the middle, salt and pepper and a dish of butter, set out in Margaret's style, the style of his mother. It was odd that. I had let myself forget how my father might have taken something from his own growing up, something that wasn't resentment. His parents had made it into his sober life in minute ways.

That huddle of condiments.

The line of shoes by the door.

The chip basket trapped in layers of old lard.

A photograph of the *Queen Mary*.

And the smell of pine, no wind in the trees, but a thick kitchen chemical, a gloop on the lino, the memory of freshness, the killer of all known germs.

The order there of a formerly married man. More tidy than clean; less proud than preserved. The marks of a man who was keen to fill his time. The home of a person of burgeoning discipline, calmer waters, fewer regrets. A life of troubles now being shushed to the gentle swing of a pedal-bin.

'Is there anybody in your life?' he said.

'I have a girl called Karen.'

'Karen, aye. Nice lassie?'

'I like her,' I said.

There was a dog barking outside. We could see it romping through the furrows of a frozen turnip field. The rain came again.

A few rocks lay on a shelf above the sink. One was a lump of coral. Another was covered in deeply engraved lines, patterns of shells. I turned them over in my hands.

'Up the road,' said Robert, 'there's a farmer I've come to know. He's hopeless at his work, but he collects these things.'

'They're beautiful,' I said.

He took the fossil in his hand.

'He gave me this at Christmas time. He said it was a common one. From lower carboniferous rocks. That's what he said at the time. He's teaching me about them.'

'The study of pressure and time,' I said.

My father was quiet. He looked out the window.

'Beautiful,' I said, turning the fossil. 'It's really great.'

We sat with our tea. The wind dashed the rain on the roof of the caravan. The noise was there all right, but the place seemed so peaceful. We just sat there. You couldn't believe this van was a real place, in a real country, in a real time, with the world all real. With that noise on the roof, and the sweet, dislikable tea, the afternoon felt more like a thought, more like a melding of things in the mind, and less and less like a scene in the world of people and fossils and rainfall and fields.

'Do you think I will ever meet the lassie?' said Robert.

'I don't know,' I said. 'There might be a day. There might be.'

'Aye,' he said.

We had both settled into not saying much. I told him I liked his place. He looked at me as he bit into his lip. He sniffed.

'I think,' he said, '. . . I think this might be all I ever wanted.'

You could tell that he found this hard to say.

'Well then,' I said, 'it's a good thing that you have it now. It's the best thing. You can't live all your life as somebody you're not.'

'This was all I wanted,' he said, as if to himself.

'Well you have it now.'

We spoke about how those fields were once full of men and coal. 'Everything in this country is cheap now,' he said. 'It's all the same way. Cheap.'

I smiled at him.

'It used to be build, build, build,' he said. 'Not that I wanted anything the fuck to do with that. I could hardly stand up myself.'

We laughed at the same time.

'Now it's demolish . . .' he said.

'It has to be done,' I said.

We put our hands around our cups. The rain now battered down. The dog that barked was running away from the field to the trees. I could feel the heat come up through my hands.

'It has to be done,' I said. 'You can't stop change from happening.'

Robert's eyes were green. They were wide in that small, airless home of his. His eyes were green and his voice was steady.

'Aye,' he said. 'I suppose that's right enough.'

Robert Burns died in Dumfries. In his last weeks he took to the water off the Solway Strand. The Brow-well was rich in iron; a bottomless, salted mud. The wind of Annandale cut to the very bone. The poet waded out: he shivered in the green cordial, knowing death, his eyes on England. The last of his letters are here in my memory.

To Jean Armour: 'I delayed writing until I could tell you what effect sea-bathing was likely to produce. It would be injustice to deny that it has eased my pains, and, I think, has strengthened me, but my appetite is still extremely bad.'

To James, her father: 'I returned from sea-bathing quarters today, and my medical friends would almost persuade me that I am better, but I think and feel my strength is so gone that the disorder will prove fatal to me.'

And to George Thomson: 'After all my boasted independence, curst necessity compels me to implore you for five pounds.'

Getting wet is a local perdition, and yet it begins the Christian life. In Annandale the people are baptised every other hour. The rain seldom halts. I was soaked on my way down Mill Vennel, along the street where Burns' last breath still hangs at the eaves of an old house, a stout place bricked and re-bricked, surpassing the buildings on either side. The street filled my head. The rain was heavy. I went into the town in my waterlogged jacket.

In the bar of the Atholl Arms I took a five-pound note from my pocket. I spread the wet note on the counter.

Culzean Castle in a soggy blue.

I asked for a whisky. There was vapour of peat in the glass, an invisible cloud of old fermentation, amber-bright, a broth of burning grass. The whisky went down in one. It burned at my tongue and my throat.

His slogans had passed me by at the time. But now I could see them. On the walls of my father's caravan, hung here and there, above the fridge, propped by his bed, a series of slogans painted on wood:

'One Day at a Time.'

'Easy Does It, But Do It.'

'There But for the Grace of God Go I.'

'You are No Longer Alone.'

And printed on a dish-cloth, under a drawing of some praying hands:

> God Grant me the Serenity
> To Accept the Things I Cannot Change
> The Courage to Change the Things I Can
> And the Wisdom to Know the Difference.

I think he had painted the slogans himself. Cut the wood, planed it off, stained it, and painted out the letters with a steady hand. I could imagine him doing it. And as he did so he might have said those words over to himself. The words became him, and he became the words. He was making a life. He had rounded the slogans with sandpaper.

I sat in the Atholl two days after seeing Robert. The sky was as grey as any in my time. Rainwater bubbled at the choking drains. The bar was golden. I was due that day to see him again. He was speaking at a convention of Alcoholics Anonymous in the Loreburn Hall. He asked me to meet him in Oughton's Restaurant, a chip shop in Barony Row.

He was there already as I came to the shop. I stood for a minute under sheets of rain. I watched him from the pavement. His head and hands were crouched over the table. With concentration, with higher hopes, he drove a bookie's pen across a betting slip. He was neat in a shirt and tie.

'Christl! You're dreeping wet,' he said.

'It's pissing out there.'

'Hang your jacket next to the fire,' he said.

He screwed his newspaper halfway round.

'There's a good Ayrshire nag running at Lingfield,' he said. 'Three forty-five. Two-to-one favourite. Corncrake.'

'Oh.'

'Do you ever have a bet?' he asked.

'A bet.'

'Aye. A bet, you know. Do you ever back the horses.'

'No,' I said.

The waitress was very young. A pair of dark glasses was propped on her hair.

She licked her top lip; she pointed at the board.

My father clearly had a way with strangers. He was able to talk to them, as if he were glad to be just himself, as if he liked to be starting from scratch. He seemed happiest to proceed where there was no expectation of him, no overshadowings, no underminings. He wished for a world without background noise. He would hate to be told who he was by anyone. That was the opposite of the freedom he craved. He wanted now to take charge of his story; he wished to present himself as he himself thought good, without complication, without the ravenous interventions of those who will always know better. Robert was his own man now. He may always have seemed that way to others, but now he seemed that way to himself.

He smiled at the girl and made her laugh. He pointed at me.

'Now don't take any messing from him,' he said.

The girl laughed; she laughed the way young girls do when

older men embarrass them in front of younger ones. I bit my
cheek and smiled as well.

'Don't listen to him,' I said.

Robert ordered hot Vimto and a King Rib Supper.

'You're just after saying they had the best fish in Dumfries,'
I said.

'But I'm not wanting fish,' he said. 'You have fish.'

'Fish,' I said to the girl.

'Two Vimtos,' said Robert.

'Not for me. I can't drink it.'

'Don't listen to him,' he said. 'Everybody likes Vimto.'

I always had a habit of denying myself things I secretly
wanted. People would ask me if I wanted another drink; I'd
say no, and then stop at a bar on the way home. They'd say eat
some more; I'd wave it away, and then watch with envy the
second-helpers. A lot of things were like that with me. I
was always suppressing appetites, wishes, dreams. Enjoyments
were a sort of danger to me. Pleasures contained an element
of risk. They could make me feel subject to some unmindly
force, swayed by something larger than me. I was afraid of too
much comfort. I don't know why. And in some dark vale I was
scared of addiction. Watching Robert eat his dinner made me
scared for him. He ate like someone helpless.

Drink, anger, sugar, potatoes, curses.

Robert was an addict; he felt at home in the storm's eye, a
swirling glut of everything. I once thought he was just like a
baby with his bottle. All his life spent proving the truth of
need over want. He had always needed one thing or another.
He was always stuffing himself. He couldn't help it. The new
excesses were bad for his body and good for his mind. He
liked chips. He liked sugar. And once I advanced past my fear

for him, and saw that he wasn't drowning, I began to admire the force with which Robert devoured things for comfort, the way he wanted it all, even as he knew that all his indulgence would one day come to devour him. He went to his plate as a nihilist. He dared his body to tumble and die. He wasn't going to let himself be in want of anything. He would have what he wanted now. So long as he managed to stay off the drink. He would have what he wanted, and now.

His life had been one long search for things he could say he needed. Once upon a time he needed a ball and a Celtic strip; he needed a wife and an only child; he needed miles between him and his father. And then, the consolation of an English strand; all the drink in the world; his home again; a hospital bed; a long silence; a room of recovering boozers. And now he needed a rain-soaked afternoon. He needed his son to come and go. He needed to feel there was something salvaged. He needed the girls there in Oughton's to like him. He needed chips with every meal.

I sipped at the hot Vimto. It coated my tongue in iron.

'Do you know,' he said, 'what your grandfather's favourite word was?'

'Progress,' I said right away.

'Nearly,' he said. 'Have another wee try.'

'Deliverance,' I said.

'No. That's not the one I'm thinking of. He used all those Moses words. But the word he used most often in his life was the word "fuck".'

'That's not funny,' I said.

'But true all the same. I was just thinking about it the other day. He used to say that the word known to all men is "love". He'd read that in one of my granny's Irish books. "What is the word known to all men?" he'd say; my mother she smiled up at him, and said "love". And I would think, what is the word known to all of us. "Fuck".'

'I would have said that about you,' I said.

'True and all,' he said. 'But I was thinking, the word I will always remember him by is a word I heard all the way through my life. He said it nearly as much as he said fuck. In the fifties, in the sixties, he said the word at least two dozen times in any day. "Municipal" was the word. "Municipal." It's one of those words that's hard to say if you're a wee boy. I used to say "Manisipeople". I didn't know what it meant. I didn't want to know what it meant, either.'

'It was the kind of word he liked,' I said. 'It described the way they wanted things to be. Municipal.'

'You don't hear it now. Why is that?'

As he asked me the question I felt a mighty swell in the pause. The air was damp with the sap of thoughts. I was filled with the sense of the long story.

'*Why is that?*'

It was the biggest question my father had ever asked me.

'I don't know. It's an old word. It's not what people know any more. It's an old word.'

'Manisipeople,' said my father.

'Municipal,' I breathed, into the dark of my glass.

The Loreburn Hall, a chamber of well-shaped granite. The door was a local wood. And chiselled above was a coat-of-arms: a ship, a hammer, a tulip, a blood-red hand. The hall was filled with blue-breathing people. Everyone smoked. Thousands of people with time on their faces; women with lipstick on smiles; old men with canes and veteran fedoras;

keen mums in headscarves, all in their rows of interminable plastic. Along the sides there were young men in tracksuit bottoms. They seemed to say nothing. They seemed on their own. They snapped out smoke-rings from the midst of their tentative whiskers. They looked shell-shocked. Their eyes were bright and Scottish.

Up on the stage there were tartan banners: THE 42ND ANNUAL BLUE BONNETS GATHERING. YOU ARE NO LONGER ALONE. My father was smart in his tie. I went for a walk outside as he spoke. I could hear them laughing; 'My name's Robert . . .'

When I came back he was down in the seats. There were people around him, shaking his hand, clapping his shoulder. They gripped at his arm; they came with a kiss and a cuddle those women, fine and laughing as they gathered round. An elderly man stood on the platform. He held a microphone. He was large-eyed standing there, a pipe in his hand, a shoal of fish passing silver in his hair. He looked down smiling at the thousand eyes.

He spoke of the first of these conventions, the first to come to Dumfries. 'How careful one should be about starting anything new in AA,' he said. 'You never know where it will end!'

The audience was keen to clap and laugh.

'In addition to our alcoholism,' he went on, 'Billy and I had a lot in common. Billy was the co-founder of the Dumfries Gathering. He is dead now. Almost the same age to a day, we had both served in the King's Own Scottish Borderers during the First World War, and had marched many a mile to the regiment's most famous pipe tune, "Blue Bonnets Over the Border".'

My father's cronies sent smiles to the platform; the speaker was very old. At the back of the hall, under a jammering strip-light, a bagpiper kissed at his chanter, busy rehearsing an old tune to come.

'A good few years after the war . . .' said the old man on the platform (he spoke so clearly for someone of that age), '. . . I wrote to Bill to tell him that members of the fellowship in Liverpool and Carlisle were coming to Dumfries. I asked him to write to all the Scottish AA groups and ask them to meet us there. I wrote: "Tell them the English are invading Scotland once more. Raise the old Border war cry, Blue Bonnets Over the Border!" This started a chain of Gatherings held once a year. Everyone who has ever attended one of those Gatherings has come away with a new store of memories and a host of new friends.'

A cheer went up from the body of the room. Whilst the Chairman spoke on, my father sat enraptured, the feet of his chair near-bending in complicity, the smile on his face going tensionless and free.

I walked to the back of the hall. The tea-urns stood like security guards; they stood at the back in their silver armour. Lemonade was stacked in packs of two dozen. Everyone you saw was carrying a soft drink. The hall was hot. But it wasn't all heat: they carried their bottles of Curry's Red Cola as passports to the Gathering, as softly-carbonated trophies, the thirst they all conquered now marked by a craving for the innocence of raspberry and vanilla, the bubblings of Tizer and Irn-Bru.

Hundreds of old men with their bottles of pop: the more they can drink, the more sober they are.

A table up against the back wall had literature for sale: *The Big Book. The Twelve-Step Life. The Jack Alexander Story.*

I wondered at the passage of these words, these bits of

wisdom from faraway places, a column of words from the *Saturday Evening Post*, a flutter of sense from forties New York, now made for this table, with the tartan cloth, and the line of communicants free with their Scottish banknotes.

I had noticed down there the way they had named each other. Danny D., or Fergus Mac., or Sheila C. My father's group marked themselves another way. They took to their occupations. There was Bricklayer Bill. Taxman Murray. Carpenter Tommy. Grocer Annie. Carpet-layer Ted. Teen the Machine. Coach-driver Duncan. Plasterer Jimmy. They all had things to do in the world. Or they once had. Or they hoped to have again.

But on that day they seemed bound by a sense of the second life. A language of self-help slogans. Recovery was the story of the moment, and they all told those stories, and listened to the stories of one another, and they brought the old stuff of wars and ideals, of history and dreaming, of enlightenment and love and deliverance and progress, and they made it serve the swelling narrative of their own improvement. They believed in a unity of needs; they had made a nationhood of self-rescue. Our fathers were dead and gone: here were the living, and every wind of tradition came about them, every breath of the past came in whispers to make them new, and here they were, a gloaming of faces in a tartan seance, a calling-down of ghosts from the greenwood side.

'Help us to help ourselves,' they said. 'Help us to help one another.'

Oh help us to live where you could not. Oh show us a place that you – father, son – have only ever dreamed of knowing.

One day at a time. My father's eyes.

They knew the ideals we had tried to know. He had found

Utopia in a community of reformed boozers. He looked up at me. Those green eyes were his father's. They glistened there in that darkness of joy. The people touched his arms. They patted his back.

He made his life by making lives. They all did. And all the rest was another story.

These people were off the drink. They had found themselves in Scotland and the world, and had made it new, for themselves, for each other. A pipe band began to play. The AAs stood up in their rows. My father too. They took out white handkerchiefs and waved them in the air.

The Legionnaire's Song.

A sea of white sails leaving for America.

'Goodbye, goodbye,' they sang.

I watched my father with his spotless cloth. He waved it high in the air.

'Goodbye,' I said to my father's eyes.

'Goodbye,' he said to mine.

And all my life I will see my father's face, and remember it there in that festival of hope. When I got to the door I looked back again. He was there. He was alive. The light was pale, the rain was falling on the old roof, and we found each other's eyes again, the same green eyes, and we smiled over the crowd of legionnaires, his army of new friends, and we waved a hand. The smile and the hand that brought light to our rooms, and passed over time, the years behind us.

Margaret's hibiscus. The leaves they were green. And the orange petals curled from the plant, a wave of Chinese, paper-thin.

She hung the pot in a wire basket. There at the window in

Hugh's old room. The blinds had gone, a breeze came in from the peaks of Arran, and the whole day long we worked together, hands filled with plaster and soil, like two young newly-weds making their house. Margaret stood on an Ottoman chest. Her face had the light of the day. With one slim hand she traced the flow of the veins on the leaves. I took her other hand in mine, and traced the flow of the veins on her.

'Why don't you come away from here, Granny,' I said.

'We'll be grand here,' she said. 'We will all be grand.'

I clamped a flower-box to the window's ledge. You could see for miles. The town and the sea, the cars and the people. We were high as any hill out there. Margaret pressed the soil in about the plants. A many-nodding-headed campanula: its blue flowers ringing the morning, drinking the light.

'At the nursery there,' she said, 'they don't call this a blue-bell. We used to call it that, or a harebell. Now you all call it by the other name, campanula.'

'Do you think they'll be able to live this high?' I said.

'We can try them,' she said. 'I'll turn them and water them. If they don't like it here, I'll take them down to the park, and start them again.'

She stuffed the edges of the box with heather. You could smell sweet muck in the tangle of its needles. I brought her a cup of tea. She blew on it and drank it.

'There is work to do,' she said.

She watched me up on the metal steps. My basin of Polyfilla; laying it into the holes. Every punch in the plaster was filled. She sat on the Ottoman and started to cry.

I went over and took both her hands in mine.

'Come away from here, Granny. You could come down south.'

'This is my life,' she said. 'My life is here.'

'It doesn't have to be,' I said.

'I know well enough,' she said. 'I'm not wanting a sheltered house, or somebody's back room. And you have your own life, Jamie.'

She put her hands into my hair. The tears came down, but her voice was strong. She whispered to me. She whispered in a long-ago voice.

'Believe in things, son. Away you go, and believe in things. And live.'

I packed all Hugh's papers into boxes. I labelled them all for Liverpool. Margaret told me to take every bit: the old plans of Glasgow; architects' drawings; photographs from the air; his mother's letters. A bag of old clippings and pamphlets.

'Take them with you,' she said. 'They'll be good to look back on one day.'

In the cupboard we found a bag of old prints. We wiped off the dust and spread them over the bed. A region of colours, undertones.

'These were mine when I was a girl,' said Margaret. 'Some of them I brought down on the bus from Muir of Ord.'

One of the prints showed a girl in a set of blue beads. Her lips were red, without caution. Her eyes were black. There was green and blue and yellow on her face. Her hair was a stroke of brown paint. The lady seemed like a champion of the world. She looked up at us, as if to say something . . .

As if to say, 'I have always been here.'

The print, of course, had never seen paint, never been touched by a brush or a knife, and only the layers of old dust were there. And yet it looked wet, and lay there as fresh as the morning. In another print the background was deepening black. At the dead centre was a red chair. Sat on the chair was a blue jug.

An orange, a lemon.

Underneath, it said: 'Cadell, "The Red Chair", circa 1920.'

Margaret looked at the pictures; she caught her own tiny breaths. Much of what she said she said to herself. She pushed back her loose grey hair. She bit her lip like an easy young lassie.

'Jesus, Mary and Joseph,' she said. 'These are the very best pictures I ever saw. You can't get over them. Look, Jamie. These are the pictures that brought me south. I wanted to see these things, these modern things.'

'Let's put them up,' I said.

The prints were just loose. We pinned them up with tacks. Ladies in red hats, with teacups. Smears of chimneys and boats. Children at play in a yellow garden. Cogs within cogs, wheels within wheels; a Cubist church in a drop of rain.

'Oh we thought they were so modern,' said Margaret.

Some of the prints were of people like machines.

'My teacher would talk of these,' said Margaret. 'These ones.' She pointed to the black-and-white ones, the abstract lines, the botched machines. 'These were to show art and science coming together. They are very good. I remember that teacher reading Hugh MacDiarmid in the class. Art was to be modern. Look at that one – pure sense it seemed. Pure sense.'

The one she lifted was called: 'Gethsemane'. A thirties man in a rough wool suit kneels in a clearing, surrounded with trees. His hair and moustache are clipped to the day. His boater is there by his side. The shadows are long and dark at the trees. There's a hint of coming wind. The man wears brogues. A group of disciples, like college students, snooze on the verge at his back. In their weakness they sleep. They can't stay awake for their master's agony. And just in the distance there's a smattering of Glasgow.

A church spire. A mound of dwellings. The time of day in a spark of light.

Margaret stood beside me and looked at the picture.

'Hugh always said your man there was an engineer. He looks like one. An angel in the garden. It looks like Glasgow — like Bellahouston Park.'

'Why is that one the only one framed?' I asked.

'Hugh did that,' she said. 'He made it his favourite. And look on the back.'

I turned it over. The back was a scribbled-on board.

'The Glasgow engineers,' it said in Hugh's pencil. 'Done accordingly.'

Someone else's writing was underneath. I didn't know it. And yet I had a memory of those loops and curves, a memory of another person, a memory of me. The words written out were not my words. They were copied out. There was something of play in the way they cavorted across the back of the picture, the way they cartwheeled under the string. The picture was strange, the words were a stranger's.

'There are ruined buildings in the world,' it said, 'but no ruined stones.'

Margaret hung it above the bed. The bed where Hugh had lain those months. The place where my grandfather had stared in the bloodless dark, the wending trail to the Scottish night, his head-oils sunk in the pillow, and his every breath going out to the world with a story of love.